White Picket Fences

Fences

A NOVEL

Kyle Ann Robertson

D1376755

Fulton Books
Meadville, PA

Published by Fulton Books 2023

ISBN 979-8-88505-756-1 (paperback)
ISBN 979-8-88505-757-8 (digital)

Printed in the United States of America

Chapter 1

My father's voice echoed in every movement of the second hand from the vintage desk clock he had passed down to his grandson. "Time. Heals. All. Wounds. Give. It. Time." I was pretty sure there was not enough time in the universe to surmount the death of my son.

I summoned strength by running my hand over the collage of superhero posters: Captain America, Spider-Man, the Hulk. After today, the walls would be bare. The slight leathery, sport-locker smell of the light-blue room elicited visions of my darling son. And so, between therapy sessions, grief groups, and the several books I'd read on loss over the past year and a half, I digested my pain as a void forever in my heart. If it wasn't going to get any better, then I had to learn to live in the now with my grief and help my family heal. I could understand that Curtis would never come home, but I couldn't accept that he was gone forever. I called the incident an accident. Surely, an eleven-year-old dying from a brain aneurysm could be nothing but a mistake.

Curtis's dearest possession, a team-signed baseball, rolled between my fingers and brought a smile to my face. On the hottest afternoon of his last summer, Curtis hit a home run in the ninth inning of his Majors All-Star Game. He tied up the longest, most boring, 1–0 game. He single-handedly brought a small stadium of zombies back to life. The echo of his laughter above the awakening crowd and his smile as he slept that night were forever locked inside my heart.

Draped over his karate trophy at just the right angle, I could easily read "Most Valuable Player" on the medal Curtis received from that game. The tears I had been holding back fell as our eight-year-old golden retriever entered the room, wanting his morning walk. Was he looking for Curtis too?

Plopping on the corner of the twin bed, I ruffled the puffs of fur behind Roger's ears as he settled at my feet. "I know, Rog. I know." Together we shared the loss, which was no less today than it had been yesterday or all the yesterdays before then.

I picked up book number eight of Darren Shan's *Cirque Du Freak*, making sure the bookmark was secure where Curtis had left it. I smoothed out the wrinkles I had created in the superhero duvet cover and flipped the matching pillow, exposing the lump of Curtis's hidden "Doggie."

From inside the pillowcase, I pulled out the threadbare stuffed Doggie Curtis never slept without. But after one embarrassing sleepover with a few baseball buddies, I found Doggie tucked deep inside the pillowcase. Close by but hidden. Had everything not happened so fast in the days after Curtis's incident, had I time to think about it, if I could have thought at all, I would have placed Doggie in the casket with Curtis.

"Come on, Rog. Let's go for your walk."

Roger sauntered in front of me down the long hallway. I paused at the door to my art studio as the early morning light illuminated the painted canvas on my easel. I would get back to my latest commission as soon as I cleared my thoughts and got through this first step toward my family's new normal. Silence came from behind the twins' closed bedroom door across the hall. The twins were either still asleep or understandably tucked under their weighted comforters to delay the start of their day.

By the time Roger and I made it to the sidewalk, pink and purple light seeped through the grays, but the sun hadn't quite snuck above the horizon. I now walked Roger every morning and understood why Curtis never complained about this one chore. The boost of energy from the brisk stroll, the silent moments for clear thought, and the apparent joy it brought Roger was a great way to start every day.

Although Roger stopped and smelled every yard, his tail never failed to wag. If only it were that easy. Stop and sniff and move on. I needed to move on, but not back to where I was before Curtis's incident. Life had gotten stale, and as good as Michael was to me, I thought I wanted more, but I was wrong.

The day of Curtis's passing, I had taken some time, just a few meaningless hours, for myself. Time to catch up with an old friend, one visit. It wasn't intended to be a secret. It just wasn't anybody's business.

Curtis's death pushed me closer to my empty nest sooner than I'd ever wished and was not what I imagined when I said I was tired of being Mom and Mrs. just for an afternoon. Would things be different if it weren't for my selfishness and for not appreciating what I already had? I'd apologized to the universe every which way since then.

I kicked a stone. It bounced and rolled down the sidewalk in front of me. Roger chased it down, sniffed, then snorted, not pleased with his discovery. As we walked, the neighborhood came alive. Lights switched on. People brewed coffee and brushed their teeth. Across the street, Mrs. Amberly rocked on her front porch, sipped coffee, and watched me with consideration. Old Mr. Pender stepped out in his bathrobe, shot up a quick wave, then searched the ground as if the newspaper at his feet had disappeared before his eyes. Mary Simon herded her three small children into her minivan. I caught her eye, but she looked away, overreacting to her oldest child climbing into the back seat. It had been more than eighteen months, and still, people felt the need to avoid me. But I understood. How many times could a person say, "Sorry you lost your son"?

Chapter 2

I rushed back to the driveway of my forever home and down the brick path into the backyard. The sound of the gate closing allowed me to breathe. That gate guarded my little world where no one could interfere or judge me. Well, no one but my family and Pamela.

Pamela Spenser, the best friend a girl could have, would soon arrive to help me repurpose Curtis's room. After months of wringing my hands and talking it out with Pamela, and our third amiga, Alicia, I decided two things. Accepting that Curtis would never return was not the same as forgetting he was ever here. And that I needed my twin daughters to move beyond their grief and create new memories, not to erase the old, but before it was too late to create new ones. I wished for them to live their best lives despite their father not wanting to be involved.

I missed our family weekend camping trips, with trail hiking and freshwater fishing. I missed movie nights with pizza and popcorn, and I especially missed game night when Michael would act goofy and the kids competed playfully. I realized it would be hard without Curtis by our sides, but I desperately wanted to add new, brighter chapters for my girls before they headed off to the local college.

At Roger's insistence, I broke my brooding as he pulled on the leash wanting to go in and I steeled myself for the unfolding day. My head and heart were ready to face the task at hand. I could never get over my son's death, but I needed to fix my family, get us back to some sort of normal, so I could get over my guilt of failing them on that fateful day. All I had to do was take that next step.

"It's my brush, give it back to me."

"Liar. It's mine. I bought it." The twins were at it again. As I entered the kitchen, I cringed hearing the girls arguing upstairs—again. Nicole and Heather were too competitive and totally opposite.

Both athletic at only five feet four inches, their similarities ended there. Brown-eyed and brown-haired Heather, the older one by three minutes, was the spitting image of me; but her personality was a little more high-spirited and more independent than I ever dreamt of being. Nicole, on the other hand, was blonde-ish and blue-eyed and very much like her father. She was relatively quiet and reserved but had my artist's soul and preferred to look at the world through her Canon zoom lens.

"Heather. Nicole. Come down now," I yelled up the stairs.

"Hey, Julie." Pamela walked in the front door without a knock and kicked off her four-inch Stuart Weitzman pumps. The tension in my shoulders subsided. She understood how I worked and was showing up to mediate between my anguish of letting Curtis's room go and how my heart pained to see a vacant room waiting for the return of its occupant.

As the youngest sister of four siblings—youngest by eight years—I would walk past the open doors of my brothers' or sister's empty rooms after, one by one, they left for college. Every two years, one sibling would leave, never to return home except for short visits. Those sad, empty rooms would be hopelessly left behind, continually shrinking my world as my father received his next marching orders, and we'd move to a new location, to a new home, each time with one less bedroom.

Pamela's energy had calmed me since the day we became best friends in our high school bathroom while I cried over my boyfriend, Chad. A natural-blonde bombshell of a cheerleader, and the total opposite of me, she somehow cared enough to put her arm over my shoulder and say, "Chad's a big flirt. He's not worth all this blubbering. You'll mess your mascara." As if my mother let me wear mascara in tenth grade.

I took the bag of fruit hanging from Pamela's wrist. "Let me help." I added the bananas, apples, and pears into the fruit bowl in the center of the kitchen table. Pointing to the box of donuts in her hand, I tutted, "No homemade goodies today?"

Before Pamela could answer, Nicole ran down the stairs and spotted the donuts. "I call the vanilla frosted."

I was glad to see a smile on Nicole's face. Today was going to be a tough day for all of us, and my heart lifted, knowing at least one of my girls was ready to face clearing out Curtis's room.

"I thought some good old lard and sugar were needed for today." Pamela centered a vanilla-frosted donut on a napkin and served it to Nicole with a curtsy. "Here you go, your majesty." She leaned forward for her expected peck on the cheek and got one.

I peeked into the box. All the donuts were vanilla frosted. "You know us way too well."

I pulled out a chair for Nicole. "Where's Heather?" I asked, anxious for the answer.

Nicole tossed her head toward the stairs and shrugged then headed into the den with her donut. At least she didn't say Heather refused to come down.

"What's up with Heather?" Pamela asked as she blew away the steam from her coffee mug and sat in the chair as if I pulled it out for her instead of Nicole.

I folded my right leg under me as I sat next to her. "Some days she seems to be coming around, and other days I feel she hates the whole world, especially me. We argue every time I drive her to and from her job. I get it. She wants to be with her friends, but she's too young to be in other young kid's cars. It's my job to drive her around."

Uncomfortable, I shifted my leg out from under me and continued, "A couple of weekends ago, I went to the mall to surprise her and take her out for lunch, but her manager said she didn't have to clock in until two p.m. I had dropped her off at ten. When I questioned her, she said she had messed up her schedule, and she walked around the mall until her shift started. Four hours? I ended up hanging around the mall to make sure she showed up at two, and I never saw her till then. The other night, I was supposed to pick her up at ten o'clock after closing, and she showed up here at home before nine thirty. Said she got off early and a friend had dropped her off."

"Hate to say it," Pamela said, "but it sounds like a normal soon-to-be seventeen-year-old to me."

6

"Easy for you to say. You don't live with her. Anyway, it's my responsibility to drive her around," I said.

"I've been by your side since day one. Give her some space. She's a good kid."

"Lord knows I couldn't have done it without you." I always felt God gave me twins so that Pamela could be involved in raising them. The day I found out I was pregnant with twins, Pamela had confided she had polycystic ovary syndrome and was never able to get pregnant. From that moment on, Aunt Pamela was part of the family.

"Heather has become quite difficult and Nicole more distant lately," I whispered. "The hardest part about the twins growing up is for me not to compare them as they each become their own person, different from one another." I had to bite my tongue so as not to let any more draining details out with Nicole in the room nearby.

"I seem to recall in high school you wanted to run away from home and move in with your sister," Pamela said. "I believe it took me, Michael, and Chad an hour to convince you to leave the bus station and go home."

"That was different..." I stumbled at Pam's mention of Chad. "Chad had joined the Navy." Something I was dead set against after a childhood of being part of a military family and moving every two years or so. "So I was upset our little foursome was breaking up. Now it all seems so silly." I couldn't let thoughts of the past permeate the moment. My family was my priority today.

Pamela popped up from her chair. "Hey, Heather."

Heather's long, uncombed brunette locks curtained her face as her thumbs rapidly texted. When Pamela wrapped her arms around the sullen girl, Heather's arms and cell phone flailed by her side. If only I could snap my fingers and have my spunky, funny, wisecrack of a daughter back.

"Grab a donut. Nicole's in the den." I slid the box of donuts toward her.

Upon Pamela's release, Heather finished her text and said, "I'm good."

"Are you excited for school to start in a couple of weeks?" Pamela asked, attempting to engage her. "What clubs are you going to join this year? Or are you going to keep working at the mall?

"Not sure," Heather said, glancing at the donuts as she joined Nicole in the den.

I rolled my eyes behind her back and threw my hands in the air as if Heather just justified my previous statement about her. I whispered, "I had mentioned her behavior to the therapist. She told me to give her time. Heather lives in fear of her life ending any minute like Curtis's did. Doctors have assured her it is abnormal for a child to die from an aneurysm, but still, she mistrusts God and the world. On the other hand, Nicole is the one the therapist wants me to watch. She is trying to stay strong for the whole family, not allowing herself to grieve." I guiltily took a bite of a donut, enjoying every bit of it. "Hopefully, by clearing out Curtis's room, it will allow the girls and Michael the closure and courage to move on." Guess I'd see. I didn't know what else to do.

"Speak of the devil," Pamela said, getting up to refill her coffee.

Michael, his blond hair wet from his morning shower, descended the stairs with his chin on his chest, focused on the bottom button of his shirt.

My instinct, still, was to blow him a kiss—as we did for years, our secret love language since four-year-old Curtis was grossed out by us being "too mushy" when Michael and I greeted each other with an embrace. But ever since the day of Curtis's incident, Michael had made it perfectly clear he no longer wanted to receive my airborne kisses.

"Morning, Pamela," he muttered and headed across the kitchen straight to the box of donuts. "What, no pancakes today, Jules? We always have pancakes on Saturday. Not like you to shake things up."

My gut wrenched as he said it. The old Mike would say nothing before he'd say something hurtful, and I'm sure he remembered how difficult it was for me to go off my routine. Since the twins were three, until Curtis's death—when everything came to a halt—we had eaten pancakes together as a family every Saturday morning. It took almost a year, and only at the girls' unrelenting requests, before I could add Saturday pancakes back into our weekends by reimagining it as a new activity for our new family.

I bit back the words wanting to spew from my mouth. Instead, I said, "We're going to address Curtis's room today, remember? Aren't you sticking around to help?" I tried to keep the irritation from my tone because I—once again—had to remind Michael of the very last thing we spoke about the evening before.

His eyes bore into mine, sending me the message that he wasn't going to discuss this. Last night, he had said if we got rid of Curtis's stuff, we'd forget all about him. He felt I was cruel to change things as if Curtis never existed. Michael didn't want to understand that if we didn't, we would stay stuck. Something had to change for us to begin to healing. Of all people, I thought he would understand the pain that empty room caused me. No matter how often or how desperately I had explained to Michael we needed him to be part of putting the rest of our family back together, he couldn't—or wouldn't—understand my intentions.

I stared into his dispirited blue eyes, pleading for him to stay. His scowl and the measured shake of his head informed me not to go there, and our gaze unlocked.

"Forgot Jeff asked me to do something with him," Michael said, taking another bite of his donut. He winked at Pamela as if she surely knew what he was talking about since Jeff was her husband.

As Michael reached for a second donut, I suppressed the urge to slap his hand and tell him those donuts were for people wanting to move forward, not for those who chose to shirk their responsibility and not accept a new normal. He should want to help, not just in honor of his lost son, but for his two remaining, grieving daughters.

He turned to face me. I pivoted my back to him and rearranged the fruit in the bowl. My spine stiffened as he passed behind me to grab a bottle of water out of the fridge. How could he not stay? I had no qualms of challenging him with Pamela in the room, but I wouldn't argue with him while the girls sat nearby. So I inhaled, exhaled, then bit my lip.

"Funny. Jeff didn't mention anything to me this morning when I left." As usual, Pamela picked up where I wouldn't go. Pamela and

Michael not only went to high school with me, but they also spent the following four years together at the same college. Treating him like an annoying little brother was her norm. She moved the box of donuts away from his reach and said, "But don't worry. We've got this. You and Jeff go find some pancakes. Julie will return to her normal duties next Saturday, Michael."

He stuffed the remainder of his donut into his mouth and plucked his finger out with a pop, emphasizing his no-comment.

Chapter 3

The day of…
Nineteen months earlier, 6:20 a.m. to 7:15 a.m.

"**K**nock it off you two," I said as I neared the bottom of the stairs. It was always something with those two. Their squabbling was like nettles under my skin. Curtis and I joked about how quiet the house would be once the girls left for college. The local campus was far enough away to not be underfoot yet close enough so they could come home for weekends or any evening in between. "It's too early for locking horns. You're twins with an internal connection. Can't you two discuss this in silence?" I tied my pink floral bathrobe and walked directly to the fridge for my beloved, must-have, morning diet cola.

Heather and Nicole continued arguing and hip-checking each other as it dawned on me my girls were cooking breakfast, something they less than rarely attempted—on a school day. Something inside me said to run. Instead, I popped open my cola for the wherewithal to deal with them.

"Mom, tell Heather you don't put vegetable oil in pancake batter. Just in waffles," Nicole said and pulled the bowl of batter away from Heather.

"Give that back." Heather yanked the bowl from Nicole. Thick golden batter splashed all over the countertop and dripped down the cabinet door below.

Unable to ignore them any longer, I yanked the bowl from Heather. Both girls froze. "Go upstairs, both of you."

"But, Mom, we need to bring pancakes for Ms. Chambers." Nicole spun paper towels off the roll and swiped at the goop.

"Making pancakes is reserved for Saturdays for a reason," I said and grabbed the towel from her before the whole glop landed on the floor. "Just go upstairs and get ready for school."

11

"Okay, but we need, like, fifty pancakes for our class," Heather said over her shoulder.

"Pancakes for the whole class?" I was dumbfounded. My two relatively intelligent sixteen-year-old girls woke up only fifteen minutes earlier than usual to make pancakes for thirty kids and failed to mention it to me the night before. They were lucky I had all the ingredients. My amazement fueled each stroke as I whipped up more batter.

The two girls raced up the stairs, shoving each other as Curtis and Roger clambered in the back door, shaking off cold January sprinkles from their early morning walk.

"What happened?" Curtis asked as he covered his mouth to hide his giggles.

"Your sisters. That's what happened," I said, squatting like a catcher to wipe batter off the face of the cabinet.

Still giggling, Curtis said, "Pancakes are for Saturdays." He hung the long red leash on its hook as he stepped around me to fill Roger's water bowl. He lingered in the pantry as if he had many choices of cereal to choose from then pulled Cheerios, the only box on the shelf, and set himself up at the table with milk and a banana. Eleven-year-old boys were so much easier, although they lacked any urgency with anything they did.

I set two bowls on the table for the girls and called them down for breakfast.

"Why so many pancakes?" I asked whichever twin I heard trotting down the stairs.

"Ms. Chamber's birthday. Nicole and I have to bring pancakes," Heather said as she pushed the bowl away, sat at the table, then cracked open a banana.

"Yep, since there were two of us." Nicole joined in on the conversation with her head in the fridge.

"Girls, you should have said something last night. At the very least, you should have gotten up a lot earlier. At this rate, you're going to miss the bus." I pulled out a second skillet. I hated when they missed the bus. When I had to drive them to school, my whole day was thrown off.

"We can't be late. The pancakes are for first period." Nicole grabbed a spatula out of the utensil jar and stood armed to flip.

"Okay. You done eating, Curtis?"

"Why do I have to get involved? I have plenty of time before my bus comes." He slurped the sugared milk from the bottom of his bowl.

"I'll drop you off at Jared's, and you can catch the bus with him." I shooed him off with my spatula.

"You wouldn't have to drive us if we could ride with our friends," Heather said with her mouth full of banana.

"Not now, Heather," I said.

"Who's riding with friends?" Michael asked as he wiggled his tie tighter and dodged a fake tackle from Curtis.

"We're not," Heather said, tossing her banana peel on the table. *"I can't wait 'til I can get my own car."*

"Let's not rush it, honey." I flipped another pancake. *"You'll get your permits soon enough."*

"Oh, nice. Pancakes on a weekday," Michael said as he tapped on my right shoulder to distract me then reached around my left to pick a hotcake off the top of the pile.

It's like I had four kids. I slapped his hand with the spatula. The pancake fell right back to its top spot. Could he just help for once instead of making everything into a game?

"The girls need these for homeroom," I said.

"Doesn't mean you have to make them." He was right, but it was easier to make the pancakes than to listen to the girls' whine. I wiped my bangs off my forehead with the back of my hand as Nicole impatiently helped me whisk, pour, and flip.

"They won't cook any faster by you waving that spatula at them," I joked in an attempt to hide my frustrations. *"Go make sure you're ready for school."*

Trying to elicit help from Michael, I said, *"Tell you what. You dig out a couple of aluminum pans from the pantry, and I just might be able to squeeze out a few extra pancakes for you."*

When a clatter of plastic trays and a few cuss words took me by surprise, I leaped like a kangaroo rat and propelled a pancake onto the stovetop as stacks of paper cups bounced and shot like cannonballs across the kitchen floor.

"What the… Thanks, but I only needed two pans." I laughed and took the stack of aluminum containers as Michael handed them to me with a this-is-not-funny smirk.

This was how they trained me, screw up so badly in hopes I'd never ask them to help me again. Michael picked up the fallen trays and paper plates, and most of the plastic cups, and put them on the counter. I couldn't be bothered to ask him to put them back in the pantry where he knew they belonged. I'd have to rearrange them anyway.

I filled two of the pans with five dozen warm pancakes, took two off the top, and plopped them on a plate for Michael.

"Hurry up, Mom. We're going to be late. Bye, Dad," Heather said as she left out the door to the garage. Nicole and Curtis flew across the kitchen, and I held up one finger as I filled my large YETI rambler, my travel cup, with ice-cold, bubbling caffeine for the short trip to the high school.

Michael forked a pancake and swiped it through the syrup on his plate. "Thanks for breakfast, Jules. Next time, can you make bacon too?"

"Sure, on Saturday, per usual." And on Friday, I'll do your laundry, Tuesday pick up your dry cleaning, and have your dinner on the table when you get home tonight. Exasperated, I tossed a dishtowel at him. He caught it and blew me a kiss. He might think it was all a joke, but I was tired. When was someone going to wait on me? I grabbed the grocery list off the side of the fridge. Since I'd be out, might as well get some errands done. I made it into the garage just as Michael threw the dishtowel at the closing door.

Chapter 4

As the new Michael left the house, my chin trembled. I yanked a tissue out of its box to catch the tears falling from missing the old Michael more and more each day. "I wish he would at least try to understand why I need to turn Curtis's room into something other than Curtis's room."

Pamela put her finger to her lips and pointed as Heather, head down, staring at her still vigorously texting thumbs, entered the kitchen.

"If Dad's not helping, then I'm not helping," she said without looking up.

Putting a lid on the gurgling volcano inside me, I said, "You don't have a choice. Helping will be good for you—for all of us. You'll see."

Heather nonchalantly continued up the staircase.

I cocked my head in disbelief. "Heather, you come back here. We need to talk about this."

"No, Mom," she yelled down the stairs. "You need to talk about this." She punctuated her statement by slamming her bedroom door.

I sunk onto a step. "See what he's doing? His actions are driving a wedge between all of us."

Pamela took my hand and pulled me away from the bottom of the staircase. "You're doing all the right things—for you and the girls. And that's what's important right now."

"Fake it 'til I make it, right?"

"Face it then you'll make it," Pamela bettered my quote.

"I miss the old Michael."

Pamela signaled for me not to speak and motioned to the back door. Roger cut me off and beat me to our exit, but it was the right move. Nicole was still in the den, and I had to vent.

"Michael used to be Steady Eddie, the pleaser, never making waves." I cringed internally, wishing I hadn't lost sight of that nineteen months ago before I took off for a day to myself. "It's sad and maddening to see him so—so uninvolved. I've tried to tell him that life isn't the same for any of us, but we should all try to make the best of it. And he said he most certainly did not." I cupped my face and shook my head. "What does that even mean?"

"So why are we turning Curtis's bedroom into his office? I'm surprised one of the girls isn't clamoring to move into their own space."

"Michael's always wished for a home office. So I mentioned turning Curtis's room into one. He said 'it was only fair since I took over the fourth bedroom for my hobby.'" My quoting fingers burned through the air.

"As if he's ever worked from home," Pamela said. "I think he's always been a bit jealous you're able to do something you love, and he's stuck with managing people. He probably just wants a man cave to watch his sports."

"Are you going to put a TV in Curtis's room, Mom?" Nicole startled us from the open doorway. "If Dad doesn't use it, can Heather and I can have our own den upstairs?"

I winced, realizing I had not closed the door tightly. "No, honey. We've always watched TV in the den down here, and we'll continue to do so."

"I bet you five bucks there'll be a TV up in that room within a week," Pamela fake whispered to Nicole and stuck her hand out for a high five.

We returned to the kitchen, and I closed the donut box. Knowing there was no time like the present, I stretched my neck from side to side and unfurled my tight fists like a prizefighter shaking his nerves.

"Follow me," I said and led Nicole and Pamela up to Curtis's room, the grand marshal of a thwarted, bereft procession.

Pausing at the twin's bedroom door, I knocked. "Heather, we can use your help." I continued with laggard steps toward the entrance of Curtis's deserted room and looked over my shoulder, confirming Nicole was nearby. She took my hand and led me over the threshold.

Pamela asked, "Where would you like to start?"

Overwhelmed with the realization of what was previously just a reasonably sound idea, I froze.

"Is it too soon, Julie?" Pamela pulled me in for a hug. "Would you like to wait and do this another time?"

I covered my face with my hands then took a deep breath. "It'll always be too soon. We're here now." I reminded myself we had been through a year of firsts: our first Christmas and all the other holidays without Curtis; the first birthday of his we didn't celebrate; the first anniversary of his death.

Nicole picked up a large plastic garbage bag and picked at its edges, trying to open it. Frustrated, she threw it into a heap at her feet. Heather strolled in and snatched the bag off the floor. She rubbed it between her palms, separating the two sides, opening it.

I couldn't help but smile to see Heather join us. "Thank you," I whispered.

Heather stared at Curtis's Doggie, and tears welled up. Wanting her to know I was there for her, I put my arm around her shoulders, but she was like hugging a cactus.

I garnered the grit my father had expected from me every time we packed up one of my childhood bedrooms before each transfer and nodded for Pamela to go ahead and take over.

"Okay. How about if we start with his clothes?" Pamela took charge. "Girls, why don't you start with the drawers. Fold everything nicely and place them in that bag."

"No, everything needs to be washed," I said and swiped the shirt Pamela had just pulled from a drawer.

"Mom, they're clean." Heather rolled her eyes.

"They've been sitting here for months. I'm going to wash them before some other child wears them." I grabbed the tall white laundry basket from the bottom of the closet and dumped the entire drawer of T-shirts and then the drawer full of shorts until the basket overflowed.

Pamela left me to my all-important nonsensical task. "Girls, why don't you sort through his toys? I'll be right back. I have a few empty bins in my car."

I stuffed the items which had fallen on the floor into the basket as panic took over. The fruition of Curtis's death hadn't seemed as real since the day he died. When I saw his baseball shirts and his yellow-and-green striped bathing suit, my heart rate quickened and reached my throat. I rushed out the door through the stifling air, trying to save all my memories of Curtis in the one basket. As time moved on, I felt as if I collected memories in a sieve.

As little black spots rushed my view, I reached the hallway and dropped the laundry basket. My hands dropped to my knees, and I lowered my head, panting, forcing air through my grinding teeth.

Pamela got to the top of the staircase with her stack of bins, startling me. Avoiding the obvious, she said, "I thought these might help."

I slid down the wall into a squat and gasped for breath as if I'd just completed a marathon. Tears hit my bent knees as Pamela slid beside me. She draped an arm around me and dragged me into her lap. I was grateful the girls couldn't see my tears flow as I curled onto my side and lay there. What if Michael was right? What if I was acting on "out of sight, out of mind"? Could I be that heartless?

I wanted to go back. Back to before. Before anything happened to Curtis. Back to before Michael became so distant. Before I manifested a karmic kickback by acting on inklings that there had to be more to life, more to being Mom or Mrs. If I could return, I'd never take anything for granted ever again. The guilt of not being available for Michael and the girls that one day would forever dwell in my heart.

Determined to take on the ache which would never go away, I vowed this would be the last time I'd break down over it. I accepted the pain as I would a war wound, a reminder of what I'd been through, and use it as strength to reassemble my family. I wiped my tears with the hem of my shirt. With a couple of pats on the back from Pamela, I retreated to the basement to wash Curtis's clean clothes.

I ran up and down the stairs, rotating the laundry from washer to dryer to baskets. I folded a blue polo shirt and wondered which eleven-year-old boy would end up wearing it. I held the soft cotton to my cheek. Curtis wore this favorite shirt to his first boy-girl party.

He called me within forty-five minutes and asked me to pick him up—something about a boy telling him he didn't have a shot with Mallory, the birthday girl. He claimed he didn't even like her. Yeah, right, Curtis. I grinned at the memory until an imagined older Curtis in a navy-blue suit with pant legs just a smidgeon too short, dancing at his senior prom, pressed the corners of my skull.

As I broke out in a sweat, the image faded into an even older Curtis, one looking more like Michael, in a traditional black-and-white tuxedo on his wedding day. Unable to breathe, I mowed through space as if breaking through a wall, smashing the images to little bits. Out of breath and quivering, I quieted my mind, repeating, "I will never forget you. You will always be a part of me." I added the blue shirt to the others and lowered the pile into a plastic bin for some other boy to wear.

While I took my time with the laundry, Pamela dusted and polished the furniture as the drawers emptied. "The baggie queen strikes again," Pamela said as she pulled out gallon-size, baggies filled with color-coordinated Legos.

"I heard that," I said as I entered the bedroom with a pile of folded clothes. The girls teased me because I'd always had just the right size baggie whenever needed. If we were at the beach, I had quart-size baggies for shells, and if we were at a restaurant, I had freezer baggies for the leftover rolls. I had large baggies in the car for trash or dirty shoes. And if a bag of chips or chocolate candies ripped open too much, I had a baggie for that. I even had a snack-size bag in my purse filled with spare change.

Nicole sat on the bed, organizing Curtis's baseball, Pokémon, and Magic trading cards into several pint-size baggies and separated the playing pieces for his Monopoly and Battleship games into snack-size baggies. I could tell she was creating busy work to stifle her sniffles.

"It's okay," I said, cradling Nicole's head to my chest. "Let it out. It's okay." I rocked my fifteen-year-old as if she were a baby in my arms.

"It's so unfair," she said between sniffs. "I wish…"

"I know, I know. Me too," I whispered into her hair. Me too. I wished Curtis was here and we were doing anything other than emptying this lonesome space.

Across the room, Heather tilted her head and, with a gentle touch, skimmed the stacks of books on the desk—each series its own tower, *Maximum Ride*, *Fablehaven*, and *Cirque du Freak*. She retrieved the book from the nightstand and slid it between books seven and nine in the *Cirque du Freak* pile. On the other side of the shelf, several books of different titles, authors, and sizes were stacked, throwing off the symmetry.

She lifted the top book, and the corners of her mouth curled up as she handed it to me. She broke her silence of the long morning and said, "*The Absolutely True Diary of a Part-Time Indian* by Sherman Alexie. Curtis wanted to become a veterinarian because of this book, because Junior couldn't save his sick dog, Oscar, and his father took him out back and shot him."

"Oscar, the dog," Nicole explained to Pamela as she took the book out of my hands. "The father shot the dog, not Junior. Curtis would read this to us just so he could say words like '*breast*,' or '*wuss*,' or '*bastard*' out loud." Everyone giggled, and the giggling turned into laughter as the girls relaxed and repeated more of the unsavory words from the book.

I clicked the bin's lid shut as the laughter washed over me, softening my tense muscles. To see the girls laughing and tossing the book back and forth so each could read different parts in Curtis's innocent voice brought a lightness to my breathing. Maybe our family would be okay after all.

No one rushed their attention to the personal mementos from the bedside table drawer I had dumped atop the bare mattress. Awaiting their final destinations were souvenir shark's tooth necklaces from different Florida vacations and several wristbands from county fairs, the boardwalk arcade, and a *Marvel Heroes on Ice* show.

I picked up a silver chain with a Saint Sebastian charm. Curtis wore it to every baseball game and practice. I kissed it, slid it over my head, and whispered into the V of my shirt, "I hope you're looking after my athlete now."

Heather stepped forward and picked up Doggie. "Mom, would you mind if I keep him?"

"Not at all. You two can keep anything you'd like," I said. Panic seeped into my voice as I looked over Curtis's packed-up favorite items. "Maybe I should just store everything up in the attic. We don't need to give his things away. We can donate his clothes and put everything else up in the attic. It'll be safe up there." I sat on my hands so I couldn't gather all the items and never let go.

Pamela stroked my hair, allowing me to take in a deep breath. But I knew what she was going to say because I had told her if I got to this point to stop me. "Jules, if you put it all in the attic, you will still one day have to go through it, and it will hurt the same all over again. You plan to let other kids enjoy Curtis's things now. I'll take whatever you'd like to wherever you want. Just tell me."

I didn't want to let go of any of it. Saying I wanted other kids to enjoy Curtis's books and games was a lie I told myself, a way to justify the unbearable actions of clearing out his room. But if I didn't clear out his bedroom, how could we move on? How would things be different if I didn't do this one thing that could reshape our future? I needed to show the girls we could move on as a family and that having too many of Curtis's things around would only slow us down.

"As kids," I said to the twins, "my brothers and sister and I were allowed only one box of items to take from our bedrooms each time we moved, so I never accumulated much. I had one doll, my Easy Bake Oven, and my sketch pad. That's pretty much what came with me from house to house. I never wanted you kids to have to throw anything away. That's why you all have way too much stuff."

"And that's why you're now a secret hoarder," Nicole said and slapped her thigh at her own wit. Heather agreed and pantomimed scooping up items and shoving them into her pockets.

"I am not." I feigned offense, having been called out, and patted my front pockets to prove they were empty.

Pamela cleared her throat. "On the outside, you're not a hoarder. Your kitchen counters are bare, your shelves have no knickknacks, and your towels are color-coded per bathroom. But God forbid I open a drawer or closet door. You hoard like a squirrel. Every drawer is a junk drawer, your closets are packed, and your garage and attic have everything from gum wrappers to anything you've ever owned even if it's broken."

I laughed because they were not wrong. It was the dichotomy that lived inside me. Moving around as my father served our country filled us with pride and patriotism, yet given the choice, I now contributed my honor and allegiance to my family behind a permanent white picket fence.

Go ahead," Pamela urged. "Go ahead and finish what you were saying."

I thought for a second before I continued and slid down next to Roger, who insisted on spreading out and resting in the middle of the room. "What I was trying to say was that I had to move around a lot. We were never allowed a pet. We could never commit to a club or a team. And with my siblings being so much older than me, they left for college and left behind their empty room. As long as I lived in that particular house with their empty room, I expected them to return."

"And Curtis isn't going to return," Heather said with an adversarial stare. "Is that what you can't say out loud, Mom? Curtis is not going to return."

Flinching, I stepped back and tripped over Roger before sinking onto the bed. What did she want from me? I couldn't change the facts. I was trying to help them. I was trying to get us all on the right track. Pamela sat next to me and challenged Heather to back down with a simple nod of her head.

"Can I have this, Mom?" Nicole sliced through the tension as she slid the MVP medal off the trophy and wrapped the red, white, and blue ribbon around the book she had yet to put down.

"Yes. Anything. Keep anything and everything you want," I said and packed up the Legos, a Game Boy, and a pile of *Sports Illustrated Kids* magazines, acting as if I was happy to do so.

"What about Dad?" Heather asked, her voice less challenging, less hateful.

"I'm sure if he wanted something, he would have already taken it," I said, although I was not sure of that at all. But if Michael wanted something to remember his son by, he should have been here to help. He made his choice. His presence today—well, any day lately—would have shown the girls that the Scotts were still a family. If Michael couldn't accept that, how could the girls?

"Maybe he'd like these," Heather tucked Curtis's baseball glove with the signed game ball under her arm and walked away from what used to be Curtis's bedroom into her own.

Pamela followed Heather to her room directly across the hall. She stuck her foot out and stopped Heather from shutting the bedroom door. "You girls grab a bag or a box and put it by the front door. I'll drop them off wherever your mother wants me to on my way home."

I counted the four bins and five bags of Curtis's belongings and puffed my chest the tiniest bit, seeing how much my own child managed to accumulate and enjoy. I squeezed the St. Sebastian charm through my shirt, counting on his help with getting my family all on the same page. Eventually. With a little bit of luck.

"I got this bin. It'll go to Goodwill," I said, hinting for the girls to bring a bag downstairs.

"I'll get this," the always accommodating Nicole answered and picked up the heaviest bin.

"Heather?" I called to her across the hall. My patience thinned, but my heart knew better than to respond to her hostility. I braced for her antagonism.

"What?" Heather approached her doorway, still clinging onto Curtis's Doggie.

"You'll go with us to bring Curtis's things?" I asked, trying not to make it a command.

"You do what you need to do, Mom. I'm all set." She retreated coolly back into her room.

I leaned in her doorway, not daring to step into Heather's territory. "All set? What does that mean? All set."

"It means you do what you need to do for you. I'm all set. I don't need to see where Curtis's things end up."

"Well, you can help us bring the stuff downstairs," Pamela said, leaving the bin she was carrying in Heather's doorway.

In a less-somber mood than when we ascended, the four of us paraded down the seldom used front staircase and dropped the bins and bags by the front door. After two more trips each, Nicole and Heather landed on the couch in the den, feet up on the coffee table, and phones in hands. I embraced this moment of everydayness and prayed there'd be many more balanced days to come.

Chapter 5

With the bins and bags piled at the front door, I dropped into the oversized chair across from the girls, waiting for our phoned-in lunch to be delivered. "I guess that wasn't too bad. I thought clearing out Curtis's room would be the hard part, but I think the hard part is what's coming next."

"I told you I will take everything to Goodwill if you don't want to," Pamela said.

"I was referring to turning Curtis's room into something other than Curtis's room. That's going to be the hard part."

"Only because it's not done yet," Pamela said, always making the best of everything. The doorbell rang, and Pamela pulled me to my feet. "Chinese feast!"

"Come and get it." Pamela whisked past the slouching girls, tempting them with the Chinese aromatics wafting from brown paper bags. I dug through the pantry and pulled out a stack of paper plates with pumpkins and turkeys printed on them from last Thanksgiving, a package of red, white, and blue napkins from Fourth of July, and a box of sparkling silver plasticware from our New Year's Eve party.

"Let the de-hoarding begin." Pamela winked at me. Pamela handed each of the girls a paper plate. "Why aren't one of you girls clamoring to get your own room?"

I interjected quickly, "We talked about it. I thought it would be a great idea. Then when you two go to Del Tech or somewhere else local, you'll each have your own space."

Heather and Nicole simultaneously glanced at each other, shook their heads, then scooped lo mein and sweet and sour chicken onto their plates.

"Mom, I told you. I want to apply to NYIP," Nicole said.

Heather gave Nicole a quick wink and pointer finger. "Good one."

"It's not a joke. I'm applying there no matter what anyone says. NYIP is the best there is, and if I can get in, I'm going."

"Okay, I give," said Pamela. "What's NYIP?"

"New York Institute of Photography," answered Nicole. "And I want to go there for college."

"Not the time nor the place, Nicole." I didn't mean to start a heated conversation about college applications. I couldn't bare their empty room if they went far away to school. They'd find faraway boyfriends, then faraway summer jobs, and faraway apartments just like my siblings had done when I was younger. I just couldn't go there.

"Pam, we can't fit all those bins and bags in your car," I said. "Let's just throw them into my van, and the girls will help me deliver them."

Nicole, Heather, and Pamela glanced at each other, but no one negated my suggestion.

During the rest of lunch, the girls gossiped about who was going to the high school fall dance with whom and, more importantly, who wasn't going with whom. As Pamela chatted with the girls, I played with the food I had dug out of the cartons. I shifted in my chair and placed my fork on my plate, my appetite lost. My hands and feet grew cold as fear of the next step took over. Turning Curtis's room into an office for Michael was like creating a forest for a polar bear. But I didn't care. I just needed Curtis's bedroom to be anything but Curtis's room waiting for his return.

The girls stretched out on the couch again and searched Netflix for a movie. While Pamela closed up the Chinese takeout containers and stored them for later snacking, I took Roger out back and tossed a tennis ball for him to retrieve. With each toss, I had a new thought. I hoped I was doing the right thing. Would Michael get onboard with his new office? How long would it take to establish our new normal? Why Curtis? When my toss became a missile, and Roger sat by the door not wanting to play anymore, I was ready to enter the house for phase two.

Pamela and I returned upstairs to convert the now barren bedroom. "Let's call it a guest room with a desk," she joked when I mentioned my doubt of Michael's usage of the room.

I had bought a comforter with navy-blue and white stripes and solid navy-blue sheets to turn the young boy's twin bed into an occasionally used, if at all, guest bed. Plus, I purchased the coordinating navy, gold, and white striped curtains. I hoped Michael liked the idea of a more-adult office. It was part white flag, part olive branch.

"Now that we're alone, I gotta ask, what is Michael doing with Jeff today?" I wrapped the brand-new fitted sheet around the corner of the mattress.

"I really don't know. But he shouldn't have given you a hard time about not making pancakes this morning. That was just heartless," she said, shaking her head and raising her eyebrows.

"Was Jeff even home when you left?" I stuffed a pillow into its case. I refused to waste one tear today on Michael. I lobbed the pillow across the room. How could he not be here with his girls? He used to be the ultimate family man, and now a person would wonder if he knew he even had a family.

"Jeff helped me put the bins in my car. He said something about going to the club to watch a college football game."

"That's it." I stomped over and scooped up the pillow. I fluffed it back into shape and tossed it to Pamela with a sigh. "I don't want to put your husband in the middle, but Michael always uses Jeff as an excuse not to be here."

She sat next to me on the bed. "What a little shit. I'll talk to Jeff. Michael can't keep acting like Curtis is out on a long camping trip and will be home in a week. Do you want me to say something to Michael? You know I will."

"No. Please don't. The therapist said for me to allow everyone to grieve in their own way and in their own time."

"And yet here we are trying to move things along," Pamela said, giving a nod to the pile of bins and bags by the front door.

"That's different," I said, tired of having to defend my actions. If Michael couldn't get over Curtis's death, would we ever be a family again? "Something has to change. She also feels as if Michael's dealing with survivor's guilt. Why Curtis and not him? The problem is, how can we move on if Michael can't? Or won't? I can't wallow any longer. And I'm sure Curtis wouldn't want us to. I'm hoping this will instigate all of us moving forward."

"Shit. Julie, you and the girls have taken a healthy approach in dealing with Curtis's death. You immediately went into therapy. You went above and beyond when you reached out to Curtis's classmates and baseball team. Hell, you've helped the whole damn town deal with it. If Michael doesn't want to be helped, then you can't help him." Pamela shoved the bed toward the window with me still on it.

"I'm not sure his attitude is totally because of Curtis."

"What do you mean?"

"We were having issues before Curtis. Well, I was anyway. Michael and I were growing apart. Parallel lives, like roommates. And now he's using Curtis's death as an excuse to separate himself from me and the girls. Part of me pities him. His life was work, work, work until Curtis came along. Then he found his mini me and taught him all he knew about soccer and baseball. And now he doesn't know what to do with the extra time on his hands."

"Um…he does have two daughters," Pamela said. "Michael's a grown man. He makes grown-man choices. Don't you dare feel sorry for him. He'll work it out. Come on. Let's finish making the bed."

"Pity's the wrong word," I said. "Maybe I'm just sad that Michael and I can't face our feelings together, support each other." The old Michael and I used to share everything. He had been my very best friend since high school, along with Pamela. She was the crazy ring-leader, and Chad, the dissenter of our party of four and my boyfriend at the time, pretty much went along with whatever I wanted. The four of us always got along. We did everything together, and I never considered anything or made any decision without their input. "I miss the days when Michael was the logical one, always practical." And now, here I was with my wise-ass friend being the logical one.

I smiled at the memories but couldn't shake how much we all had grown and changed. "I'm sad for Michael because he lost his best friend when he lost Curtis."

Pamela and I made the bed then centered it under the window. I arranged the pillows like my interior designer friend, Alicia, taught me—fluff, place, karate chop. I stood back, taking in the vignette.

"The bed's perfect under the window. I just need a couple more pillows to make it look more like a day bed."

"I have some gold and navy pillows at home. A couple different prints to go with those stripes. I'll bring them by tomorrow," volunteered Pamela, then out of the corner of her mouth said, "Not that I want to share my pillows with Michael."

"Not to worry. I don't know that he'll ever step foot in here." I grunted as I attempted to move the desk away from the wall and into the middle of the room. I dragged in the worn navy-blue rug with gold nautical knots from the hallway alcove and scooted a floor lamp next to the desk.

"Need any help, superwoman?" Pamela grabbed a corner of the desk I was trying to wriggle into place.

"Yes, thanks. Lift and rotate."

The desk ended up in the middle of the room, facing the day-bed and the window behind it. I rolled the desk chair behind it, and Pamela sat, crossed her feet atop the desk, and clasped her hands behind her neck, bumping the wall behind her.

"This will work just fine," Pamela said two octaves lower than normal. "But where's the TV?"

"Ha. Ha," I said and left to retrieve some of Michael's books from our bedroom.

"Pamela, could you go get the rest of the books I left on my bed?" I asked as I lined the books I had brought back with me on top of the dresser.

"Do you want me to move Michael's clothes in here too?" Pamela semi-joked on her way out.

As Pamela arranged the rest of the books on the shelves above the dresser, I dragged an old gray linen armchair from the now-empty alcove. The once light-blue superhero room had matured into a nautical themed office.

"And I won't be too embarrassed if a guest has to sleep here," I said, proud of our day's work. It was hard keeping my heart at bay and my head moving forward, but it was time.

"Put a TV in here, and with a little luck, maybe Michael will move in," Pamela added one more jab.

I laughed, but that was the last thing I wanted. I wouldn't care if he did put a TV in here. I just prayed he'd like the room and hoped he'd be comforted that it used to be Curtis's. But somehow, I felt it would do just the opposite.

"Go on down with the girls. I'll be right there," I said to Pamela, knowing she'd understand that I wanted to be alone one last time before Michael took over.

As I leaned on the corner of the desk, I pulled out the St. Sebastian charm and kissed it. "I love you more than all the M&Ms in the world, Curtis, and I always will."

Hoping karma was done with me, I went downstairs and anchored myself to the front door threshold as Nicole and Pamela carried Curtis's possessions down the driveway and farther from our home, stabbing at my heart. I was helpless as I leaned in the open doorway and watched as they walked back and forth, carrying Curtis's items to my old, well-used family van, the only car Curtis had ever seen me drive. We had bought it used the year I was pregnant with him so that we could fit all five of us. Added bonus, I could deliver my own art pieces. Michael had offered several times to buy me a new van, but I never saw the need.

Pamela placed the final bin in the back and, like a period on the end of a sentence, slammed the back hatch shut. The end.

I bolted outside. "Okay. Goodbye. Love you, girl." I wrapped my arms around her. "Thanks for your help. I couldn't have done this without you. I've got it from here."

"You okay?" Pamela's brows furrowed, but I just wanted her to leave.

"Just tired." I could feel the panic rising, and I clenched my fist so I wouldn't physically help her into her car.

"I can go with you."

"No worries. You've done enough," I said then called out to the girls. "Nicole, Heather, Pamela's leaving. Give her a hug," I said and hugged Pamela again. The deep pressure of her bear hug momentarily calmed my strained nerves. "Really, thanks for your help."

Heather never appeared for our farewells, and after Nicole retreated into the house, I waved until Pamela backed out of the driveway. I just wanted to sit alone with Curtis's things for a little bit. His treasured belongings were never supposed to have to leave this house. They were supposed to collect dust in the back of his closet, forgotten as he replaced them with cherished new teen items like electronic games, joysticks, and a guitar.

I squeezed the latch to the back of the van and stepped back, expecting it to pop open. I pulled on the trunk handle again. Nothing. I ran to the driver's door and pulled on the handle. Pop. A purple fingernail whizzed by and landed on the cement driveway.

I pounded on the window with both fists and exhaled. If I was going to take Curtis's things to Goodwill, I needed to do it now. Every moment delayed, with his items in limbo, was another moment I delayed beginning my recovery of his loss all over again.

I rested my head on the window, and the car keys sparkled, winking at me from the middle of the driver's seat. Heat emanated from my ears as I released my vexation and kicked the tire. I muffled a groan with tight lips.

"Screw you," I yelled in defeat and kicked the tire again, punishing the van one more time.

I leaned heavily against the ramshakled car. Curses seeped through my gritting teeth until tiny bubbles rose from my gut, dismantling my anger.

The tight grip on my heart released, and in my exhaustion, I tipped my head back and laughed at the sky as I ran around the van, trying to open each door one more time. Yes. They were all locked. This had to be a sign that I was supposed to keep all of Curtis's things.

I ran into the house and dug through the junk drawer in search of the spare key. I listened for the girls—nothing, no TV, no talking, no arguing. A bit suspicious, but I took advantage of the quietude and ran back to the driveway.

I unlocked the van and looked around. My nosey neighbor, Mrs. Amberly, was not in her rocking chair for once. I scanned the windows of houses up and down the street for anyone peering out, including my own, for anyone who would dare stop me from bringing every bit of Curtis's belongings up to our attic for safekeeping.

Chapter 6

Sleep eluded me for most of the night as I stared at the ceiling separating me from Curtis's belongings. What did it hurt to save everything upstairs in no one's way? Then again, it was silly not to bring at least his clothes to Goodwill. But what was the rush? Maybe I'd donate his games and books near Christmastime when it would feel more joyful.

I opened the two adjacent windows in my studio, appreciating the warm morning cross breeze, and took a moment to rub my temples, uncoiling my anxiety and brain fog from lack of sleep. When I pushed off my toes to sit on my stool, a moan escaped, and I switched to massaging my tight calves fussing from my many treks up and down the stairs yesterday.

I leaned on the window frame, pulling my ankle to my rear end. Across the street, Mrs. Amberley sat alone on her front porch, yet it looked like she was talking to someone. I thought about going over and thanking her again for all she had done for our family when she had organized neighborhood meals and helped with our lawn care after Curtis's death. But the thought of walking down the steps and all the way across the street to her home overwhelmed me and my sore legs, so I decided to stay put and stretch my other leg. Stretching my legs felt good, and it reminded me to sign up for yoga—something I knew I needed to do but never quite found the time. If the girls wanted to practice yoga, I'd be banging down the door to sign them up. Maybe I'd ask them to do it with me. We could do it together, but the tickle in my tummy suggested that it wouldn't be such a good idea. I'd just be setting myself up for disappointment.

Shaking my head to rid my brain of random thoughts, I addressed my studio. The house felt different today, as if it changed purpose, comfortable but not as welcoming. The soul of our family changed the moment Curtis passed, but the soul of the house changed today.

I fell in love with this old worn-out house when I realized what a perfect family home it could be. We bought the center entrance colonial knowing it would be our forever dream home. A home our kids would grow up in and never want to leave until they bought their own home down the street in the same neighborhood so we could always have Saturday breakfast or Sunday dinners together. I never wanted my children to have to leave their childhood home, school, and friends the way I had. Michael knew it was vital for me to create a forever home for our family. He worked long hours so we could afford the renovations, and he gave me the green light to do as I wished. We were young back then, and the future was all so bright.

Closing my eyes, I fought to hold on to the feelings of yesterday when things were simple, and we were fearless. But then, the accident happened. We lost Curtis, then Michael lost faith in me. How could he ever forgive me when I could hardly forgive myself?

Goosebumps raised as the window sheers rippled across my arm, caressing me. A titter of Curtis's laughter echoed in my brain.

I so wished I had a recording of his deep belly laugh and his snort of a giggle. As the refreshing breeze, as well as my goosebumps, dissipated, I became lost in images of the past countless months.

The first several months without Curtis, the four of us followed the same path—silence and avoidance. Still shocked, none of us wanted to believe Curtis was no longer with us. Next, it was like each took personal inventory, reassessing how to live in our new world with our new pain. And me with my new guilt. Then everyone chose a different direction. Michael stayed on reassessing the accident, with me anchoring his anger. Heather rebelled, testing me and the world, daring it to fill the hole in her heart. Nicole hid her depression with the need to protect the rest of us. And me, the only way I could survive was to ignore the pain and guilt or at least learn to live with it and feign acceptance. Someone had to bring our paths back around to each other so we could be a family once again. I had to believe we all wanted it, but I knew some of the journeys were going to take longer than others.

The fresh air picked up again and whispered Curtis's name in my ear. Maybe Curtis will help me get through this. I rubbed the St. Sebastian charm through my T-shirt.

"Please, help your sisters and father too," I whispered back to him.

I returned to my easel at ten hundred hours—as my father would say—when the sunlight perfectly lit the hues of my painting. The cool breeze and warm morning sun lifted my spirits and brought back my gratitude. For years, I kept my fingers crossed, hoping one of the twins wouldn't want a room of her own as she grew older. I would have had to give up the studio. Thankfully, the girls never felt the need to separate. I always appreciated having my own private, spacious, well-lit studio—until Michael said he should have his own office since I had a room for my "hobby." My studio lost a bit of appeal when guilt took over the space.

Just as I began to add highlights to my current painting, an argument escalated between the twins. I was having none of it. I pushed open their bedroom door just as Heather threw a book at her sister.

"This has to stop," I screamed like a banshee, my fingers clenching the hair on top of my head.

The girls froze, Heather in midstance and Nicole squatting behind her desk chair. I even stunned myself. I should be grateful they were even talking to each other. They'd had a few long months when not one word was shared between them. The girls used to be as close as twins could be, but lately, they disagreed a lot. I had long since learned to stay out of their arguments, let alone raise my voice to such a level. Yet their lack of consideration for the people within earshot required reckoning.

I signaled for the girls to sit on the edge of Heather's bed. I was the boss, and it was getting a bit old to have to keep reminding them. "You both are in for the weekend. Don't even ask me to go for a walk."

Neither girl moved a muscle. I stomped back to my studio and slammed the door, more disappointed in myself for losing my temper than angry at the girls for quarreling. Now I was stuck with them for a weekend filled with whining and pouting, punishing myself more than them.

I groaned at my selfishness and reminded myself I was a better person than that. But I hadn't the strength to step out of my indifference. I had developed a pretense of patience lately, but the real thing had been all but nonexistent. A person would think I would appreciate the girls bickering over not having them around at all. I would do my best to contain myself until school started back in a couple of days. Between the twins' after-school activities, jobs, and looking into local colleges, their senior year would be over before I knew it.

Hiking my hip onto my stool, I grabbed a paintbrush to finish the last touches on my commissioned piece named Peach Blossoms. I just needed forty-five more minutes of morning light to finish this painting. Forty-five minutes with no interruptions.

From somewhere in the distance, my phone rang. "Crap," I said, never wanting to miss another phone call. My pulse raced even though I knew the girls were safe in their bedroom, but Michael had left early in the morning before we even woke up. I prayed he was safe. I listened harder as I left the studio in a half run, following the sound of the ring.

I lunged and grabbed my cell phone off the nightstand then flopped back onto my previously wrinkle-free bed. "Hello?"

My head rolled to the left. Michael's dirty socks and T-shirt were in a heap, near—but not in—the clothes hamper. It used to be cute, my messy husband out earning the bacon for his family, and I didn't mind picking up after him. Now I felt like he left a mess on purpose so I would earn my keep. Or maybe that was my guilt talking. Frustrated, I turned over and faced an unwelcoming stack of half-read magazines spread on the floor next to Michael's nightstand. Inhaling to stay unnerved by the mess, I sat up to a full view of the left-up toilet seat.

I exhaled into the phone. "Pamela?"

"What's wrong?"

"Nothing. You called me." I sighed.

"But I can tell something's wrong." Pamela waited for an answer.

I took the silence as a cue I might as well tell her what was on my mind, or she'd just keep bugging me. "Michael's a slob, and I just broke up another fight between the girls. They seem to be fighting all the time now." I rubbed my temples again. "I can't even focus on painting anymore, which used to be my one saving grace, the one thing I could get lost in to get away from everything else. It's as if every little thing is adding to a runaway snowball."

"Michael's always been a slob, and the girls will be back in school soon enough. But either way, you need to get out of the house. Get a job or volunteer somewhere. You're doing everything you can for your girls. Maybe even too much."

"Don't start with that." I grimaced. "You sound like Michael." I lowered my voice an octave and mimicked, "'You do too much for the girls. Just because your mother did nothing to support you as a kid doesn't mean the polar opposite is the correct thing to do for our kids. Find a happy medium.'"

"Well, don't listen to him, except for the part about finding a happy medium. The twins are going to be out of the house soon enough. You need to start thinking about yourself."

"Pamela, I didn't think I'd be alone in the house with Michael for at least six more years. Now I'm thrown into this soon-to-be-empty nest. I'm not ready."

"I know, honey. Think about what you have, not what you don't have. Maybe once the girls are out of the house, you and Michael will remember why you got married in the first place."

"Ha. I'll have to do a little digging for that." I traced the center medallion on the cream matelassé bedcover. I didn't mean that. I remember exactly why I married Michael. He understood my need for stability. As my best friend, he knew I wanted to raise my family with roots in one place, something Chad would never have been able to give me once he joined the Navy. And luckily, Michael and my friendship, steeped with the same philosophies and values, turned into love for each other. I did love Michael, but I was afraid he'd lost his love for me.

"Promise you'll think about volunteering once school starts back up. I know the hospital is always looking for volunteers. I'm sure I could…"

As I half-listened to Pamela, I rolled over and buried my face into my pillow. I couldn't think of someday in the future. I couldn't even plan today. It was the end of summer, and the girls would be going back to school soon. I needed to plan the Labor Day cookout which I held every summer on the last day before school started, which was the day after tomorrow. Last year, Michael grilled, and the girls came down to eat burgers in silence. We kept the tradition, but then again, we didn't. There were no guests, no music, no games. I thought this year might be different. I had brought up having a version of the cookout again, with other people, a couple of times with not even a nod for a response from either of the twins. Was it that they wouldn't miss the thirteen-year tradition, or was it they just assumed it was going to happen? We had gotten through Mike's yearly March Madness birthday party, something Curtis and Mike used to go all out for, by Mike leaving the house by himself and watching the games with Jeffery at his club. Then he came home to a whipped cream frosted angel food cake the girls had made for him. He had hardly thanked them.

We all together skipped our annual spring-break trips and our Florida summer vacation weeks that always took place between spring baseball championships and summer ball. This past spring, we had cancelled our annual reservations for Mother's Day and Father's Day. Neither Mike nor I desired to go out for dinner, but the girls cooked a meal for us—well, ordered our dinners—and we observed the holidays at home. I wished it was written somewhere how and when to evolve into normalcy. With a little luck, the new school year would be the perfect time to start over.

But no. I was too exhausted. The cookout took a lot of work, and I hadn't even grocery shopped for it. So, no. If they wanted the cookout, they could ask for it.

"Julie? Are you there?" Pamela asked.

"Yes, sorry." I put thoughts of the barbeque out of my head for the time being. "I'm sure you didn't call to hear me bellyache. Again.

Why did you actually call?" I got up and smoothed the wrinkles I created in the bed cover.

"I'm meeting some friends at the club next Thursday. It's Iris's birthday. Remember her? You've met before. Anyway, I'd like you to come with me. I need to discuss the fundraiser."

Pamela could drive me to drink. What she really wanted was for me to be her back up when she tried to garner big-ticket items for the fundraiser she ran every year. We'd played this dog and pony show before. She stroked her wealthy and competitive type-A friends' egos and got them to up the value of their donations by starting with one of my paintings, which she swore would bring in well over five thousand dollars. Then she would wait and watch the women compete among themselves—not to be outdone. Each wanted to be the highest donator. Actually, her plan was genius.

"Come on. We'll have a blast. In fact, you've met a few of them before. You can turn on your charm and fit right in," Pamela said.

Maybe I didn't want to fit right in. Perhaps I didn't give two hoots about Pamela's country club friends or her fundraiser. Maybe I did have something better to do than be Pamela's sidekick for the day. Ye of such little faith.

Usually, my social life consisted of avoiding supercompetitive mothers at the kid's activities. I had only so much time, money, and energy—and nice outfits, for that matter—and I coveted spending them on friends and family, not with people I didn't know.

What was Pamela thinking? She knew I didn't even go to office dinner parties with Michael if I didn't have to. "I'm really behind on my painting." I threw the words out, knowing they wouldn't fly.

"Jules, that's not going to cut it." Pamela's smirk came through the phone loud and clear.

Yup. I'd end up going to Pamela's luncheon because we both knew I had nothing better to do. Maybe it would be fine going out with women who knew nothing about me. I wouldn't care if they judged me.

Not even a minute after I hung up, Pamela texted, "And go out and buy yourself a cute dress. I don't want you wearing any of your comfy athleisure wear or baggy, artsy linens. Love ya! Ciao."

I snickered. Pamela never let up. She knew I only owned baggy, artsy linen and yoga clothes. She teased me constantly, claiming I was the only person in the world who owned enough yoga outfits to fill a warehouse yet didn't do any yoga. I defended my choices. I enjoyed painting and housecleaning in comfy clothing. Not to mention grocery-shopping and driving the kids all over town. Plus, I genuinely did want to take up yoga. One day. If I could find the time.

I kicked some of Michael's magazines under the bed on my way back to my studio. I'd always gone for comfort over fashion, and Pamela knew it, but recently it was just one more thing added to my failure bucket. Would it make a huge difference in my life if I began wearing Betsy Johnson or Ralph Lauren? Would Michael even notice?

Chapter 7

I returned to my easel for the third time that morning, very conscious of my tight yoga pants and oversized T-shirt, and stood back from the painting in front of me. I lost the impetus to paint due to the girl's interruptions and Pamela's call, but as I absorbed the image in front of me, I felt it was complete. My focus of late was minimal and limited by my desire to fix Michael. I wiped my brush on a cloth and took a sip of diet cola, which was now warm and flat, a sure sign I should quit the stuff, again—but I won't.

Like everything else in my life, I went back and forth about creating art for commission. I wished I could paint just for myself, then if Alicia wanted to buy my art for her clients, great. If not...so what? Maybe I could sign up for some of the local art festivals. But I didn't have the luxury to buy paints and canvases and not be guaranteed return on my money. I couldn't afford "if nots." I was blessed to have Alicia paying for my art. It nudged me to keep painting, and I'd be lost without my creative outlet. I believed she knew that from the moment we met.

Alicia Benitez lit up a room anywhere she went with her generous smile and rich brunette Latina curls. She offered a refreshing break from all the bottle blondes around town, and unlike those bottled blondes, Alicia was a great car-pool partner. She'd been my only other close friend ever since her daughter Lizbeth, Liz, met my daughters at the local park when they were five years old. She was thrilled to gain two friends at once.

My first commissioned piece for Alicia's interior design clients was a six-by-six-foot modern landscape in acrylic. Aquamarine, salmon, and white weren't the most natural colors to work with, but those were the colors requested. Alicia's client loved my rendition of an abstract, color-blocked beach scene, and the rest was history. After forty-plus commissioned art pieces over the last twelve years, my heartfelt personal diversion had become an almost dreaded daily job.

This particular piece of art looming in front of me, commissioned through Alicia by a local banker who happened to see one of my paintings on her friend's living room wall, was to be the permanent floral arrangement in her office. The dark thick branches and the delicate pinkish flowers contrasted. Male/female. Yin/yang.

Ugh, my lack of concentration, my ease of being distracted, and reminiscing time away depressed me. I used to pride myself on my ability to uni-task. I multitasked all the time. But I loved doing one thing, doing it with my whole being, and then being done with it—feeling accomplished.

I dipped the tip of my brush into burnt umber acrylic paint, my standard signature color. I leaned back to view my work one last time before signing it over. Melancholy used to take over every time I signed my completed artwork. I used to think of it like signing away a baby. But actually, there was no comparison. As I signed the lower left-hand corner, I easily made my peace with delivering the painting in a couple of weeks, per my contract.

I switched my thoughts from art to my list of chores for today. As I trudged downstairs, thoughts of scrubbing bathrooms, readying the laundry for back to school next week, and preparing today's meals weighed me down. The more I thought about my dutiful penance, the heavier my legs became as I passed by Michael in the den, feet up and newspaper held at shoulder height, TV babbling sports information.

What if I lounged all day and caught up with magazines like my mother used to do? How accomplished would I feel? Assuming the goal was to decrease the number of magazines in a pile, I'd win. But would it fulfill me? Absolutely not. If Michael's goal was to gather statistics for no reason other than to have something to discuss with the guys around the watercooler, then I felt sorry for him. Was this his priority in life now that he no longer devoted his spare time to Curtis's extracurricular activities?

I sat at the kitchen table and attacked the laundry like a soldier on a mission, making sure all the girls' new school clothes were ready to wear, but my mind continued to wander. Weekends used to be family time. How could he turn that off? Was he not comforted, as I was, by the four walls of our kitchen, the kitchen we devoted our hearts to, knowing it would be the center of our family's forever home? He used to sit at the kitchen table and chop veggies or whatever I needed while I cooked in preparation for the week ahead. I wanted to go back to then, when we were invincible after getting married and buying our house. We knew exactly what we wanted and were determined to make it happen.

I called Heather and Nicole down to help with the laundry and to ask them about the end of the summer picnic. Should I bother to hold it? Maybe now would be the time to change traditions.

Nicole arrived, having taken the steps two by two. I gave in and asked, "Do you girls want to have our Labor Day cookout?"

"I don't care," Heather said and passed in stealth behind her sister then poked her head around the corner to ask her father if he would take them out to practice driving.

"Not today, hon," he said without taking his eyes off the page in front of him.

"But, Dad, this is the only time I have to practice this weekend."

"Ask your mom."

Heather trudged up the stairs, whining about no one willing to teach her how to drive without even asking me.

"Hey," I called. "Come back here and take a pile of clothes up." She huffed down the stairs, returning for her pile.

"Does everyone want to have the end-of-the-year picnic? Girls? Michael?"

Heather grabbed a pile of her clothes off the table.

"If you want to," Nicole said.

"We gotta eat," Michael responded.

"Want me to take you driving?" I asked Heather before the girls left the kitchen with their piles. I wanted her to know that if she had asked me, I would have found the time.

Heather rolled her eyes as if I told a corny joke, then turned and stomped back upstairs.

Fine. I didn't need them driving anyway or borrowing my car. I could drive them wherever they needed to go. In fact, I enjoyed driving them. Ever since they deemed themselves too old for the bus, it was practically the only time I had with them as a captive audience.

Upstairs Heather's complaining turned into an argument with Nicole. They were at it again. How could they not know just how much they would miss each other if they didn't have one another? Their grief for Curtis concealed the love and camaraderie they held for each other. And I was the last person they would want to point it out.

Had I gotten an answer about the cookout? Miffed, I quit folding laundry and leaned back in my chair. The baseball announcer in the background brought me to the many nights of stretching the grocery budget for takeout meals while watching the Baltimore Orioles. We ate sitting cross-legged on the floor as the twins crawled around us. Michael worked overtime and took on a weekend job at the golf club to accrue the budget for new cabinets, countertops, and appliances. Some of my favorite memories were sitting in our bare-bones kitchen and dreaming of a large family, Michael's promotions, and our daughters' weddings.

Looking around the kitchen I had gutted myself, my heart sang. My children knew only one kitchen, one I had painted after stripping layers of wallpaper. I recovered the old chairs to set around this large oak dining table we bought from a neighbor for twenty dollars, where Sunday meals were rarely missed. And it was where I prepared our end of summer party for the last thirteen years. Defeated by happy memories from so long ago, I went to see if the girls wanted to go for a walk with Roger and me.

I brought a basket of more folded clean clothes up with me, an excuse to knock on the girls' door. I blinked to soften my eyes then put a smile on my face. I was determined to create a new happy memory. As I got to the top step, the girls' door was slightly opened, and I heard Heather say, "She's going crazy, you know."

I stopped short. My smile instantly faded. I leaned on the wall as the vibrations of her words jackhammered my heart into my gut.

"She's doing her best," Nicole responded. "Problem is, she doesn't know how controlling she is. Alicia says it's the only way she knows how to cope with Curtis's death. She's afraid to lose us."

Nicole talks to Alicia about me? I knew Heather talked to Pamela, but she was like an aunt to them. Even though Alicia was my other best friend, Nicole talking to Alicia about me invaded my privacy. I spoke with Alicia from my point of view. She was my champion. Where Pamela added humor and sarcasm to get her points across and often defending the twins, I depended on Alicia's unwavering positive advice. Couldn't I have anything to myself? The girls got my time, energy, and money. Do I have to share my friends too? The basket slid to the floor, and I stroked my throat as if air needed assistance getting down to my lungs.

"Lose us? She's going to drive me out of the house. I can't wait until I'm eighteen. I'm out of here," said Heather.

My vision wavered as if looking through water as Heather's words uprooted the hometown feeling of belonging I fought to create for my children.

"Give her a break. And Dad's not helping. He's totally shutoff," Nicole said as she neared the door.

I flattened my back against the wall as the abstract painting hanging on the wall in front of me broke into a million pieces. I squeezed my eyes shut, attempting to expunge the kaleidoscope view.

"Give Dad a break. At least we can leave in a couple of years without involving the court system." Heather laughed at her own joke.

Did they think Michael wanted to divorce me? Where would they get an idea like that? Did he say something?

"Not funny. You could make things a little easier for her, ya know," Nicole said.

"Why? She doesn't make anything easy for me," Heather said.

My fists tightened the more Heather spoke. With my view cleared, I took two steps forward, wanting, but not wanting, to hear more.

"You're impossible." The squeaks from Nicole's side of the room suggested that Nicole sat on her bed. At least she wasn't about to come out the door. And Heather better not, or I might have smacked her.

"I don't care anymore," Heather said. "Mom's out of hand. Her grip is so tight. I feel like I'm choking. I'm working as much as I can so I can move out of here as soon as possible."

My throat tightened as her words shocked me. I was choking my daughter? I was driving her out?

"You wouldn't," Nicole said. Her voice sounded as shocked as I felt.

"I most certainly will. You watch. I get it that you need to stick around so they'll pay for your college. But I don't want anything from them. I'm not going to college."

"They won't have to pay for anything if they don't let me go to school in New York," Nicole said.

"It'll never happen. Mom will never let you go that far away. How on earth could she control you?"

Nicole's silence frightened me. She didn't argue the point with Heather, as if she totally understood. My stomach dropped, and I couldn't listen to any more. I snuck into my studio, grabbed my earphones, then grabbed Roger and took him out.

I left the house, needing to find a spot to scream at the heavens. How was I the crazy one? I'd had my shit together for a while now. I was the one who wanted to move forward to a new normal so happiness and appreciation for each other could be part of our family story once again.

The air held an autumn breeze, but the late summer sun was bright and warm. I walked around our neighborhood for fifteen minutes. How could every one of my good intentions turn into a chokehold? What was I missing? My pillaged head ached from shaking back and forth with every "No. No. No." How could this be?

Roger led me down the main drag to our little downtown. I looped his leash around a bench outside the local coffee shop, The Daily Grind, and went in to order a diet soda.

After leaving Pamela a nonsensical message, something about being stuck in quicksand and someone needed to throw me a rope, I called Alicia, who said she'd be right there.

"Get in," Alicia said when she pulled up in front of the coffee shop.

Roger leaped into the back seat, and I handed Alicia a luke-warm coffee.

She pulled to the side of the coffee shop, parked, and lowered her convertible roof. "Tell me what happened."

As we sat and rehashed my morning, Alicia insisted that the words I overheard were typical teenager speak, my best was good enough, and I wasn't going crazy.

I shook my head. "You don't understand. I can't quite put it into words. I was here before, and well, I didn't want to be…" My thoughts wouldn't organize into coherent sentences. "The day Curtis died…that morning…I wanted to run away. I wanted to leave the monotony of my life just for the day. But then…"

Alicia leaned over and hugged me. "Honey, it's okay." Alicia patted my hand. "It's okay. Take a breath. Believe me, all mothers look for an out from time to time. It's normal," Alicia said, never one to let a life lesson pass by.

I took in a long breath and slumped back in the car seat. "But does unconditional love for my teenage children mean I have to accept feeling underappreciated and taken for granted?" How did keeping my family together become viewed as strangulation by the others? The pressure inside me gurgled as I listened to and agreed with all of Alicia's reassuring words and semi-valid justifications but knew they were only a tarp over a ticking bomb.

Once my rant was over and my frustration waned, I asked Alicia to drop me off at the front of my neighborhood. I needed more time to walk. I pulled out my phone, and it read 3:23 p.m. I was gone for nearly three hours, and not one person texted or called me, except Pamela, who was at the day spa and would call me when her nails dried. Her response to my desperate message convinced me she thought I was crying wolf. Everyone's lack of interest regarding my whereabouts proved my theory of out of sight, out of mind until they needed something from me.

As soon as my house came into sight, I stomped and pumped my fists like a two-year-old mid-tantrum. I wasn't as ready to go home as I thought. Anger and hurt simmered inside me like hot, molten lava. With three more winding laps around my neighborhood, my pain dissipated, defeating my anger, and my overriding guilt returned. I was their mother—unconditional love and all that.

Somehow, I needed to loosen my grip, a grip I didn't recognize as tight, just maternal, and become a better mom. I'd listen harder and figure out what they all expected from me. I could make this work. I would stay positive, so karma didn't have a chance to bite back as it did with Curtis. I would not lose my girls.

After considering my list of pros for the cookout: thirteen years and running, continue to shape our family values, create new lasting memories; and cons: Is doing the same thing year after year choking the girls by forcing them to attend? Does anyone care about lasting memories anymore? Should I be worried about our values when none of us are on the same page? It dawned on me, indecision fueled my stress.

Best to just do it. Admittedly, I'd be more wrong if I didn't have the cookout than if I did, even if no one showed up for it. I'd find out after the fact if it was the right choice or not. I would do it, but do it differently. Why not make pulled pork sandwiches instead of hamburgers and hotdogs? Grilled veggies instead of chips and dip? Pasta salad instead of homemade French fries? I had all night to prep for tomorrow's Labor Day cookout. I'd do it for the girls, but would they see it as our family tradition or a habitual chokehold?

If Curtis was here, and for some reason, we were having this dilemma, he'd say, "Who cares what the girls think?" and ask a hairbrained question like, "Can Jared and I do the grilling?" I so wish he were here to lighten my mood. But mostly, I wished I had yelled, "I love you," out the car window that morning.

Chapter 8

The day of...
Nineteen months earlier, 7:15 a.m. to 7:50 a.m.

A *heated discussion about which kid was bringing what to Mrs.*
Chamber's breakfast party volleyed between Heather and
Nicole in the back seat of the van as we rushed to get the pan-
cakes to school, if not warm, at least on time. I pulled into Curtis's best
friend Jared's driveway, and he couldn't get out of the tumultuous car fast
enough. My "Goodbye" got caught in the slamming door.

Eleven minutes later, I pulled up to the front of the high school. Tins
of pancakes, book bags, and long tresses flew out of the car before I even
shifted into park.

"Bye. We love you. Thanks, Mom. You're the best. Hope you have
a good day," I said to the rearview mirror framing the empty back seat.
I reached for my travel cup for a comforting sip of my morning mojo.
"Shit." My YETI still sat on the kitchen counter between the fridge and
the empty cola can. It was the last thing I did. How on earth did I forget
it?

I grabbed the steering wheel at ten and two and stared at the skin
stretching over my knuckles then squeezed my eyes shut.

Silence.

I should feel guilty for loving the quiet as much as I did.

My thoughts were already rushing to the hours ahead. Michael
would pick up Curtis and bring him to dinner between soccer practice
and his baseball game. The girls had afterschool activities, and I didn't
have to pick them up until 5:00 p.m., then we'd grab some fast food and
meet the boys at Curtis's game. I had all day to myself. I leaned my fore-
head onto the steering wheel as my brain put the three kids' itineraries
away until pickup time.

What was on my calendar for the day—if anything? I couldn't even
think which day of the week it was. Ah, Tuesday. Lunch with Pamela,

but first, since I was out, I'd go to the grocery store. I opened my eyes and stretched my arms overhead.

"Shit, shit, shit," I growled as I caught sight of my pink floral bathrobe.

I threw the car into gear and sped away before anyone saw me.

"Shit."

I wasn't sure if I was angrier that I hadn't realized I left the house in my floral robe or that not one person in my family was courteous enough to stop me, let alone allow me to drive them to school. I'm sure they'd have a good laugh, if they noticed me at all.

Chapter 9

Light violin music gathered tempo and volume as my alarm clock woke me up at 6:30 a.m. Today was the cookout, and I wanted it flawless. I slid out from under my covers, not wanting to wake Michael, lumbered into the bathroom, and threw on yesterday's linen pants. I'd shower later after I got everything set up.

I first mixed brown sugar, ketchup, and baked beans in a stoneware bean pot then added two slices of raw bacon on top before I set it in the oven. My mom used to say, "The longer in a low oven, the better the beans." Next, I heaved an eight-pound Boston butt out of the refrigerator and into my large cast iron skillet. I caramelized the floured sides, opened a can of stewed tomatoes, sliced a Vidalia onion, then threw it all into the crockpot.

At nine o'clock, two-and-a-half hours into cookout prep and cleanup, I ran upstairs to take a shower. Michael sat on the edge of the bed, towel drying his hair. My timing was perfect.

"What are you cooking? It smells delicious," he said. He threw on a T-shirt over his wet hair. "Is it for the cookout?"

"Thought I'd do something different. No hamburgers or hotdogs this year." I hoped changing up the food would add a twist to our tradition of old. "Is that okay with you?"

"Sure. Do whatever you want. I can always throw on a burger."

I shut and locked the bathroom door before I let out any curse. I still wasn't used to this new Michael. I should have realized Michael would do what Michael wanted to do.

Twenty minutes in a hot steamy shower didn't melt my rigid muscles or loosen my tight jaw. I wanted to be angry, but instead I was sad. I wanted things to be different, but they weren't. I threw on cropped leggings and a colorful tunic and went downstairs with begrudging positivity, my third attitude adjustment of the day.

As I flipped the Boston butt in the crockpot, Heather strolled into the kitchen in pajamas and a messy bun bobbing on top of her head. "Mom, I just got a text, and they need me to come into work today."

I wiped my hands on my apron, the front a spattered casualty of my attempt to keep this end-of-summer tradition alive. "Today? What about the cookout?" Echoes from yesterday's con list that no one really cared about the cookout rattled in my head with mocking laughter. "Can you tell them you can't work today?"

Nicole skipped down the stairs and past Heather. "I have to call Liz and Alicia. They asked me about the cookout yesterday, and I didn't know what to tell them." She pulled her phone out of her backpack.

"Why aren't you mad at Nicole?" Heather wanted to know. "She was just going to walk out the door?"

I turned to Nicole. "You were?"

"Just to the park to take some pictures." She turned away to talk on the phone. "For Photography Club."

"Wait. Aren't you both grounded?" I threw my hands in the air.

"It's just a damn cookout," Heather said. "The same one we have every year. I'm pretty sure I won't miss anything."

My jaw dropped. The same every year? Wasn't that what it was supposed to be? They were clueless. When I was younger, nothing was ever the same. Not my school, not my friends, not even the color of my room. Growing up in a different house, in a different neighborhood, in a different state every two years didn't allow for traditions to take hold. And here I was, fighting for that very thing.

As Heather turned to go upstairs, a flash of bright yellow and orange ascended the steps with her.

"What the hell is that?" I squelched. A black-and-white cloud partially covering a bright-yellow and orange sun on the back of Heather's neck nearly knocked the wind out of me. My girls weren't tattoo girls.

"What?" she asked, continuing to walk up the stairs.

"What is on your neck?" I took the stairs two at a time and met her on the second floor. How on earth could she say my grip was too tight when I never noticed a five-inch tattoo on my daughter's neck?

And didn't she need a parent with her if she wasn't eighteen? I swear, if Michael knew about this and didn't tell me…

Heather pulled the rubber band from around her bun and let her brown locks fall over her shoulder blades. "It's nothing."

I grabbed her arm. "When did you get that?" I spun her around and lifted her hair. The tattoo didn't look raw or new. The outlines were flat and smooth. She had had it for a while, and I never noticed.

"Too late to do anything about it now." She entered the bathroom and shut me out.

She had a point. There was nothing I could do about the tattoo. I would address it later, when things were calmer and we wouldn't have a house full of people in an hour or so. One thing at a time. I knocked on the door.

"I'll drive you to work. What time do we need to leave?"

"Don't worry. I've got a ride."

"I said I'll take you. In fact, you can drive. You said you need to add more supervised driving time for your permit." I stayed outside the bathroom door, still astounded over the tattoo. "Anyway, you're not getting in some kid's car. I have no problem taking you and picking you up." Why did I lie like that? It absolutely was a problem to drive her to work. I would be in the middle of a damn family cookout. I inhaled and tightly closed eyes. I'd made my bed; now I must lie in it. "What time do you need to leave?"

Heather opened the door, walked out of the bathroom, and into her room.

"In case you didn't hear me, I said I'll take you," I said one last time and left her in her bedroom, knowing she'd have to pass by me in the kitchen to go out.

I made it to the bottom of the stairs just as Michael waltzed in from the den, adding his two cents, "We should just get them a car. At least you wouldn't have to worry about her in some other kid's car."

I glared at him. Now he decided to interject parental wisdom? If he was not going to offer to take her, then he could just stay out of it. It wasn't as if the girls' needs were going to affect his schedule. Anyway, the twins didn't even have their licenses yet. Discussion closed.

"Did you know Heather had a tattoo?" I asked his back as he ransacked the pantry.

"Bye, Mom," Nicole said as she walked through the kitchen, again.

I spun around. "I thought you already left?" I felt like Elasti-Girl, limbs and thoughts pulled in all directions.

"Forgot my notebook. See ya," she said.

"But what about the cookout?" I headed toward the front door and called out to her as she flung her backpack over her shoulder. I heard the back door open, and I spun around again as Michael walked out. "Wait," I yelled.

"What?" Nicole said as she stepped back into the house holding the door wide open.

"Not you, your father." The back door shut with a click. "Oh, never mind. Where are you going?"

"I told you. To the park to take some pictures for photo club. Anyway, I didn't know you were having the cookout for sure 'til right now. I just called Liz. They're coming."

I had already called Alicia, my own friend, and invited her, thank you very much. "But we've always had the end of summer picnic on Labor Day before school started."

"You never said anything about it," she said.

I most certainly did mention it. When would they learn that I couldn't read their minds? We needed to communicate. My fear of their answers was why I didn't ask further questions, so I remained in my skewed world of maternal assumptions, my kaleidoscope of instinct and reason.

"We thought you didn't want to have it without Curtis."

My heart skipped a beat. "You guys never mentioned it, so I wasn't sure if you wanted to have it. And by the way, I did mention it."

"Well, you should have asked us." Heather said, skipping down the steps, headphones in place, cell phone in hand.

"I di—"

"Well, we are having it, so it's all good," Nicole said. "I'll be back in half an hour to help." The front door closing behind her snapped me back to Michael and Heather's tattoo.

"Wait right here," I told Heather. I went out the back door, but Michael was nowhere to be found.

Again, having to deal with teenage shenanigans by myself, I said, "I'm making your lunch. Then we can leave," I said to her back. I layered pulled pork, hot out of the crockpot, lettuce, tomato, and pickle slices on whole-grain bread and sealed it in a baggie. I rinsed an apple then tossed it in a paper bag with a bag of chips.

She stood, headphones in place, and thumbs scrambling. I was pretty sure her senior photos would be a great picture of the part down the center of her scalp. As I poured my diet cola into my travel YETI, she raced past me and out the front door.

"Wait." I grabbed her bagged lunch. "I said I'd take you." By the time I reached the driveway, Heather was nowhere in sight, and a black BMW was halfway down the street.

I stomped back into the house, threw her lunch on the counter, tearing the bag open, and the apple rolled into the sink. I just told her not to get into some kid's car. Why was it so difficult for kids to understand that parents were here for two things? To teach and to protect. I seemed to be failing at both.

Michael entered with an empty cooler and began placing beer in the bottom to be covered in ice.

I stared at him, miffed at how he meandered through life so unaware of the chaos around him.

"What's up?" he asked as he straightened a kink out of his back.

"Heather just took off in someone's car, and did you know she had a tattoo?"

"Let's not let Heather, who won't even be here, ruin our day. Okay?" He returned to his cooler and pulled it out the backdoor.

By the time I gathered my fourth wind, Pamela was already in the kitchen, tearing apart the tender Boston butt with two forks. "This pork is going to melt in our mouths. I'm ready for your delicious barbecue sauce."

"It's your recipe," I said and gave the brown sugar, ketchup, and special spices one last stir then drizzled it over the pulled pork.

"I haven't made it in ages," Pamela scooped and tossed until every mouthwatering piece of pork was drenched in sticky sweetness.

An hour later, Alicia and Liz arrived, bearing trays of Alicia's famous grilled shrimp and charred corn salsa. "Julie, you've outdone yourself once again. Everything looks so delicious," Alicia said. She placed mini tortillas on a paper plate for the shrimp taco appetizers.

The backdoor flew open as Michael raced in, hollering over his shoulder to Jeff out on the deck. "I'll be back before the second inning starts. You just watch."

He ran behind me and pulled out hamburgers and hotdogs from the meat drawer and tossed them onto a tray with bags of buns. My spine straightened as every cell in my body clenched.

"Appetizers," he said, grinning.

The pan I had just washed made more noise than I intended as I dropped it into the drying rack. "What are you doing?"

"We always have hamburgers and hotdogs for the end of summer cookout," he said, digging his grill spatula out of its drawer.

My fingers strangled the spoon I was washing. "Can't you see I made pulled pork?

"Yup," he said, "Can't wait," and breezed out the door.

He would have had the cookout with or without me. Part of me regretted I wasted time and changed up the menu, but secretly, part of me was happy to learn that yes, my family wanted our traditional end of summer cookout. But then I suddenly didn't like the feeling of being so predictable. Clearly, it wouldn't have bothered the girls if Michael just flipped burgers and drank his beer on the back deck without anyone else. He wanted to keep the tradition. Why couldn't I just let things be?

Alicia must have noticed my cheeks bulge and my nostrils flare because she lifted one finger, signaling me to stay calm. Then she opened the refrigerator and casually handed me mustard, ketchup, and relish to put on the table.

I noted that only Jeff and Michael ate hamburgers. None of the girls would have betrayed me like that; however, both guys dumped large spoonfuls of pulled pork on their plates and returned for seconds. I tingled with vindication.

I opened another bottle of wine and followed Alicia to the lounge chairs under the pine trees in the backyard. Pamela preceded us with a plate full of her homemade snickerdoodles and chocolate chip cookies. She practically ran a professional bakery, sweet and savory deliciousness, out of her kitchen. At no time did one need to worry about desserts if you've invited Pamela to your party.

I relaxed, finally content with the decision to have the cookout, and sent out prayers of thanks that just maybe our lives would settle. We laughed as Liz and Nicole tossed horseshoes, with cookies in hand, entertaining us with their many missed shots.

A loud bang drew everyone's attention, and we all startled in trepidation as Heather pushed open the gate, hours before she was meant to be home.

"Hi, everyone. This is Tucker." Heather spun around and pulled a very tall, very slim, moppy-headed boy from behind the fence. Her laughter was loud and unfamiliar as she hung on his arm and pulled him toward the deck.

Chapter 10

Nicole, happy her sister was home, dropped her horseshoes and ran over to Heather. I expected Michael to jump up and introduce himself to the tall, lanky boy Heather hung on to, but instead, he looked them up and down without missing a word as he spoke to Jeffery then returned to watch the game on TV.

The enthusiasm on Nicole's face changed to furrowed brows as she stopped short and took a step back. She glanced back at me, like she hoped I wasn't looking. But I was.

I scooted out of my lounge chair with my glass of wine then grabbed the bottle, thinking I just might soon need the rest of it. Pamela followed at my heels. I walked past Michael, wishing he'd feel the heat from my glare burrow into his back and follow me into the house, but he never even turned around. I couldn't look at Heather. Hearing her alien laughter was bad enough.

I slid into the kitchen with Pamela and shut the door. "Is Heather drunk?" I asked, knowing the answer. "She practically fell into the backyard. And she brought home a boy?"

Before Pamela could make a humorous, snarky remark to break the tension, Heather walked in. Her eyes glistened and were barely open. Tucker, whose eyes couldn't be seen through his floppy curls, followed close behind her.

"Hello, Heather," Pamela said, standing between me and her. "Who's your friend?"

"Wow, so much food," Tucker said as he pulled up a chair to the table where the food was set out buffet style.

Heather picked out a clump of shells from the pasta salad with two fingers and stuffed it into her mouth.

"Here's plates and forks for each of you," Pamela said, handing them some manners and pushed the trays of food away, making some space for them to eat like normal polite humans. I froze as I watched

Heather giggle and hip check Tucker. Heather was drunk, or stoned, or…and she had a piercing in her nose.

"Heather Elizabeth Scott?" I squelched out her name. "What is in your nose?"

"Isn't it cool? I just got it," Heather said and giggled as she fed the boy a shrimp.

Pamela handed me my wineglass and helped carry it up to my lips as I shrunk into the corner cabinets, trying to disappear. Was Michael not the least bit concerned? He saw his daughter barge into the backyard, with a boy, and acting foreign. Where was his unwanted parental input now?

"Look at that chocolate cake. Did you bake it, Aunt Pamela?" Heather picked up the knife beside it.

"Whoa. Cake's for later," Pamela said and slid the cake stand off the table, replacing the dome, protecting the whole, untouched cake from any chemically induced appetites.

I couldn't watch the unfamiliar teenager anymore and abruptly turned to lean over the sink and look out the window. In the middle of the yard, Alicia wrapped her arms around a crying Nicole. Liz, with arms tight across her own body, nodded her head in agreement with whatever Nicole was saying.

I pointed to Heather as she and Tucker giggled over the shapes of pasta and said to Pamela, "That one's yours," and headed out the door.

I marched passed Michael, who seemingly hadn't a care in the world except who won the baseball game, then slowed as Alicia lifted her hand, warning me off. She clearly didn't want me to interrupt while Nicole was speaking. I listened from a few feet away.

"She came home stoned the other night. I should have told Mom, but she made me promise not to," Nicole spat out the words between sobs. "She's been lying to Mom about work too. Sometimes she leaves early, and sometimes she's not even scheduled."

"Where does she go when she's not at work?" Alicia asked.

"She goes over to Tucker's. He picks her up. His parents are never home."

"How did Heather meet Tucker?" Alicia rubbed Nicole's back.

Nicole seemed to calm down with each truth told. "At some party. A couple of months ago, she told Mom she was with me and Liz at your house."

"We've never met him until today," Liz clarified.

"Nicole?" I interrupted, unable to stay out of the conversation any longer.

"Mom," Nicole flinched and turned around to face me. "I'm sorry. I should have told you. But you already have so much on your plate."

"You could have said something too, Liz," Alicia added, clearly expecting better from her daughter.

Pamela joined our group, only to tell me that Heather had taken her new friend upstairs.

"Oh no, she isn't." I ran past Michael, and this time I didn't give him a choice. "Michael, follow me."

I took the steps two by two, my thighs fueled by anger. My inner voice countered my fury by telling me to chill. When I reached the top, I sucked in a well-purposed inhale and paced, waiting for Michael to appear behind me. As I approached Heather's bedroom door, uncertain what to do, I heard giggling coming from Michael's new office, which he had yet to use.

"No," I murmured as her disrespect slapped me in the face. The nerve of her to use Curtis's room, as if it were a free for all. I took in a slow breath. Maybe she went into the office to avoid Nicole's wrath, not mine. As I contemplated running down and physically dragging Michael upstairs, Pamela's head peeked up from the bottom of the staircase.

"Go get Michael," I whispered loudly, jabbing toward the back of the house, knowing Pamela would make it happen.

When Michael arrived with a beer in hand, I wiped away my tears. "Really, Michael," I said, pulling him behind me and putting his beer on the bathroom counter as we passed. "What took you so long?"

"I figured you'd handle it, like you always do. Anyway, what's the urgency? So she's got a boy in her room. She's a good kid," he said as he stopped in front of the girls' door. I pulled harder on his hand and could see his demeanor harden as I walked him to Curtis's bedroom-turned-home-office door.

Without hesitation, Michael knocked on the door, called out Heather's name, and pushed right through all at the same time. Heather and Tucker scrambled off the daybed, kicking pillows across the floor. Their surprise was almost comical, and I was relieved they were fully clothed.

"Hi, I'm Michael, Heather's father." He shot his hand out and gripped Tucker's then led him out the door by the elbow, never releasing him. Heather took a step to follow, but Michael stopped her. "You stay here, young lady. I believe your mom would like to talk with you, and say goodbye to your friend. He'll be leaving now." He closed the door behind them when they left.

Heather puffed out a sigh as she plopped on the daybed. In her silence, I was sure she was thinking exactly what I was thinking— what the hell was Michael saying to Tucker, and what the hell was I going to say to her?

I threw my hands in the air. Here I was, right where I didn't want to be—interrogating my daughter alone, without her father.

"What was that all about?" I asked as I picked up the pillows and put them behind her on the daybed.

"I don't know. Ask Dad." Heather headed for the door.

I grabbed her arm and helped her back to the daybed. "Don't be fresh. You have a lot to answer for." I found myself wringing my hands again and immediately dropped them by my side. I needed to be the adult here and not second-guess my maternal responses and knew that Heather deserved consequences for her conduct. "Are you drunk?"

"Nope," she said, avoiding my eyes.

Sadness entered my tone as I pitied my sweet, independent, daughter and mourned her loss of adolescence. I wasn't ready to treat her like an adult. She still had so much to learn, yet at the rate she was pushing me away, I was losing opportunities to teach. But she was here with me now, and I had a chance.

"Do you realize how much you embarrassed yourself?"

"You mean how much I embarrassed you?" She stared straight at me then.

My pity hardened. "We're not talking about me. It's your behavior we need to discuss." I sat next to Heather and placed my hand on her thigh. She turned, angling her knees away, and pulled her arms around herself.

"Heather?" I didn't want to have this conversation in this room, but in a strange way, it gave me the courage to ask, "Would you like to go back and talk to the therapist?"

"About what?" She abruptly turned, almost frightening me, and stared. "About how you don't like my behavior? How I disappoint you? How badly you need to control me and everyone else? Maybe you need to go back to the therapist."

I began to shake, but I would not let her flip things around and start blaming me. This was about her. About her choices and her behavior. I got up, turned to face her, and grasped her arms with my hands. My grip hopefully punctuated the seriousness of the situation.

"Honey, I love you. You aren't a disappointment. I just don't know how else to say it. You've become argumentative and disrespectful and no longer the responsible girl I can trust. It's not like you."

"Like I said, disappointing sums it up."

My heart reached out for the little girl who had lost her way. "You don't disappoint me, but you have changed. My god, Heather, you're drunk, you have a tattoo, a nose ring… I just think you might want to talk to someone, go back to the therapist and…"

Heather jumped to her feet. "You'd like to blame everything we do or don't do on Curtis's death. I'm the same person I've always been deep down inside, Mom. Maybe I just don't care to spend my energy on trying to hide myself to please you and perform for you anymore. What's the point?" Heather opened the door to leave. "But you, you're the same exhausting person now as you were then. This is about you, Mom, and not Curtis. When are you going to stop using him as an excuse for everything we do and face yourself? Maybe everything is back to the same as before, and that's your problem."

Several silent, empty, wrenching moments passed before I took a breath. As I crawled out from under the Mack truck that flattened me, I gathered up strength despite great pain and anguish and walked out the door, past the cheerful voices flowing up from the kitchen, and into my bedroom. Maybe she was right. Would my actions have been the same before Curtis's death? Would Heather have still gotten a tattoo and piercing if Curtis were here? How would I ever know if my reactions were based on my new fear of losing the girls versus my need to protect them? I would never know. As vacant and hollow as one could be, I lowered myself across my bed and sobbed.

Chapter 11

Daybreak streamed through the unshaded windows, waking me as I went to bed—sprawled across the top of the covers, a fully clothed empty shell of a human being. Nice of Michael not to disturb me. He didn't take my shoes off nor throw a blanket over me when he came in for his pillows, which were no longer on the bed. Hints of flashing lights, distorted images, and fractured thoughts of my dreams remained with me as I stumbled through the morning with no intent, like a zombie from *The Walking Dead*, adrift, with little eye contact, and using only one-syllable words.

I said a quick prayer of thanks to my girlfriends for the spotless kitchen with no signs of the previous day's cookout. It seemed Michael had already left for work as the remnants from his sleep on the couch remained.

Both hands held on to my diet cola for dear life as I sat at the table where bagged lunches the girls, apparently capably, made on their own. Nicole informed me that Alicia, who must have foreseen how my morning would be, was here to drive them to school as trendy outfits and new school supplies flew past in a blur. An echo of goodbyes lingered in the house after the front door slammed shut. I appreciated Alicia foreseeing my need.

September, with the first day of school, and new timetables, routines, and activities, was always the beginning of the year for me. The past eleven years of front porch first-day-of-school pictures, some happy, some with tears, ran through my mind. But there would not be a twelfth first-day-of-school picture. My heart okayed ending that tradition today.

Heather's words from last night filled the room. She had made her feelings quite clear, and I had no clue which way to run with that ball. There had to be repercussions for her behavior. My job was to not let her get away with it, right? She was screaming out for help, wasn't she? This morning, she never really looked at me nor addressed me, but she didn't tilt her head toward me, snort, and paw at the ground either. Maybe she just had to get her anger out. After all, being a sounding board was one of the prerequisites for being a mom.

I strummed my fingers on the side of the cola can and studied a drip of condensation as it eased its way to the tabletop. As it reached its goal, I felt a little lost not driving the girls to school, a bit scared because I didn't have the energy to truly care anymore. Roger fake sneezed to get my attention, and my fog lifted.

With a wagging tail, Roger headed toward the back door, and a sense of determination crawled up and straightened my spine. I raised my can into the air to no one. "To new beginnings, new goals." With my newfound energy, I popped open a second diet cola and took Roger for his walk before I settled down to paint—my form of meditation.

The first week of school went smoothly, however quiet. I kept a smile on my face and occasionally asked if either of the girls wanted to play cards or watch a movie, pretending not to notice how little time they spent in the house. I cooked their favorite meals only to spoon them into Tupperware and freeze them due to the absence of diners at my table. The weekend dragged as Heather's behavior during the cookout, let alone the ring in her nose, simmered beneath my skin. As if by not punishing her, we gave her permission to come and go as she pleased. Monday couldn't have come fast enough.

By midweek of the second week of school, I resigned feelings of being chastised as I drove the girls to school in silence. It seemed the girls had a pact not to talk in the car, not even to each other. When I picked them up, asking how their day went was like pulling teeth, so gradually, they won. I stopped asking. But I did take advantage of the girls not being around in the evenings to try to connect with Michael.

"Hi," I said to him as soon as the next round of commercials began on the television. I had a cold beer for him as an ice breaker and sat on the coffee table in front of him with wine in hand.

"What's up?" he asked, taking the beer.

"Just checking in with you. It's been awfully quiet around here."

"Didn't notice." He sipped his beer, then asked, "Do you want something?"

"Just to talk," I said and looked directly at the remote control in his hand. "While the girls are at dance rehearsal."

His thumb quivered, and his eyes darted to the TV. I could tell he was processing his options. "Hold on," he said and paused his show.

"Thanks," I said. "About Heather at the cookout last week. Did you talk to her about her behavior?"

"No. I dealt with Tucker. You had Heather."

"You didn't say a word to her about having a boy upstairs?"

"No. I thought you took care of that."

"Michael, I can't do this alone."

"What? I took care of the problem. I removed the boy from upstairs." Michael set his beer on the coffee table next to me and sat up in his seat.

"Yes, you did," I said, not wanting our conversation to become confrontational. "But there should be consequences for her actions."

"Again. I thought you took care of that."

"Michael, she doesn't want anything to do with me. She thinks I'm the bad guy on a good day. It would be nice if you had my back with her."

"So she had a boy upstairs. She's almost seventeen. You might not ever have had a boy upstairs, but I recall several times you snuck out of the house at night to meet me, Chad, and Pamela to go downtown."

I stared at him. Was I really the only one bothered by Heather's behavior? "What about her being high or drunk or whatever?"

He picked his beer up and clinked it with my wineglass. "And that's not calling the kettle black?" He winked.

I stood. I would have loved to have gone down that path and reminisce about our high school days when we were out looking for innocent fun. Either because I was the youngest of four and my mother had already seen it all or maybe she just didn't care, there were few consequences for my actions. But I was never drunk. And just because we might have gotten away with harmless teenage behavior didn't mean there shouldn't have been consequences for Heather's actions.

"Listen," he said. "I told Tucker I had my eyes on him."

"But did you tell him Heather wasn't allowed in his car?"

Michael shrugged his shoulders. "If it helps you out…"

"What about the tattoo or pierced nose? Did you give her permission? Go with her?"

"I didn't know anything about them until you pointed them out." I could tell by his smirk he didn't have a problem with either issue.

"Great," I said. My heart raced. I would soon be the one escalating the discussion if I didn't leave immediately.

As I turned away to leave, Michael grabbed my wrist and said, "Listen, next time just tell me exactly what you want me to say or do, and I will. I just don't see what the big deal is."

He didn't get it. I didn't want to be in charge anymore. It made me enemy number one.

Chapter 12

My good mood from delivering a well-received painting to the bank president's office vanished, and my ire piqued as I pulled into the driveway behind Michael's two-seater sports car. "Crap it all. What's he doing home on a Thursday afternoon?"

The sight of his car instantly squashed my desire to jump into my studio with my newly found motivation. He was seldom home in the middle of a workday afternoon unless he had to change for golf. It's a wonder he didn't store a change of clothes and his clubs in the trunk of his car. I stepped out of my van as an upstairs window slammed shut.

"Shit." I prepared for an earful. Whenever I could, I opened the windows and shut off the air-conditioner in the morning, allowing fresh air to stir through the house. But I usually closed them and turned the air back on long before Michael got home.

I cringed when I heard another window slam shut. I hadn't planned on being home this late. But after delivering my painting to the bank and the long lines at the grocery store, post office, and dry cleaner's, my day became severely delayed. I'd have to pick up the girls in a couple of hours, and I had to put away groceries, pay bills, and—*slam*. A third window shut. I entered the kitchen through the garage door as Michael stomped down the stairs.

"Why are all the windows open?" He glared at me as if I was the devil himself hefting the groceries onto the counter.

"I was out delivering another painting. Thank you for asking." I shoved boxes of pasta and loaves of bread into the pantry.

"Do you know how long it's going to take to cool off this house?"

Actually, I did. "It was so nice this morning. I wanted to air out the house. I didn't realize how long I'd be gone." I folded the paper bags as I emptied them and threw them on top of the several dozen already on the shelf in the garage. "What are you doing home now anyway?" I asked, trying to divert his anger.

"We're going to dinner tonight. I sent you a text. It's at the Frazier's, and you don't say no to the CEO," Michael answered.

"Tonight? And you're telling me now?" I glanced at the clock on the wall. It read "14:37" on the outside circle and "2:37" on the inside circle.

"Don't tell me you missed another text from me. At least this time it wasn't life or death."

My breath wouldn't move in or out. He was kidding, right? How could he even jest about that day?

For a split second, our eyes locked. "Anyway, dinner is at six," he said. "The guys decided to meet early for a cigar and a drink, so I wanted to come home and change my clothes."

Michael stood near the base of the steps, watching me put away the groceries, not recognizing he had now pushed me into a time crunch. I could use some help. "I'm wearing khakis, so nothing too fancy," he said and hoofed it up the stairs.

As if I had anything fancy to wear. Guess there'd be no time for any of that survival stuff—give myself oxygen first so I can help others after. There goes the checklist I had created for today, now my choice was to rush through the list to complete it or fail once again. I was really good at breaking promises I made to myself.

I checked my cell phone, and yes, Michael had sent me a text while I was in the bank. Sick that I had missed his text, I pulled the Saint Sabastian charm from beneath my blouse and kissed it, silently thanking him for keeping my family safe.

"The girls need to be dropped off for six p.m. dance rehearsal and picked up again at eight p.m.," I said as he jaunted back through the kitchen to the den. For some silly reason, I expected Michael to understand the dilemma he dropped me into and discuss a solution or at least empathize with me. The old Michael would have.

After reappearing from the den, he briskly walked past me to the front door with a pocket full of cigars and a bottle of bourbon in hand. "Okay, I'll meet you there."

I stared after him. Had he even heard what I just said? I stomped in his footsteps and slammed the door he had left open a crack. I couldn't leave a window open when the air-conditioning was off, but it was just fine if he left the damn door open when the air-condition-ing was on.

Just once, I would like him to say, "It would mean a lot to me if you'd come with me to this work dinner, even though I know it isn't your thing."

I swallowed hard and once again consoled myself with the man-tras Alicia had given me to settle my temper. "Pretend you are a sin-gle mother. Expect nothing from anyone. Your expectations are what lead you to disappointments. You got this, girl."

Roger approached me and pushed the top of his head into my palm. I ruffled behind his ears as he pressed his head on my leg. "I can always count on you, Rog. Thanks for the love." I squatted and gave him a big hug.

By the time I picked up the girls from their afterschool activi-ties, I had managed to make a pot of spaghetti, pay three bills, and fold a load of laundry. I'd be damned if I didn't check off every item on my list for the day, even if I didn't quite get all the clothes put away.

As soon as we got home, I made a couple of calls to see if one of the other moms could drop the girls at home after dance rehearsal. The first mom said she and her family were going out for dinner afterward so she couldn't help, but "maybe next time."

The second claimed that her daughter "wasn't even in school, so of course, she wouldn't be going to dance class." As if I should have known better.

"This is why I don't depend on anyone and just do things myself," I said to the phone as soon as I hung up.

"This is why we need a car of our own," Heather said as she pulled out her history book and took over half the kitchen table with her backpack and notebooks.

My heart leaped, and I snapped my head to look at her. It was the first thing Heather had said to me in days. She obviously forgot she wasn't talking to me, for when our eyes met, she quickly turned and looked at the open page in front of her.

"Yeah, Mom," Nicole said as her books slapped the table on the way out of her backpack. "Just think how much better your life will be when we can drive ourselves around."

I would just pretend she didn't realize they were eligible for their driver's licenses in a couple of weeks. I shook my head. "I need my car," I said, disappointed that this was the first topic they chose to discuss. When were they going to understand I had no problem driving them around? "That's why you can't take it to school or work. I need my car here for me."

"Why? You don't work," Heather said and couldn't have turned a sharper knife.

What did my girls think I did all day? Even if I never had to use my van to deliver paintings or pick up supplies, did they think our groceries magically appeared? Shaking off Heather's clueless jab, I focused on the fact we were having a conversation.

"You won't have to buy one for each of us. We'll share," Heather said, chewing a nail on her left hand.

"We've discussed this. It's expensive to own a car. There's gas, and insurance, the upkeep. Nicole, you'd have to get a job. Plus, you'll be leaving for college soon, then who'd get the car?"

"I won't need a car if I go to New York," Nicole said.

My delight with having a conversation with my daughters plummeted. It would be better to say nothing than to start a sparring match now. I would call a family meeting this weekend and get all of these issues out of the way.

"I can call someone to come pick us up for dance practice. No problem," Heather said in a helpful tone.

Snap. "You know you aren't allowed in your friends' cars until they turn eighteen and have been driving for a year. Let me call Meegan's mom."

"Ugh, not her. She's such a snob. Tucker won't mind driving us. He's nineteen." Heather suggested with such confidence and nonchalance it stopped me in my tracks. The girl had guts. And nothing had changed.

"You are not allowed in a car with a boy. You're only sixteen. I thought your father made it clear you couldn't hang out with Tucker."

"Really, Mom. We'll be seventeen in less than a month." Nicole surprised me with a rebuttal.

"Today you're only sixteen."

Meegan's mother was happy to bring the girls home and suggested I could pick Meegan up and bring her to class. Great, another commitment between now and tonight's unwanted business dinner.

"Spaghetti's on the stove. You have less than an hour. Be ready to leave before 5:30. I've got to get dressed for dinner."

I took a diet cola upstairs and closed the door to my room. Ah, alone at last. Disconnecting myself from the rest of the world, I wrapped my hair up in a towel, not wanting to wash and dry it for the second time that day. I stepped into the hot, steamy shower, dissolving the tension constricting my muscles.

I scrabbled around my closet for something decent to wear and caught sight of my pink floral bathrobe tucked in the corner of my closet and shoved it far into the clothes around it. I didn't want to catch sight of it again. I grabbed the dress hanging nearest to me and threw it on. It didn't matter what I wore. There would be no impressing the insufferable, high-maintenance Stepford wives of Michael's corporate circle.

Chapter 13

The day of…
Nineteen months earlier, 8:10 a.m. to 11:00 a.m.

I entered the kitchen after dropping off the kids and ran into Michael on his way out. Two ships, per usual. *"Nice outfit. Pink does wonders for your complexion,"* he said.

I lovingly punched him in his arm. "Why didn't you stop me from going out in my bathrobe?"

He grabbed my hand and pulled me toward him for a hug, but I twisted my way out of his grip and picked up the dishtowel he had previously thrown at me off the floor where I knew it would still be when I returned. Michael left for work, blowing me a kiss, and I headed straight to the YETI I had left on the counter. Dreading to face the pots, pans, and dishes from our whirlwind of pancakes, I sank into a chair. Across the kitchen, my phone rang. It took me a few moments to dig it out from the bottom of my purse.

"Hi, Pam."

"Just checking in. Let's have a quick lunch then go shopping. Boutique du' Claire and Violette's Home and Décor are having sales today."

"I haven't had a moment to remember my name this morning." I returned to my chair and my YETI. "I had to make fifty pancakes and drive the girls to school."

"Pancakes? On a school day?"

"Exactly. What's up?"

"I'll pick you up at noon," Pamela said, not giving me a choice.

"Yea, yeah." I nodded and hung up the phone. "That means I have to take a shower today, Rog."

Roger pulled his ears back when he heard his name. After washing and drying, wiping, and putting away, the kitchen was spotless—ready for the kids to come home and mess up.

73

Exhausted, and it wasn't even 10:00 a.m., I plodded my way upstairs and looked forward to a nice, long, warm shower. I stepped over the heap that was Michael's dirty socks, underwear, and damp bath towel. With both hands, I scooped up the pile and threw it at the laundry basket, hoping for a three-pointer. Not even close. Still miffed that my family let me leave the house in my bathrobe, I slid it off and tossed it toward the basket. Made it.

My phone dinged as soon as I turned on the hot water to steam up the glass-enclosed shower. A message from Facebook Messenger was usually someone trying to sell me something or join a group. Knowing my family would contact me by text or a phone call, I said, "Not now," to the app I seldom used and turned on my favorite playlist—spa music.

I sat cross-legged in the middle of the shower floor. The hot water pelted my stretched out back as I leaned forward and let the luxurious steam swallow me up. In the mist, I planned a day at the beach alone or maybe a girls' trip with Pamela and Alicia. Michael was so busy at work this time of year, and as long as I organized rides and meals before I left, the kids probably wouldn't even miss me. Even dreaming of such a day helped me break up the monotony of my trivial life.

I leaned my head back and ran my fingers through my hair as the water rolled down my face and chest like I was in a tropical shampoo commercial under a waterfall. Minutes drifted as I inhaled steam and sat until the scorching water felt good. I didn't open my eyes. I didn't want to see the box-store faux travertine tiles on my shower wall. I needed to stay on this imaginary island, alone, with no kids and no husband. I did consider having Roger with me. He'd enjoy the calm. The music from my phone faded as another ding came through, putting an end to my reverie.

Reluctantly having left the solace of my steam shower, I applied mascara and lip gloss and finished my diet cola by the time I figured out what to wear. Or rather, what not to wear. I eliminated everything in my closet except for loose-fitting, comfy clothes. If I had to spend time with Pamela's frivolous shopping romp, I might as well be comfortable. I chose khaki linen pants and an oversized off-white button-down.

I heard the front door open and, assuming Pamela was super early, called out, "Come on up." I gathered my damp hair into a ponytail and called it a day.

"Thanks for the invitation," Michael said, surprising me when he entered the bedroom and gave me an automatic peck on the cheek.

"I thought you were Pamela," I said.

"I need to grab a change of clothes. A client invited us to golf, so…" He held up a couple of shirts.

Without much thought or care, I pointed to the shirt on the left. "I'm going to lunch with Pam," I said, even though he didn't ask. As much as I was happy for Michael that he could take some time for himself, it wasn't quite the same as me going to lunch with Pamela.

Going to lunch with Pamela once a week had been part of my routine since I left college. Which I shouldn't complain about. I loved Pamela and the time we spend together, but it was just so status quo. The only variety in my life was when I painted. At least every painting was fresh and unfamiliar. Even if I knew the outcome, like for a commission, the journey through color, texture, and design was always a new experience.

I grabbed a scarf and my phone and followed Michael down the stairs. He said, "Goodbye," over his shoulder. I didn't bother to respond. He didn't wait for one anyway. We took each other for granted, not in a bad way but a comfortable, not-needy way. Our relationship had a we'll-always-be-there-for-each-other confidence that sometimes left me lonely. I clicked on my phone and saw it was only 11:15 a.m., and my Messenger app had three unanswered messages.

Chapter 14

The one good thing about being late for dinner at the CEO's house was I got to park my faded-blue family van with its dented fender in front of a stranger's house down the street at the end of the row of Range Rovers and Bentleys. On my way up the long driveway to the front door of the small mansion, I passed by Michael's white Audi in the driveway. He must have been one of the first to arrive.

The dinner went as expected: the food superb, the men ignored the women, and the women got drunk on prosecco. I was not cut out to be a corporate wife. First of all, I preferred cabernet. I didn't care if it stained my teeth. If I were going to consume the calories, then I damn well would drink what I liked.

Secondly, the other women didn't work—at all. They had nannies and housekeepers, gardeners, and personal shoppers. I did all that, plus chauffeur. I had absolutely nothing in common with these women, except what assholes our husbands could be. But I was not about to admit that to perfect strangers. Who knew what they'd hold against me, or Michael, for that matter? I just smiled when they smiled and laughed when they laughed, taking note of how commendable Michael seemed compared to their husbands' asshole-ness.

As fabulous as the food was, if I ate two bites of the chopped salad, an eighth of the broiled white fish, and the fondant potato, which I actually thought was a scallop, I would have eaten twice as much as any wife there. Obviously, their caloric intake came strictly from the bubbly wine.

The women chatted, and I checked my watch, hoping the twins made it home okay. I mentally reviewed my calendar for the morning, but still giggled when I heard the others laugh. With a grin of thanks, I slid my hand over the top of my glass as one of the caterers tilted the bottle of cabernet in my direction. If I had more than one glass of wine, I'd fall asleep face-first in the Flan.

After dinner, when I'd heard enough petty gossip and reached information overload from way too many people I didn't even know, I found Michael lounged with the guys in the wood-paneled cigar room off the front foyer. I knocked on the French door's beveled glass panels to get his attention and wave goodbye. He responded by raising his rock glass with barely a glance. My hand remained flat on the glass as if I could draw him to me. I watched him cajole and gesture with the group of men, wondering how he could appear so friendly and social yet at home could barely string a whole sentence together.

A few men, distracted by the ogler in the windowpane, glanced at me as if I were the one in the fishbowl. Once Michael noticed their distraction and followed their eyes, he said something. All the men broke into laughter. Michael had regained their attention. Mortified at being the butt of a joke, I let myself out the front door.

With a shiver, hurt took over my embarrassment. I couldn't get to my car fast enough, wishing I had the smarts to have called in sick to the dinner party. I reached for the Saint Sabastian charm beneath my blouse and prayed for him to help Michael get his priorities straight.

My house glowed as I turned the corner of my street. Every light in every room was on. Nice to know the girls weren't worried about Michael's wrath any more than mine when it came to saving electricity. I hoped the girls had at least cleaned up from their pre-dance spaghetti dinner and post-dance snacks. I was in no mood to pick up after them. The twins wanted to be treated like adults, yet still be dependent enough for me to be their maid, cook, and secretary. Well, until they could get their dishes to the sink, I'd make sure I was their chauffeur too.

All was quiet as I entered the relatively—I could see the attempt—clean kitchen. I had gotten myself worked up over nothing this time. I walked around the house, shutting off lights. I left the front exterior lights on for Michael then checked on the girls. Neither looked up when I peeked in as each was in bed with their own form of digital entertainment.

I reached back and knocked loudly on the door to get their attention and blew them kisses good night. Nicole slightly waved in response. Heather's eyes never left her phone.

Comfy in my nightgown and slippers, I poured a glass of my favorite cab and attempted to empty my mind. I tried not to think about how crazy my day had been by purposely avoiding how angry I was at Michael. But of course, his behavior was the elephant in the room.

I tilted my glass and swirled the cabernet, seeing how close I could get it to the edge without spilling it. 'Round and 'round it went. The focus it took to keep the wine in the glass was refreshing. I remained hypnotized until I heard one of the girls upstairs shut the bathroom door.

Once out of the trance, my heavy heart wished Michael, the old Michael, was sitting beside me. I wanted to curl up next to him on the couch, watch a football game or whatever sport played across the TV screen, and appreciate his random knowledge which I had no interest in.

Michael. In high school, he was the best friend a guy could be without being a boyfriend. He loved to go to the beach like me, listen to the same music as me, and play the same board games as me. Even though Chad was my boyfriend, and Michael occasionally had a girlfriend, we always included each other. It wasn't until he went to college that Pamela set us up as a couple, and it was perfect. A match made in heaven. According to Michael, he had waited for me to get Chad out of my system.

Michael had won me over when he invited me to his campus for a picnic on the lake behind his dorm, in a rowboat. It was there, after we had been on half a dozen dates, he asked me to be his girlfriend. With the oar across his lap, he poured me a glass of our favorite wine.

He was so sweet and just wanted to please me. And eventually, I fell in love with him through his desire to make my dreams come true. I needed stability and a forever home, and he couldn't have been happier to oblige me. I should have appreciated him more, not taken him for granted. Was this new behavior some sort of retribution? More karma? Life had a funny way of kicking me in the butt.

Wanting to dump the questions from my head, I dug out the sacred remote control tucked into the side pocket on Michael's La-Z-Boy, the one chair in the middle of the room, smack in front of the TV, as if no one else was eligible to see any show head-on. I hit the red button to turn on the large over-the-top smart TV and settled on HGTV.

A kink in my neck woke me from a not-really-asleep-but-not-awake snooze. By the time I straightened up, corked the rest of the wine, it was after 2:00 a.m. Where was Michael?

I let Roger out and followed him onto the deck. I stared up at a cloud as it navigated over the moon and replaced my anger with a prayer for Michael's safety. To have something happen to their father would be the last thing the girls needed. And even though we were not on the best of terms, Michael's presence kept me from being alone, if not lonely.

I crawled into my cold, empty bed and focused on the shadows swaying on the ceiling from an oak dancing in the wind outside my window. My brain emptied as I followed the bobbing images formed by the filtered light from the streetlamp below. On the edge of falling asleep, the smell of cigar smoke preceded Michael as he attempted to tiptoe across the bedroom into the bathroom pulling me back to consciousness. He turned the blaringly bright overhead light on just before the door closed.

I huffed, pulled the covers over my head, and rolled over onto my side. "Hi, sweetie," I said into my pillow. "Thanks for coming tonight. Everyone loved seeing you. They were so impressed you managed to be only twenty minutes late considering you had to drive the girls across town, which is your number one job, your priority, and get to the CEO's house all during rush hour traffic."

"Did you say something?" Michael asked as he came out of the bathroom. "I thought you were asleep."

The towel he had used hit the bathroom floor with a *wallop*, and the light switch shut off with a *whack*. Michael climbed into bed, then leaned over and pecked me on the cheek. "What a great dinner."

The stuttering in my head held me captive, and I choked on my response. Did he not see that not one woman addressed me in any conversation? That I couldn't relax among a group of cliquey rumor-mongers? And that I could have used a friend?

"Guess you don't agree," he said as his bedside lamp clicked on and magazine pages began to rustle.

Incredulous, I swung my legs over the side of the bed and turned on my lamp. "We need to talk." Confrontation here we come.

"Now? I'm drained. How about tomorrow?"

"With you, tomorrow never happens," I said, the stink of cigar smoke fueled my frustration.

"Seriously, Jules. I'm pooped."

"We can't keep doing this. I miss you. I miss us being partners." I pictured him chatting comfortably with his coworkers, a cigar in one hand and a drink in the other, and my hurt became jealousy.

"I don't know what to say…" He chucked his magazine on the floor then sat on the edge of the bed with his back to me.

"I want you to say I miss you. We can fix this. I want you to want to work toward what we had before Curtis passed."

The bed bobbled as he stood up. "Okay. I promise to do better." He tossed the words out as if to placate me.

"I don't need a promise. I need action, Michael. You have two daughters who miss you too." I sat back and pulled the blankets over my legs, the weight of them comforting me. "Why didn't you give me more than a few hours' notice about the dinner? Paul's wife knew about this specific invitation for over a week. Does it ever occur to you that I cannot read your mind, and I don't have a fortune teller on retainer?"

"Is that what all this is about? You not knowing sooner about the dinner?"

"I can't help but feel you didn't even want me to go."

"I'm surprised you did go. I know you hate those things."

"I went for you. I found the girls a ride home from dance, for you. I sat through that damn *Real Housewives of Wilmington* episode, for you."

"I don't know, Jules," Michael said as he paced the length of the bed.

My lower lip began to tremble, and I stared at his back. "You don't know what?" There were so many words I wanted to put in his mouth, but I knew, in doing so, things would only get worse.

"I'll just try harder. I promise." He added sincerity in his tone as he looked at me, but his earnestness didn't reach his eyes.

"Let me help you." If I could only show him that his role in this family hadn't ended with Curtis. That we all needed him.

His shoulders slumped as he faced me with sad, red-rimmed eyes. "You can't," he said and snatched his pillows and the blanket on the bench at the foot of our bed. "It should have been me."

What should have been him? "Michael. Wait. Don't," I begged as he left the room. I held my breath, hoping he would turn around. "Michael, we can fix this."

Pressure built in my chest as I imagined Michael entering Curtis's room and pulling down the bedcover. The beginning of the end of Curtis's bedroom. I remembered reading something about never go to bed mad, but if you do, then at least go to bed in the same bed because once you've allowed the first time to happen, which we did the night of the cookout, the easier it would be to continue in separate beds.

He had made me feel as if I was doing all the wrong things, like wanting to move forward was wrong; like wanting him to be part of working together, eating together, just being together was all wrong.

The kaleidoscope returned with unnerving images, jarring colors, and tail-spinning words. Each fractured image rotating in my head represented a connection I'd broken and didn't know how to fix or a must-have that I'd created yet now didn't know how to live with. My thoughts escaped through my tears. I squeezed my hands over my mouth to contain my sobs. Then I threw myself face-first into my pillow. There were no answers. I feared the reeling and jarring would never end.

Chapter 15

I woke up from a surprisingly deep slumber devoid of any thought, having to recall the scene with Michael last night piece by piece, as if my mind had tried to tuck it away. I quickly dressed and peaked into the open office door. Not a pillow out of place. Michael hadn't spent any time there.

But as I passed the den, my curiosity was pacified. A pile of pillows and blankets filled the sofa, his slippers stuck out from under the coffee table, and a couple of magazines were open and upside down on top of it. That was more like it. The mess he left didn't bother me. But did he go to work naked? I ran back up the stairs as the girls ran down.

"I'll meet you in the van," I said.

As soon as I reached our bedroom, I saw Michael's pajama bottoms on the floor in front of his side of the closet. I exhaled with relief. His dirty clothes on the floor was such a typical sight I hadn't even noticed it as I got dressed.

I drove the girls to school and rushed home, anxious to talk to Pamela and Alicia over coffee. I had made early morning calls to move our Friday morning weekly debriefing coffee to my house, needing support and advice from my friends. By the time I returned home, my besties had let themselves in, made their coffee and tea, and set out baked goods.

"I just can't believe, well, I guess I can. It's just that he makes me feel like I'm the bad guy here." Pamela handed me a diet cola in a coffee mug that said, "All I need is coffee and a paintbrush."

"I busted my ass to even show up for that dinner. And did I tell you Paul's wife said she knew about it for over a week? I got the feeling Michael didn't even want me to go."

"There's nothing wrong with standing up to him," Pamela said, slicing a cinnamon crumble coffee cake.

I cringed at the thought of challenging him at 2:00 a.m. My need for immediate answers didn't help the situation. "But I did it all wrong. I really wanted to talk to him about us, not about last night's dinner."

"You didn't do it wrong," Pamela said. "He missed the point. Men are good at that."

"No. I'm really worried about him." I stared out the window over the sink. "He said something about wishing it was him that died instead of Curtis."

"Survivor's remorse," Alicia said.

"What do I do?" I asked and returned to the table.

"There's nothing you can do," Pamela said. "He needs professional help to see that there was nothing he could have done to prevent Curtis's death, and he certainly couldn't have traded places with him. Curtis was born with his aneurysm. Michael's logical mind knows it. He'll come around. Listen, you created him. He's your monster. From the beginning, you did everything to make his life easy. Mrs. Suzy Homemaker with no expectations of Mr. Bacon Winner."

"Focus on yourself," Alicia said.

I pursed my lips and shook my head. What would make me happy was to see my daughters happy, and I didn't know how to do that anymore. How could putting my needs first really help my situation? I knew where Alicia was going with this. Everyone knew I put all my time and energy into my desire for the perfect forever home and family. I couldn't admit that I now painted for an escape from daily stresses, and to avoid dealing with the very reality I'd created. If everything was so perfect, I wouldn't need an escape, right? Kaleidoscope thinking—justifying then rationalizing thoughts and images as they merged and broke apart, shuffling to make sense.

"When's the last time you talked to him, I mean, really talked to him?" Pamela asked. She cut a muffin and placed half on my plate next to the uneaten coffee cake, always the consummate hostess. "Have you two talked about the day of Curtis's aneurysm?"

I froze mid gulp. My diet cola went down like splinters of glass. I looked from Pamela to Alicia. I hadn't discussed where I was that day with anyone, and Pamela knew it because if I had, I would have discussed it with her. My silence answered her question.

I struggled to not feel guilty over taking time for myself that day. Weren't they just saying I should make time for myself, put myself first? I owed no one an explanation.

Pamela stood and walked to the coffeemaker as if she didn't want to see the reaction in my eyes when she said, "If you don't want to discuss it with me, that's one thing, but I think something broke in Michael that day when he couldn't reach you. I say his issue is with you, not Curtis's death."

My breath hitched. Michael's loss of trust and respect for me was obvious to everyone, not just in my imagination. I had added to his grief. It was easier to think he blamed me for Curtis's death, which I knew was unrealistic. No one could have predicted, let alone have prevented, his death. I knew Michael was disappointed in me, but it never dawned on me that Michael still carried a lack of faith in me after all these months.

Behind Pamela's back, Alicia waved the comment away, silently telling me to let that go. "We're talking about last night. What did you talk about last night?"

"I tried to explain my feelings. He promised he'd try harder."

"Promises made in the morning are broken, promises made at night forgotten," Pamela muttered.

I took a second to peel the wrapper off the half banana-nut muffin, one of Pamela's most requested baked goods, and let what Pamela said soak in. Even if I explained to him where I was, it wouldn't change anything. I wasn't around for him.

"How would you feel in reverse?" Pamela asked.

"He's not here for us now. He is so unavailable and distant now. Do you mean how would I feel if he weren't there when I desperately needed him?" Tears welled as I realized he would never forgive me.

"I'm sure he's doing his best," Alicia said. "Grief has as much to do about new beginnings as it does about letting the past go."

"Hold on here," Pamela said in her devil's advocate voice. "Grief aside, he isn't in dire straits. He's working and golfing and hanging out with his buddies. You told Michael the girls had a busy schedule, and he didn't offer to help you. He's not an idiot. He wasn't going to make it his problem. I'd say he's pretty much back to normal." Pamela took the spoon from her coffee and tapped it loudly on the lip of her mug. "That's"—*tap*—"what"—*tap*—"men do." *Tap. Tap.* "They ignore and purposely don't inquire to ensure it doesn't become their problem."

"There's more going on than that," Alicia said.

I sat back in my chair in thought. I knew I wasn't going insane. I just needed my girlfriends to point it out to me. I'd love to believe that Michael was just being…a man. A man that needed some help dealing with something I unintentionally did. Again, back to being my fault. And I'd gladly take the blame if he'd just come around to loving me again.

"You can't let him get under your skin, Julie." Alicia took a sip of her tea. "You have a good life, and Michael's a good provider. He does love you."

"We all enjoy being together," Pamela said. "We'll keep an eye on him. Give him time. He'll work it out."

"You could have it a lot worse, you know." Alicia tilted her head and raised her eyebrows at me, reminding me that she knew what she was talking about. She'd been there, done that, which was why she was a single mother.

"There are different kinds of abuse," mumbled Pamela, bringing her coffee mug to her lips.

"Oh, geez. It's not that bad," I said directly to Pamela. "I probably expect too much from him. Nothing he does is intentional. He's just become a little self-centered and doesn't see how much his actions affect the rest of us."

"Men are clueless about how their actions, or lack of actions, affect the people around them on a good day. So there's that."

"Pamela." Alicia shook her head, preferring to hover in the positive.

"Michael's no different than Jeff," Pamela continued her banter. "As a bank president and leader of the community, Jeff's a great person, but as husband and father, he is, well, absent." She stirred her coffee, hitting the sides of her mug in a regular rhythm, breaking up the silence.

"But Michael is different than Jeff. Michael used to be present. He used to drive me crazy, calling two or three times a day to see what was going on. I'm afraid he won't need me anymore once the girls leave home." I folded and refolded the muffin paper over my plate. Michael and I had rarely discussed our future. Why would we? I planned on painting forever and living in my forever house. We would have had ten more years before Curtis graduated from college, and Michael wouldn't retire for at least ten years after that. We had plenty of time to discuss what we would do after retirement. I felt like the future Michael and I would have planned had all but evaporated.

"I think the best thing you can do is something for yourself. Don't be so available for him or the girls. Take care of you," Pamela said.

I pressed my lips together and shrugged. "That doesn't work out so good for me."

"You know what I mean. Do something for yourself. Just keep your phone with you," Pamela said. She had tried to get a hold of me as many times, if not more, than Michael on that fated day. Maybe she felt jilted too.

"Okay, enough pouting about the past." Alicia sat up in her chair, a smile spread across her pretty face. "I have a blind date tonight!"

"What? Tell me everything." Pamela loved to sink her teeth in every detail.

"One of my clients in Rehoboth Beach. Her brother is in town, thinking of moving here, so she wants me to be their fourth at dinner."

"Have you seen pictures? What does he do?" Pamela wanted more.

After Alicia left and Pamela reminded me about our fundraiser meeting tomorrow, I cleared the table and imagined being Alicia, single, with no man to plan a future with. I felt blessed to have Michael, even such as we were at the moment. We had committed to each other, and we'd see it through. Alicia answered to no one but her one daughter, who would be leaving soon for college. She'd be alone preparing her empty nest. I guess I should start planning myself. I couldn't imagine my future after the girls left for college, but the thought of being without them was no lonelier than I felt at the moment. And I had no one to blame but myself.

I began to dial Michael's number to see if he could find time to talk tonight, but recalling Heather's voice saying, "She needs to give Dad a break," stopped me. If Michael wanted to make time to talk, he would, and I would do my best to be prepared.

Chapter 16

The next morning, as I geared up for lunch with Pamela and her country club pals, I mulled over the silence of the night before. Michael had come home, already eaten dinner with a couple of work buddies, and sat himself in front of the TV. I retreated to the bedroom and read until I fell asleep. I heard him come in to shower in the morning, but I stayed under the covers and allowed him to dress in peace, wondering how many nights I'd have to go through with no answers, no clues as to which direction to take. How long should I sit back and allow the silence? As soon as he left the bedroom, I got ready for my day, but questions I couldn't or shouldn't ask kept circling.

"Jules?" Pamela startled me as she let herself in the front door, getting me out of my head. I had expected her to honk as per usual when she picked me up.

"Be right there," I answered from the kitchen as I coaxed Roger in from the sunny backyard. Then I ran through the house, shutting windows.

Pamela rounded the corner and greeted me with a frown. "This is exactly why I didn't have you meet me in the car. I wasn't letting you out of the house without seeing what you were wearing." Pamela pointed up the stairs. "Come on."

"What?" I said as Pamela grabbed my wrist, dragging me toward the kitchen to the staircase. "This is a perfectly fine black linen dress, and look, I'm wearing heels."

"Technically, those are wedges, and I can live with the dress. But let's make it look like you gave it at least a bit of thought."

I hurried as we traipsed through the kitchen past the den. I didn't want her to see Michael's pillows and blanket still on the couch. But nothing got past Pamela. She stopped in front of the den entrance. "You or Michael on the couch?"

My chin trembled, stopping me from forming words, and I shook my head. I put up a hand, not wanting to discuss it, and ran up the stairs.

"Ahh, honey. I'm sorry." She met me at the foot of my bed, grateful she allowed me the time to get the words out without bombarding me with questions.

"I never thought he'd go this far… What am I going to do? Lord knows what the girls are thinking. I told them he keeps falling asleep in front of the TV. But they're not stupid. He'd always nodded off down here, but he used to wake up and come to bed."

"It's okay. It's all going to be okay," Pamela said as if she could predict the future. She rummaged in my top-left dresser drawer where she knew I kept my jewelry and handed me my turquoise necklace.

I balled up the plagued gemstones in my palms. It held on to accusations and guilt from the last time I wore it—the day I fractured my family.

"Oh, honey, I'm sorry. I wasn't thinking. I just thought of jazzing up your dress. Here, give it to me."

I handed her the necklace just as I had in the hospital waiting room that fateful day. I tied the scarf she gave me in exchange around my neck.

Pamela brushed a tinge of blush on my cheeks then took me by the shoulders and turned me toward the mirror. She loosened the scarf, making it look just right. "Geeze, you would think an artist of your caliber would know what a little color can do." Pamela winked, her half-smile acknowledging my pain.

"Will it all really be okay? I'm giving him his space. I just hope it brings him around."

"It's all you can do," Pamela said, meeting my gaze in the mirror.

At least, that was an answer. But by not speaking to him, was I allowing him to pull away?

Pamela pulled into the parking lot of the Flagstone Country Club, where she and Jeff had been members for more than twelve years. Pamela was cut out for the country club life. She relished the social, philanthropic, and exclusive lifestyle—something I had no desire for. The only people I needed to impress were my family, and I wasn't doing a very good job at that.

"It's always so beautiful here," I said, putting on a Cinderella-finally-made-it-to-the-ball demeanor as I stepped out of the car.

The grounds of the club were beguiling. I hadn't been here since their Christmas fundraiser, and the club was all decked out in holiday wear. Now the multi-levels of fall-colored chrysanthemums, gaillardia, coneflowers, and zinnias layered with a variety of greens were stunning.

"It should be beautiful for what we pay," Pamela said with a snort, tapping a tall purple coneflower.

The few times a year I entered the club, always with Pamela, felt like I was sneaking into a castle while the Royal Family was out of town. It was pure elegance. The exquisitely ornate staircase instantly reminded me I was one of the stepsisters, not Cinderella.

I stopped in front of an oversized landscape in sepia tones which I had painted and donated to last year's big fundraiser when Jeff was at its helm. I placed my hand on the forgotten wind-worn picnic table left among the dunes behind an old, abandoned house. It was our high school go-to hangout and a memory that would never be forgotten thanks to the painting. The left end of the wind-worn bench, broken and hanging by shards, brought a smile to my face. In high school, Chad had climbed up to dive off the end into the dunes when the rotting board cracked under his weight. Michael had ribbed him about it for days. I was proud this simple, personal memory found a home in such a lavish location.

The hostess greeted us with a warm smile and an upturned hand flowing to the right toward our table. "Hello, Mrs. Spencer. Let me show you to your table. And Mrs. Scott, we've received so many compliments about your painting. The members all love it. Glad to have you here."

She knew my name. I felt like a celebrity. I decided right then and there I might not belong to the country club, but I was damn sure going to enjoy it while I was here.

The room was quite large, with a subtle elegance about it. The tables, arranged far apart with cream taffeta tablecloths, white linen napkins, shiny silverware, and sparkling crystal glassware, displayed expertly arranged centerpieces of white hydrangeas, white roses, and baby's breath in low sterling vases. Each table, no matter what size, had its own crystal chandelier above it. It was magical. Around the outskirts of the room were several seating areas with silver silk chairs and round cocktail tables. Walking through the room intimidated me. Thank goodness Pamela spruced me up for the luncheon.

The hostess arrived at a large round table in the corner of the room surrounded by a curved bay window overlooking the eighteenth hole of the prestigious golf course.

Two women were already seated in the two chairs directly in the center of the window, framed by the floral cream-on-cream drapes as if they were the centerpiece of the room itself. Clearly, the women chose their seats so they could see who entered and exited the dining room. Their conversation continued out of the sides of their mouths as Pamela and I approached the table. Their faces were inches apart, their eyes followed Pamela's every step, and their lips never stopped moving. Maybe it was going to be hard to have a good time here after all. Women like these two gossipmongers were the exact reason I didn't want to attend today.

"They must be the dreaded Georgina and Patty," I said without moving my lips.

"Bingo, but don't worry. They'll be so busy talking about everyone coming and going you won't have to chat with them," Pamela whispered. She put on her five-star smile and greeted her guests.

"Hi, Georgina. Patty." Pamela acknowledged the two women. "This is my dear friend, Julie Scott. Julie, meet Georgina and Patty."

Pamela introduced each lady with a nod of her head. The hostess pulled out the chair directly in front of me, and I instantly sat across the table from Georgina, the farthest seat. I scooted my chair a bit to the right as she leaned to her left to see the entryway, not so subtly suggesting I had just planted myself and blocked her view.

Directing my gaze toward the window, Pamela gushed, "Doesn't that make quite the picture? It's the best view from the dining area."

Georgina and Patty twisted to see what was so beautiful behind them. Apparently, they were not impressed. They returned to their conversation about a woman named Norma.

I knew instantly Pamela was making a point, so I agreed. "Yes, the flower gardens are so colorful this time of year. It's a perfect view."

The conversation continued with general topics of weather and golf. It was evident, as their eyes continually wandered toward the doorway, that Georgina's and Patty's hearts weren't into this luncheon.

"Oh, here comes Iris," Patty said as she waved toward the entrance. Pamela and I turned our heads and saw a familiar tall brunette, with two others following behind.

As the hostess approached with the three ladies, Georgina muttered, "Cindy wore that dress last month to the Junior League luncheon. I guess she needs her money's worth." Patty giggled in response. These women had too much time on their hands and not enough substance occupying their brains, which was precisely why no one could pay me enough to be part of a country club. I couldn't be bothered.

If the old Michael was here with me, we'd be commenting about these ladies' conversations and attitudes by sending each other subliminal messages through eye movements. I missed the days we would accompany Pamela and Jeff to an event and feel perfectly comfortable out of place together.

Pamela didn't have to make introductions as the three newcomers made their way around the table, giving partial hugs and cheek-to-cheek air kisses, and introduced themselves to me. Pamela greeted Iris with a big Happy Birthday hug and reminded her of when she had met me before.

"I remember. I met you when they hung the picnic table scene in the main foyer."

"That's right, and at Pam's Hasting School event," I said.

Iris slipped into the empty chair to my right, and her company instantly relaxed me, reminding me how I enjoyed her conversations about our kids. She asked how my family was but didn't bring up Curtis. She was kind enough to realize this was not the time nor the place to feed the gossipmongers.

Patty broke away from Georgina long enough to ask, "You painted that gorgeous picture?"

"I did, Thank—"

Cindy interrupted, obviously not interested in my painting, and ordered two bottles of chardonnay and six glasses from a waitress behind me. Pamela called the waitress over and whispered that I would prefer the house cabernet. That's my girl.

Most of the ladies ordered grilled salmon over a bed of mixed greens with a lemon vinaigrette. Salmon was definitely not one of my favorites, so I ordered the citrus shrimp and avocado salad. As I slid my cabernet over when my shrimp plate arrived, Cindy was just sweet enough to ask if I wanted to switch to white.

The old Michael and I used to joke about meal combinations that didn't sit right with the rest of the world but we both liked— things like pizza with ranch dressing and dill pickles, macaroni and cheese with potato chip crust and ketchup, and red wine with seafood. The one food he would never touch was avocado, and I wouldn't go near olives. So I always ate his guacamole, and he always stole the olives off my plates. The last time we did that seemed so long ago.

Pamela's brilliance at conversation kept Patty and Georgina involved in the current exchange. Every time their attention was drawn elsewhere, like when Carmen Lumas came in carrying the latest Bottega Veneta leather tote, Pamela mentioned Patty by name to bring them both back into the fold.

"It's like herding sheep." Pamela once told me when she explained how she kept things smooth at Jeffery's business dinners with those type of women. "You make each one feel special as if their comments are desperately on point per the conversation. Even if you don't give a flying F what they have to say." Pamela was definitely good at what she did, luckily for Jeff.

"Have any of you girls seen the flyers for the Wilmington Pediatric Cancer Center fundraiser?" Pamela had waited until the third glass of wine was poured before bringing up the charitable event. Once Pamela had each of their undivided attention, she continued, "I'm the chairwoman, and it's just around the corner. I'm assuming you girls already sponsored a table and are planning to attend?"

"I can't go," Lisa stated. "But I'd love to put together a gift basket from my bookstore to donate for the auction."

"That would be wonderful. Thank you." Pamela pointed her pen to her right as if expecting one answer at a time. "Julie? You'll donate a painting, won't you?"

And there it was. This was why Pamela insisted I came to this luncheon with her. This was where the dog and pony show began. "Sure. I'd love to."

"What are your paintings going for now? Five, six thousand dollars?" Pamela said, flinging a casual hand as if six thousand dollars was nothing.

I tried not to laugh and managed to keep my eyes in my head and said, "For the bigger ones, yes."

"Great. That's a couple more items. You girls have any ideas?" Pamela asked, writing notes in her little Louis Vuitton notebook. By the end of the luncheon, Pamela accrued a week in October in Georgina's 6,300-square-foot gorgeous house on Bethany Beach; and not to be outdone, Patty offered her beach house for two weeks in the summer. Cindy donated a dinner for eight with a full wine menu at her husband's restaurant, Crabcakes, and Iris offered a year's worth of monthly floral arrangements from her flower shop, Bloom.

The six women raised their glasses to each other as a slice of triple chocolate cake with six spoons appeared in front of Iris.

"Cheers," Pamela said and put away her notebook. Her mission complete. "Happy Birthday, Iris."

Thirty minutes later, glad to put the luncheon behind me, I absorbed all the color and fragrances of the flower beds around the club as Pamela exited the parking lot.

"I'm really excited to get started on this painting for the fundraiser." I'd been waiting to find the time to paint one of my favorite places—the side garden at the Ranford house in New Castle with the Delaware River flowing in the background. I imagined budding spring flowers, a white picket fence, and a lavender sunset.

"I'm sure it'll be beautiful. And don't forget, it's a donation, so you'll be able to claim it on your taxes." Always the practical Pamela.

But it was more than that. It gave me permission to paint something I wanted to paint with no guidelines, no restrictions. "I love having the freedom to paint what I want. In fact, I miss it. Don't get me wrong. I appreciate and need the commissions Alicia sends my way, but it's becoming work."

My right foot pressed into the passenger side floor as if I could speed up the ride home. I couldn't wait to face a blank canvas and paint what my heart desired, an escape from all the drama at home.

Chapter 17

The anticipation of feeling joy when picking up a paintbrush for myself instead of for one of Alicia's clients all but disappeared when I arrived home to a quiet house full of people, each in their respective corners like roommates, not family. There wasn't angst in the air nor heated avoidance—just a dolefulness, like living in a ghost town. For the rest of the weekend, I served meals buffet style from the stove because I didn't know when anyone wanted to eat. No one offered to help me cook or clean up. No one thought to walk or feed Roger. I kept the machine running, but to what purpose?

As a new week began and the girls returned to school and Michael to work, my time became my own, a strange thought since no one interfered with my time anymore. I went in search of an available piece of unused canvas rolled up and stacked in a basket in the corner of my studio. I separated the largest from the smallest and found the beginnings of a small eight-inch-by-eight-inch painting of Curtis when he was two years old. I couldn't remember why I never finished it. I vaguely remember starting it. My best guess was, I needed to paint some commission work and make money for the girls' activities and that I'd get back to painting it someday, which never came. I unrolled other canvases, and they all turned out to be other uncompleted "someday" paintings.

I found a substantial sixty-by-sixty-inch piece of canvas which I had discarded after a frustrating round of painting. The bottom third had been painted with the beginnings of a seascape. I could paint right over it, and the irregular lines of the ocean meeting the shore would give texture underneath the flower garden I planned to create over it.

In the garage, I found one-by-twos and constructed a sturdy frame with corner braces to keep it square. I stretched the canvas over the frame and began attaching it with a staple gun when Michael entered the garage, startling me.

"Whoa, don't shoot," Michael jumped back.

I shut off the pneumatic weapon as Michael pulled his golf clubs out of their stand in the corner of the garage.

"That's a large painting. Another commission?" he asked while he dug through his golf bag, checking which clubs were there.

Appreciating his attempt at conversation, I didn't want to just give him a yes or no answer. "I'm going to donate it to the…"

"Donate? A painting that large?"

I looked at the frame, thinking it wasn't that much larger than the painting I had donated for the past fundraiser.

"You've spent so much time in your studio I assumed you had a lot of commissions lined up." Michael polished the head of one golf club and then another.

"What do you mean? Where should I be? No one in this family wants to be in the same room with each other, especially with me. Where else would I go but to my studio?"

"You have it wrong," he said. He pulled out a club and wiped it down with a towel.

"Well, exactly what am I missing?"

Michael shook his head. "You don't get it."

"I get that you need help, Michael, and I am not the one able to help you."

"What the hell are you talking about?" He didn't move, but his stance was defensive.

I inhaled to calm my nerves. "I'm worried about you, about what you said the other day."

His arms wrapped around his torso as he leaned against the wall. "You're making a mountain out of a molehill like you always do. I said I wished it were me instead of him. And I meant that, but I also know I can't change it. You…" He shook his head and reached for a couple of golf balls then stuck them in a side pocket of his bag. "You just don't get it."

"Guess not. Why don't you tell me?" I put the staple gun down and lowered my hackles. I wanted him to know I was there to listen. I needed to keep him talking and share his feelings.

"What would you like me to say?" he asked.

This felt like a trap. All these weeks, I stayed quiet so I wouldn't put words in his mouth, and now he was asking me to? "Thank you for doing your best. That you really want to be part of our family. That you love the girls and me…"

"Of course, I love the girls." He slammed another golf club into his bag.

The girls. Not me. I let his sting soak in. For the first time, I could see the pain I caused him. He didn't know what to do with me. This truly wasn't about Curtis's death anymore. This was about me and how I failed him. I decided to stick to the girls.

"Michael, you're losing them. We all feel like we don't matter to you. That without Curtis, we're nothing to you."

"I'm still keeping a roof over your heads, aren't I? And putting food on the table and keeping the electricity and water on." The last golf club slammed into the bottom of the bag. Always the provider, and a good one at that, but he missed the heart of the matter.

"They need more, Michael. More attention from you."

"How'd this get turned on me? I just asked if you had the time to devote to a donation of that size?"

I hung my head and swallowed hard. Anger rose from having to fight off the guilt of wanting to do something for me.

"I need to do something for myself." What I really wanted to say was, "Isn't that what you do all the time?" and point to the golf clubs he was ready to take out. With unwarranted strength, I shoved his golf bag over. It hit the floor with a loud clang, sending clubs sliding across the garage like missiles. My stomach sank at the violence of it.

"Nice. Real nice, Jules," Michael said. He slammed his clubs back into the bag one at a time. "Maybe I'll move out. Maybe then you can do whatever you want for yourself, and maybe then you'd appreciate what I do for you and the girls."

"You wouldn't." I snorted as if he were joking. There was no way he'd move out.

"Watch me." Michael took his golf clubs and threw them into the backseat of his car. I cringed at his words, at the mere fact that he even said them.

As I watched him screech out of the driveway, I scolded myself for my juvenile behavior. He would never move out. He just reacted to my stupidity of knocking over the golf clubs. It shocked me as much as him. What had gotten into me? All I wanted was for everyone to be happy. The old Michael wouldn't care if I painted a picture for the auction. He would never have questioned it, and he wouldn't have cared if I enjoyed it. What had gotten into him?

I paced, angry with Michael for leaving without finishing our conversation. Maybe it was good he went to play golf. It would give us both time to calm down, and when he returned, I would grovel.

Not wanting the morning events to deter me from my goals, selfish or not, I finished my newly framed canvas, packed up my paints, and threw them into the back of my van with my well-worn easel. Sick to my stomach by the time I arrived at the Ranford mansion, I pulled under a large, shady chestnut oak. I checked my phone, making sure the ringer was on, and tucked it into my art bag.

My mind raced, along with my pulse. Surely, Michael wouldn't leave. He wouldn't. He knew how much I hated that my father was never around. Here I was, trying to keep my family together, and he threatened to leave?

My stomach growled. I grabbed the plastic grocery bag in the passenger seat and pulled out my sandwich and an orange. As if justifying my need not to feel selfish, I reminded myself this painting was for Pamela and her fundraiser, defending it as another commission of sorts. Knowing that settled my soul and took the "self" and the guilt out of self-serving.

I held the orange in my hand, lifted it to smell the sweet citrus aroma. It conjured my mom's hand resting on the phone in its cradle at my childhood house number six.

"Who was that, Mom?" I was fourteen years old and still glued to my mother's side. I pulled out a chair and sat next to her.

Mom stood and handed me an orange from the celadon bowl in the center of the table. I accepted the orange, knowing I was supposed to eat it, whether I wanted to or not.

"It was Carole—"

"Ah, I wanted to talk to her." I was disappointed I had missed a chance to talk to my older sister.

"She's all settled in her dorm, ready for fall classes to start on Monday," Mom mumbled as she rummaged through the freezer.

"How was her bus ride? Were there bunk beds? Did she get stuck with the top bunk? What's her roommate like?"

Mom turned around, a package of frozen chicken in her hand, "Honey, she just got there. She'll tell us all about it when she comes home for Thanksgiving."

"Thanksgiving?" That was three months away. I had stared at the orange in my hand. I shoved my thumb in the center and peeled away the first bit of rind. CJ, Christopher Jr., my oldest brother, left for the University of Florida four years before when we lived in Pensacola. Then my dad received a transfer to Corpus Christi, Texas, and CJ never lived at home again.

I peeled another piece of skin off the orange and set it on the tabletop next to the first one. Two years later, Thomas got left in Austin at the University of Texas, and I got to see him only that next summer. Why didn't he go to the University of Florida? At least my brothers would be together. Now Carole had left for the University of Virginia.

I tossed the last orange peel onto the table and plucked off the fragrant white strings one by one. My mother, still standing in front of the sink, was staring out the kitchen window.

"Thanksgiving will be here soon enough."

I knew then that would be the last time I saw Carole in my home. They would leave Carole behind in Virginia when Mom and I moved to Delaware. My father had already told me to prepare. I stared at the pile of the picked off white strings gathered on the floor and made my twelve-year-old self a promise.

I would never, ever, ever move my family around. My husband would have a nontraveling job, and I would have a forever home, where my kids would make forever friends and belong to forever groups and raise their families nearby in their own forever homes.

I carefully placed the three orange peels into the palm of my hand and scooped up the white strings. I threw them into the sink on top of the package of thawing chicken. On the way to my room, I passed my mother rocking in my dad's old brown corduroy lounge chair with absolutely nothing better to do than read her *Better Homes and Garden* as the chicken thawed.

Back then, I couldn't wrap my head around the fact that she had no other aspirations other than following my father around the country and keeping his house. She did nothing for herself and had nothing planned in her future barring a dentist appointment. I was thankful my life was different than hers. I had made sure of it.

Now, sitting in my van, staring out at the Ranford gardens, I picked the orange peels off the floor and returned them and the orange to the paper bag. I had lost my appetite.

Not wanting to waste any more of the beautiful day, I jumped from the van and took photos of the red brick three-story house with Federal period architecture, including gabled roofs, dormers, and arched doors and windows. I found the shot I wanted to recreate, just a bit of the hardscape at the southeast corner of the mansion, which would contrast with the informal English garden, in the style of Van Gogh—with my brushstrokes hopefully depicting movement, surrounding walkways and statues all contained by a white picket fence. On my laptop, I googled the historic house museum, looking for pictures of the garden with springtime and summer blooms of various colors and textures.

Just when I popped up the trunk of the van to set up my easel and begin sketching, the alarm went off on my phone. I bookmarked the pictures I would recreate. Right now, it was time to pick up the girls. And I would pick up a bottle of Malbec for when I apologized to Michael tonight.

Chapter 18

The day of…
Nineteen months earlier, 11:00 a.m. to 11:20 a.m.

Not wanting to start any project I most likely wouldn't get finished before Pamela picked me up for lunch, I poured myself a diet cola and sat on the back deck, wrapped in a blanket while Roger tended to his business. I turned my face to soak up the warm winter sunshine and checked the messages I had missed while in the shower.

Message number 1 from Chad Knight: Hi! Thank God for Facebook. I found you. I'm in town for the day.

I sat up and the blanket rolled off my shoulders. *Chad Knight? I hadn't heard from him in almost twenty years.*

Message number 2 from Chad Knight: Jules?

I ran into the house and plopped into the closest kitchen chair.

Message number 3 from Chad Knight: I'll be at Harvey's Diner for lunch a little after noon. Meet me?

My heart pounded in my chest. I wasn't sure whether to be honored or offended that he contacted me after all this time. The old high school Chad came to mind. Tall and lanky, good-looking with salty-blonde hair. Chad was a dream boyfriend. All the girls were jealous of me having won over the quarterback as soon I arrived in tenth grade.

I reread the messages. What harm could it be to meet him for lunch? I put the phone facedown on the table. Ridiculous. I was a married woman with three children. I had no business meeting him. I didn't even know him anymore. I wondered if he had married and had kids. Did he stay in the military?

What would Michael think? He and Chad were practically best friends in high school. He wouldn't care. It's not like he ever asked me what I did during the day anyway. The images from earlier in the shower came flooding back—me, alone on a tropical island, with no one to answer to. For one day, just for a few hours, I didn't have to be Mom or

Mrs. Scott. What could it hurt if Chad and I had lunch together? I could spare an hour for an old friend.

My next text was to Pamela: Sorry, have to skip lunch today.

I ran upstairs, dried my hair, and put on a chunky turquoise necklace. I burrowed into the back of my bathroom drawer and found some foundation and eyeshadow. My hands shook as I applied them, but my face did appear brighter.

Excited but nervous to do something different, something out of character, I checked myself in the rearview mirror then shut down my phone, tucked it into the glove compartment, and backed out of the driveway to have lunch with my long-ago high school boyfriend.

Chapter 19

Rushing from the Ranford house, I pulled into the school just a few minutes late. Nicole was already waiting at our usual spot across the street from the school entrance near the crosswalk.

"Where's Heather?" I asked as Nicole slid into the passenger seat beside me.

"Don't know," she said, pulling her earphones out of her ears.

We sat and waited, expecting Heather to run out any minute. When the doors finally shoved open, a police officer pushed through. He walked past his white car with its blue stripe and bar of lights across the top. My heart began to race as he headed in our direction.

"Where's your sister?" I asked Nicole again, this time an octave higher.

"I don't know, Mom," Nicole huffed. "I usually see her at lunch, but she wasn't there. Maybe she had a test to make up or something."

"Well, text her." My chest tightened, and heat crept up my neck. No, no, no. Not again. In my panic, I attempted to convert karma over to my side, I explained, once again, I just needed that day to myself. That one day. And today, today was to paint a painting for a fundraiser. It wasn't really for me, and I had my phone with me, turned on. I even checked.

My heart stopped when a knock on the window curbed my rampant thoughts. The policeman stood next to the driver's side window. Something had happened to Heather, and I couldn't catch my breath. No, no, no. I pleaded in silence. I took the day to plan for a painting for the fundraiser. Don't punish my family and me. I hadn't done anything wrong.

"Mom?" Nicole pushed on my thigh as if checking to see if I were alive. Then she reached over me and rolled down my window.

The officer said something sounding like the teacher from a Charlie Brown cartoon. "Wa-wah, wa-wa-wah."

Nicole placed her hand on my shoulder and shook me. She asked the officer, "Is Heather all right?"

"Mrs. Scott?"

My self-protective bubble popped when he said my name.

"I'm Officer Mills, the school's truancy officer. The Waffle Bakery downtown called me to collect a few kids who had skipped classes. Your daughter Heather was one of them. If you don't mind, would you come to my office so we can talk?"

"So Heather's with you?" Nicole asked.

"Is she all right? She's not hurt?" I asked as my fingers got caught up in my keychain, and I floundered turning off the ignition.

"She's fine, ma'am," the officer said as he held up an oncoming car when I opened my door and stepped out of the car. We waited for Nicole to exit from the slider and cross the street with us. With each step toward the school, anger extinguished the fear in my heart.

We entered the school and found Heather and two other boys sitting on benches outside Officer Mills's office. Heather had her earphones in and stared at me, expressionless, as I walked past her. She scooted over for Nicole to sit while I entered the office.

Officer Mills called Heather in before he closed the door. "Please sit."

Heather entered, removing her earbuds. She shoved them in her pocket and continued to stare at the floor.

"Mrs. Scott. Heather and her friends skipped school and were behaving in a disorderly manner in the Waffle Bakery. The manager didn't want to cause any problems. He just wanted them to leave. He'd asked them several times without any of them responding, which is why he called me. This is Heather's first offense. I'd like to give her a break since she's such a good student. But she won't get a second chance."

"Thank you. I understand." I was grateful my daughter was okay, there was no car accident, she was alive, and he was giving her a second chance. But once again, I was uncomfortable with Heather's choices and her lack of respect for our family and me. I churned with gratefulness and disappointment at the same time.

The officer looked at Heather. "Next time you leave school grounds during school hours, I will be forced to write up a report, and you will face a suspension."

"I get it." Heather looked up with a lack of sincerity as if she would agree to anything just to get out of there.

I shook the officer's hand then grabbed Heather's elbow. Nicole followed behind as we passed the boys on the bench, and both girls put earbuds into their ears.

When we reached the car, Heather glanced back at a black BMW in the parking lot. Tucker. I yanked the wires out of Heather's ears.

"Give me your phone. We'll figure out your punishment when your father gets home."

Instead of rushing home like a dutiful mother so the girls could get their homework done, I purposely ran my errands to free up my day tomorrow. I stopped at the grocery store, the pharmacy, and the liquor store, leaving the girls in the car to stew at each stop. Maybe Nicole could talk some sense into her sister.

After putting away the groceries, I threw grocery store-made subs and a bag of chips on paper plates and let the girls take them up to their room. I sat at the kitchen table, turning through the pages of *Coastal* magazine, waiting for Michael to come home from another previously scheduled work dinner that I thankfully didn't have to attend.

I heard each girl take their turn in the bathroom and head to bed around 9:30 p.m. It was a school night, and where the hell was Michael? He usually was home before nine when he had work dinners. Was he testing me to see if I'd text him and ask about his whereabouts? Would it anger him if I interrupted him as if I were checking in on him? Or would he be relieved that I cared enough to make sure he was fine and not in an accident? Should I text him about Heather's escapade, or would that add to his stress? I ended up texting him that I was waiting up for him, but for him to take his time. Having dinner and drinks with a work buddy and client could be a good thing. If he came home relaxed, he might be more willing to talk.

I was usually in my pajamas upstairs reading by 9:00 p.m., but I needed to be taken seriously when Michael and I discussed Heather. I opened the bottle of Malbec and poured two glasses, kicked off my shoes, slipped my bra out of my arm sleeve, and waited. Undoubtedly, Michael would be home any second, and I'd like to greet him with a truce before we got into Heather's ordeal.

There were times, when the kids were younger, Michael would come home with a bottle of Malbec, and that became our "special occasion" wine. We'd celebrate silly things like Curtis's soccer game wins or us surviving a four-hour-long dance recital. There were times Malbec welcomed in a new promotion, my first payment for my artwork, for winning $500.00 from a lottery scratch ticket. We found joy in the little things like when Michael would bring home a vase of flowers. He had snuck them off the conference table after he stared at them all day during a long, boring meeting and knew they would give me a week of joy. Once Michael opened a bottle of Malbec in the middle of the day because he didn't get picked for jury duty, and he played hooky from work.

It was almost 11:00 p.m., and still no Michael. I didn't know whether to be angry or worried. I texted him again with just a "Helloooo?" then swallowed the last sip of wine in my glass and began drinking the one I had poured for him. I wanted to apologize to Michael. I wanted to tell him how much I loved him and appreciated him for all he'd done for our family and me. I wanted him to know how sorry I was for putting my phone away in the glove compartment on the day of Curtis's incident. I wanted to ask him how I could fill the void in his heart, even though I knew there was no way I could.

I prayed I'd keep my mouth shut and not say anything while I hoped he said the words I needed to hear from him—that he needed help. I could suggest we do what we did when his father died. We spent an entire day hiking in his father's favorite park while Michael shared family stories for more than six hours until he got them all out. That was the night we made Curtis.

The bottle of Malbec was mocking me as I poured my third glass. "There's nothing to celebrate," it seemed to be saying. I took a sip, willing for something joyful to pop into my mind to justify drinking the smooth, rich wine. I leaned back in my chair, and through the archway into the den, Heather's school-year picture frame hanging on the far wall caught my attention. I stroked the framed glass over the eleven oval cutouts filled with pictures of Heather throughout the years. I circled the large center oval image of an infant Heather with her soft blankie—soon to be replaced with her senior picture. Then I moved over to Nicole's frame. In the center photo, she held her binky in her hand. The twelve smaller photos from kindergarten to eleventh grade confirmed the speed of time.

But then, there was Curtis's school-year frame where time had stopped. Kindergarten through sixth grade were filled with toothless smiles, changing hairstyles, and multiplying freckles. In the center, his chubby infant arms wrapped around Doggie. Five ovals to be forever empty.

Should I take the frame down? Should I keep it up on the wall? Would it matter to anyone? Maybe I'd just get a new frame with eight cutouts. Tears formed as I was unable to determine what to do. Michael would know. I'd ask Michael. I took down Curtis's frame and glimpsed the other two. How do I guarantee those picture frames would be complete in a year?

Too tired to have a discussion with Michael, I put the two empty wineglasses into the sink and hugged Curtis's frame to my chest as I climbed upstairs. I pushed the door open with my foot and stopped short. Sliding from my hands, the frame crashed to the floor. The closet doors were wide open, and the left side cleared out except for a couple of suits and some single hangers. I ran to Michael's dresser and pulled open the top drawer. Empty. One drawer after the other, all were missing the clothes I had folded and put away just yesterday.

I ran to the office, expecting to find Michael had moved in there, needing his own space with a door to close, but the room remained as vacant as the day Pamela and I converted it from Curtis's bedroom.

Heather came out of her room, rubbing her eyes. "What's going on?"

"Go back to bed, Heather," I said as Nicole stepped out beside her. I ran back down the stairs. "Everything's fine. Go back to bed, both of you."

I grabbed the corner of the entrance and swung myself into the den, slowing down my run. Michael's pillows and his stacks of magazines were gone, but the blanket was folded right where I had left it. Why hadn't I noticed?

When I turned around to get my phone off the kitchen table, the twins were at the base of the steps. Nicole stood with the broken frame in her hands. Wide-eyed, she asked, "What's going on?"

Heather walked into the den and picked up her father's blanket. "Dad's gone. I told you she'd run him out of here."

"No. No, that's not it," I said, ashamed Heather felt that way. "He needs to figure things out...he really hasn't dealt with..."

"Stop using Curtis's death as an excuse for everything." Heather let the blanket plummet to the floor. "You're a control freak, and you're not happy unless you have your hands around someone's neck."

"Stop," Nicole screamed. Her hands covered her ears. "Just stop." She slid to her knees, crying.

Heather whisked by her, kicking the blanket out of the way. "You're both insane."

Chapter 20

After a night of repeating, "I can fix this... I can fix this..." to woo myself to sleep, I woke in fear of facing the day. I dropped the girls off in front of the high school and said, specifically to Heather, "Stay in school today. I'll pick you up after." Neither girl asked about their father, and I was thankful. I needed time to repair what was broken and get Michael back in the house.

I called his number and left a clear message. "Michael, it's me. We need to talk. I'm sorry about the other day, but we have more serious problems. Heather got into some trouble at school yesterday. I need you home. We need you to come home."

I headed directly to Pamela's house for an impromptu debriefing coffee. I followed her to the patio kitchen on her back deck and helped myself to a diet cola from the mini fridge.

"Spill it," she said as she turned on the outdoor heater.

"Heather was all but arrested yesterday, and Michael left us," I spewed the words.

Pamela wrinkled her brow in disappointment, yet she didn't seem surprised.

"You knew?" There were times like this that I hated that Michael and Pamela's friendship went back to before I knew either of them.

"He told Jeff, but just in conversation. I thought he was just blowing off steam."

"You knew last night?" She could have called me and given me a heads-up.

"No, no. Jeff might have known last night, but he didn't say anything to me 'til this morning. I figured that was why you were coming over."

"He didn't know about Heather last night. Was he blowing off steam about me?"

"Not really. About himself. Nothing that you didn't already know. He's sad and confused and knows he needs help. He doesn't have a plan. That son of a bitch. He can't just leave you. Call him right now and tell him to get his ass back home." Pamela pushed open the slider to her kitchen.

"I've been calling. I just left him a message. He hasn't returned any of my calls or texts." I followed her into the kitchen after grabbing another diet cola out of the fridge.

"Chickenshit," Pamela said from behind her kitchen counter.

"We had a blow out the other day. I might have giggled when he threatened to leave, and he might have taken that as a challenge." I grabbed the door handle and slid it closed as Pamela put triple-chocolate muffins on the table.

"No, you didn't," Pamela said with a proud Mama smirk.

"Maybe I did. Out of nervousness. And right after that, I shoved over his precious golf clubs." I winced, hearing my own words.

"I'd be proud of you if I wasn't so shocked." Pamela pressed the back of her hand to her forehead in a dramatic style.

"Stop it. This is serious. What am I going to do? Do you know where he stayed last night?"

"Jeff didn't say, but I could ask him. Alicia would say to give Michael some time to cool off. So let's go with that while we deal with Heather."

I explained the details of Heather's adventure, thinking of all the days in high school I wanted to skip but didn't have the guts, which brought me to the one day when I did skip out on my life. The one day I went against the rules, my rules.

"Okay, let's think. First, you ground Heather's ass for two weeks. No phone, dance, or work. Then you tell the girls Michael needs time alone. Then you get Michael's ass on the phone and tell him to get some serious help before he even thinks of moving back in."

I rocked with my face in my hands. This couldn't be happening. Hadn't karma paid me back enough? "When will this end? I just wanted a couple of hours for myself."

"There's nothing wrong with that," Pamela said.

Did I say that out loud?

"You're not blaming yourself for Curtis again, are you?"

I crushed the empty diet-cola can. "No, Pamela. Just mumbling."

"Julie, talk to me."

I could see Pamela putting pieces together. How could I possibly admit that my life was unraveling because I took one day for myself almost twenty months ago? My son died, my daughters were acting out, and my husband left me all because of one stupid, totally harmless decision.

"Julie, where were you that day?"

"It doesn't matter. We all know where I wasn't." I don't often get upset with Pamela, but when I did, I clammed up.

Pamela didn't ask any more questions. "I'm sorry I brought it up."

I felt a "but" coming on, so I threw my cans into the recycle bin and hugged Pamela goodbye. Time to clam up. On the way home, I called Michael.

"Please, please, please…"

"Hello?"

"Michael?" I didn't expect him to answer.

"Julie," he said with a sigh. "What do you want?"

I couldn't think straight. I wanted so much. I wanted him home. I wanted him to want to be home. And then there was Heather.

"Heather got in trouble at school yesterday."

"I know."

"You know? How do you know?"

"I talked to the girls this morning."

That's why the girls didn't ask any questions. Of course, Heather talked to Michael and gave her version of the story.

"Heather promised she'd never skip school again," he said.

And that's it? "What did you tell them about us?" I asked. "About you not coming home last night?"

"Nothing. They didn't ask."

Of course, they didn't ask. As long as they knew he was okay, they could blame me for him leaving. "Well, we have to tell them something." I was not going to let them blame things on me without a fight.

"Tell them whatever you want."

His indifference scared me more than his absence. "Michael, please come home."

"Bring them here tomorrow night. I'll talk to them. I'll explain everything."

Here? Everything? Why did that sound so threatening? Everything, as in things I don't even know? Or something I don't know he knows?

"Where's here?"

"Drop them off at six. I'll text you the address." Michael hung up.

I was still stuck on "everything." I looked at the address he texted me, the local Flagstone Inn and Suites. A hotel? He can comment about me wasting time and supplies on a donation, yet he can afford a hotel down the street?

For the rest of the day, I wandered around the house, if one could do that in their own home. I meandered in and out of rooms. If I saw dust, I dusted with my sleeve. I wiped toothpaste out of the girls' sink with toilet paper. But I did nothing orderly nor completely. I thought of my mom after my dad had died. Her sole purpose for living had been taken away by his heart attack, and she wandered for weeks. She had walked throughout her house, taking in every bit with new eyes. She threw out half of what little she owned and surprisingly sold the house. It meant nothing to her. It held no memories of her kids who had never lived in that last house. She ended up moving into a small home with a large garden in my neighborhood to be part of my family's hometown.

As I wandered, I saw baby Curtis crawling on the den carpet and a five-year-old Nicole standing on a stool, stirring the cold water "cooking" Jell-O. I saw Michael on all fours giving a six-year-old Heather a pony ride across the kitchen floor. The day Roger entered our home, we all sat crossed-legged and played pass the puppy from lap to lap.

I pinched the bridge of my nose and prayed with all my might. I carefully chose my words, not wanting to misconstrue my feelings to the universe. "Please put my family back together under one roof. Under this roof."

I picked up the girls and let Nicole drive home. It was childish, but I felt like rewarding her in front of Heather. Nicole drove exactly three miles under the speed limit and counted to four before driving through a stop sign. With everything I needed to talk to the girls about on the tip of my tongue, I was more silent than ever before. I was sure Nicole was grateful when she clipped a curb as she made a right-hand turn, and all I did was grimace.

As soon as we landed in the kitchen, I started, "Girls, we have to talk."

"Here we go," Heather mumbled.

"Not everything is about you, Heather. Not yet anyway. Sit," I said. I waited for the girls to notice the silence and look up at me. "Your father has decided he needs some time alone. He's going to be staying at the Flagstone Inn and Suites."

"What did you do?" Heather accused.

"What do you mean, what did I do? I didn't do anything. Your father just decided this on his own."

Heather rolled her eyes.

Through tight lips, I said, "This has little to do with me." I checked myself. Parents separating had to be high on the stress scale for teenagers. "Hopefully, your father will take this time to grieve for Curtis finally. He's been having a hard time."

"He's having a hard time because you want him to do things your way. He left so he could do it his way." Heather did not give up.

"What are you talking about? Did he tell you that?" Again, I had a hard time restraining my anger.

"He didn't have to tell us. That's what you do to all of us. Your way or the highway."

Was this how they saw me? A tyrant? Couldn't they see that every decision I'd ever made was to keep them safe and help them grow into reasonable adults? "He wants me to bring you over tomorrow evening and spend some time with him."

Nicole's silence was punctuated with sobs. I handed her a napkin without taking my eyes off Heather.

"No," Heather said.

"No, what?" I asked. Was this child going to argue against my every statement?

"No. If he wants to see us, he can come here." Heather stood up.

I didn't think that was unreasonable and wished I had thought of it when I was talking to Michael earlier, but I really couldn't call the shots at this point. "Okay, I'll suggest it to him. I'll be out with Alicia tomorrow evening to measure for some commission work anyway. So I'll try to make it work."

"Don't bother. I'll text him." Heather took a few steps toward the stairs. "Are we done?"

"Funny girl. Have a seat." It was hard not to smile at Heather's attempt to escape. She knew better. "Nicole, you may leave if you want. I have some things to discuss with your sister."

Nicole clasped her sister's hand in hers and stayed seated. Okay, so that was how it was going to be. Two against one. Heather sat and scooted her chair closer to Nicole.

"Since your father isn't here, I guess I get to take matters into my own hands. I'm very disappointed with you, Heather. You're much smarter than this. I can't believe I have to have a conversation with one of my daughters about the reasons not to skip school. If you wanted the day off, you should have asked. You've done that before."

"And?" Heather says.

"And I think you should be grounded for two weeks."

"She can't miss dance class." Nicole defended Heather. "We're auditioning for roles for the Christmas recital this week."

"And I'll get fired from my job if I can't work for two weeks," Heather said, always one step ahead.

"So what do you think I should do? What you did is not acceptable. I won't even mention that you were with Tucker. Skipping school is one thing, but underage drinking is another."

"I wasn't drinking," Heather protested.

"Don't add liar to your résumé. You didn't clean your bathroom up very well the next morning."

"I got sick, that's all."

"Whatever. Should I ask your sister for the truth?"

Nicole shook her head. "Please, don't get me involved."

"I feel for you, Nicole," I said. "But you chose to stay in support of your sister. How many times are you going to have to lie or hide facts for her? That makes you just as guilty in my eyes."

"That's not fair," the twins said simultaneously. Nicole cocked her head toward Heather as if signaling her to answer my questions.

"Okay. I had one rum and coke, but I wasn't drunk," Heather admitted.

"Hopefully, you haven't been drinking long enough to know the difference. Anyway, you're grounded for two weeks." I put my hand up when the two began to protest. "Since it seems you have to go to school, dance, and work, your punishment will be two weeks with no phone, and you have dish duty all day, every day, for those two weeks. Starting today. Every dish, do you hear me?"

Heather looked at Nicole, and I made sure Nicole was not taken advantage of. "And Nicole cannot help you. Even if you want to, Nicole. If you do a single dish, you'll be grounded."

"That's ridiculous," Nicole said with a huff of resignation.

"No phone?" Heather's puppy dog eyes hadn't worked on me for a long time, but I gave her credit for trying.

"No phone." I knew how tough that would be. I knew better than most what could happen when you didn't have your lifeline available. I knew how it felt not to be able to talk to a friend or a husband when you needed to. I felt like the cruelest mother on earth.

Heather didn't respond, but the droop in her shoulder's let me know she had surrendered.

Chapter 21

The day of...
Nineteen months earlier, 5:00 p.m. to 5:10 p.m.

*A*fter my visit with Chad and hours of introspection, I was pleased that I took a day to myself. With a new lease on life, I was happy to go back to being "Mom" and "Mrs." Ending my afternoon alone with a walk on the beach, the short break from being myself was all I needed to snap me out of my rut. I had a new appreciation for all that was mine. I finally saw the grass was actually greener on my side of the fence.

I adjusted my sideview mirror and stared at the oncoming vehicles blocking me into the parking space. I put my blinker on and waited for the line of cars to pass. A day without family, without Pamela, was just what I needed to set my head straight and move forward with my life. I had what I always wanted and couldn't see it for the rut of it all. I had let my white picket fence lock me in instead of securing my forever home dream. Realizing I was going to be a few minutes late picking the girls up from their after-school activities, I dug my phone out of the glove compartment.

I had missed nineteen texts and phone calls.

One from Curtis's school.

Four from Michael.

Eight from Pamela.

One from Heather.

Five from Nicole.

The first text from Pamela: *Call me. Michael thinks we had lunch together. Call me.*

First call from Michael: *Where the hell are you?*

Last text from Michael: *Curtis is hurt. Meet us at Wilmington Trauma.*

Chapter 22

Nicole made arrangements with Michael to pick up the girls from their after-school activities and have dinner with them at home. It was all I could do not to cook something they would all like before Alicia picked me up to go to her client's home in Bethany Beach.

"Hi," I said as I slipped into the passenger seat of her convertible. "What a beautiful day." Hiding behind the windshield, with our side windows up, scarves tied under our chins, and the sun warming our faces, we drove through the late September air Thelma and Louise style.

But as beautiful as the weather was, it was hard to savor. As we motored south, my gut filled with worry for Michael and Heather. I stressed over Heather's phone hidden in my kitchen desk drawer. How could I be so cruel and take away a lifeline? And I prayed that Michael was getting the help he needed. I couldn't lose him. A thought crept in and made me sit up straight. What if I had to support the girls by myself? Was I prepared for that? The closer we got to the shore, the more I realized a renewed purpose for this latest commission.

The trip down to Bethany Beach took a little over an hour through farmland and beach towns. Silence prevailed comfortably with Alicia. If you were happy, or at least not complaining, she was happy. So I leaned back and set aside my worries. I released my thoughts into the breeze, leaving them in our wake.

"Here we are," Alicia said as we pulled into a crushed shell driveway.

The sweet smell of the beach breeze kindled a warmth in my soul. The three-story, grey cedar-shingled home with white trim was the epitome of a beach cottage; however, the 5,700 square-foot house was far from a cottage. The front of the home had a large gambrel eyebrow above an oversized arched window, with Endless

Summer hydrangeas underneath and a wraparound porch leading to the beachfront. When we got up to the front door, all glass with white trim, I could see straight through the living area to the Atlantic Ocean. Alicia unlocked the door and presented the view across the room framed by flowing sheers on either side of a wall of hidden opened sliders.

"This is mind-blowingly gorgeous," I said, standing in the middle of the room. I turned in a slow circle, taking it all in.

The entire room included the living and dining area and an eight-foot island separating the kitchen. Everything was white—a white linen couch and white-on-white paisley high-back chairs in the living room. White-on-white ticking covered the parson chairs in the dining room. The large round pedestal table was rustic white with an antique glaze that was similar to the kitchen cabinets. But it was the choice of accent colors that made the room pop. Alicia chose bright navy and yellow, with a little bit of red. It was exhilarating! Blue and white delft pottery, yellow sunflowers on navy silk and blue-and-white stripes for pillows, navy enamel side tables with glass lamps under yellow shades. It was glorious. It would be hard to be in a sour mood in this home.

"You did a great job with this space," I said and melted into one of the paisley chairs.

"Yep!" Alicia proudly admitted. "And I had a ball doing it. The budget was wide open, so it was easy for me to make it perfect. The homeowners are down on the beach," she said, pointing to the red umbrella shading two people lounging in shorts and sweatshirts at the ocean's edge. "They are the sweetest couple. They've given me free rein. They haven't been here much. Just arrived yesterday. I told them I was bringing you by but for them not to change any of their plans. I wanted you to be able to come in and soak up the way they live."

"Well, I'm glad I'm here. I'm not sure I could have imagined its fabulousness by descriptions or even photos."

I wandered through the open doors onto the deck, past the outdoor dining table adorned with a blue-and-white striped ticking table runner with bright-yellow cushions in the seats. Three fresh sunflowers reclined in a large white ceramic bowl as if lounging in a tub. The ceiling above me, encased in white beadboard with brass nautical lighting, was coverage offered from the deck above. I continued to the edge of the deck, where sunshine inundated me.

I watched the couple on the beach, sitting side by side, reading magazines. They had all this and could probably afford to be anywhere in the world, yet here they were, together on the beach, now holding hands. I wanted that scene for me and Michael. I turned, leaned on the railing, and looked back into the house.

I had nothing to worry about. There was plenty of inspiration here. "Show me where you need some artwork," I said and walked back into the house.

After gathering all the measurements and ideas for each room, it was still too early to go home. I explained how Michael needed time with the girls, so Alicia was happy to bring me to one of her favorite local seafood restaurants with an ocean view and catch me up on her life.

"Sounds like things have been building up between you two?" Alicia said after listening to my grumbling.

"We hadn't really been talking before he moved out. If that's what he's done. Not beyond pleasantries anyway. He didn't ignore me, but he never addressed me."

Alicia grinned. "One of the reasons I have such a struggle with marriage and commitment is the longer I date someone, the more I have to overlook. It needs to be a two-way street. I can only compromise so much. We usually create our own monsters. The more you compromise, the more you build a world you can't live in."

"Believe me, I think of that every day. But how do I change things now? The precedents have been set." I stared out the restaurant's window at the waves crashing on the beach and frowned. "Things were falling apart even before Curtis's incident. Back then, when we went to a restaurant, I would want to eat outside, and he would want to eat inside. I'd want a booth. He'd want a table. If we were out, say, on the boardwalk with the girls, I'd want to walk in the sun. He wanted the shade. I'd go to bed early. He went to bed late. We didn't even eat on the same schedule. Now, when I look back, it's been going on for a long time. I just didn't see it. It has gotten to the point where I no longer want to compromise, and the three of them see it as me creating problems. How could we have so little in common now?" I didn't want to speak ill of Michael, but my hands were tied.

"Before, he had two responsibilities: providing for his family and instilling life lessons into his son. It's like he saw you as responsible for the girls because that's what you did. Maybe try to get him involved with them?"

"I do try, but the girls hardly need me anymore, let alone him. I put food on the table, do their laundry, and drive them around. They're getting their driver's licenses soon, but we only have my van at home. Michael thinks I could let the girls drive themselves to school, but that would leave me at home all day without a car. Anyway, as long I can drive them around, I can keep some sort of handle on them, whether they talk to me or not. I wish I could be as emotionless and pragmatic as Michael."

Heather's words to "give Dad a break. At least we can leave in a couple of years without involving the court system" echoed in my head. My stomach sank as I thought of Michael and the twins sitting around the kitchen table, sorting out what was going on in our family, without me.

Chapter 23

When we pulled into my driveway after our peaceful, moonlit ride home from Bethany Beach, Nicole sat, shoulders slumped, on the front porch steps with, of all people, Mrs. Amberly from across the street. I ran through the front yard before Alicia turned off her car.

"Nicole?" I called out as she met me halfway. With an arm around her, I lifted her chin. "What's going on?"

"Heather. As soon as Dad left, she took off with a couple of kids. I told her not to, and we got in a huge fight here in the front yard."

I gave her a second hug, then remembered Mrs. Amberly, who had walked over to the sidewalk and stood. When our eyes met, it was as if I gave her permission to approach us.

"Mrs. Amberly heard us fighting and came over after Tucker screeched out of here," Nicole said. That explained what Mrs. Amberly had seen, but not quite why she had been sitting on my front porch.

"Hi, Julie. I apologize for interfering, but I could see Nicole was quite upset. I'll leave you two now." She patted Nicole on the shoulder and said, "Remember, the angels are watching over all of you."

I stood hand in hand with Nicole as Mrs. Amberly walked away and waved to Alicia in her car.

Alicia, oh my. I forgot about Alicia. I waved her over, and we walked into the house together.

"So what was that about angels?" I asked as I pulled three bottles of water out of the fridge.

"Nothing really," Nicole said. "She just sat with me until I calmed down then said something about my angels wanting me to focus on myself, and they'll watch over Heather."

"Humph." I rolled my eyes. Where were my angels the day Curtis died?

"She said the angels had been with Curtis, making sure he remained comfortable, out of pain, until he passed."

I plopped down, depleted, knowing I should be asking about Heather but was intrigued by the angels. "I guess I am grateful for the angels then?"

Alicia looked straight in my eyes, nodding her head as if agreeing with my acceptance and gratitude.

After a few moments, my thoughts came full circle. "How long has Heather been gone? It's after nine p.m.," I said.

"Dad left around 7:30, and she left a few minutes later. She said they were going to the county fair. She invited me, but I think the boys were drinking. Didn't want to go with them. Plus, she's grounded, isn't she?"

Exhaustion blanketed me. The liberating feelings from the ride along the beach after the highs of working in my creative zone came crashing down to the overwhelming lows of parenting teenagers alone. The pure weight of the day began throbbing in my temples.

"Text her and tell her to get her ass home."

"I can't. You have her phone." Nicole pointed out.

"Crap. Do you have Tucker's phone number?"

"No," Nicole said.

I dug my phone out of my purse and called Michael. After a few rings, it went to his voice mail. I pictured him staring at my picture as his phone rang then silencing it and putting it facedown on his desk or table or whatever the hell he was sitting near. "I'm going to go look for her." I stuffed my phone back into my purse. "Thank you for today, Alicia. It was just what I needed. We'll talk tomorrow."

"Do you want me to come with you?" Alicia asked.

"No. Thanks though. Go on home to Liz." I hugged her as she left. "Nicole, stay here and do your homework. Text me if you hear from Heather."

As I drove through town in the dark, occasional streetlights guided me toward County Road 13 toward the mall and the county fair. I slowed in front of coffee shops and ice cream stands to look for Tucker's BMW. I hadn't a clue what I'd do once I found Heather, but I knew for sure I couldn't sit around, waiting for her to come home.

These were the times I missed Michael the most. We used to be such a great team, and the girls never seemed to challenge us as a pair. When did it all begin to go wrong?

But if I were honest with myself, if we could go back, I wouldn't go back to where we left off before Curtis's incident. I'd go back to when Curtis was just born. Since then, it was almost like we used the kids' activities, homework, and schedules as a distraction from each other and as excuses for not being a couple.

But the day of Curtis's incident, I had reconciled it all. I recognized all the blessings in my life and was grateful for Michael and the kids. Those few hours I had checked out, when no one could find me, led me to a renewed appreciation of all I had. I was ready to reinvest myself in my marriage and family. But then, all hell broke loose.

Flashing blue lights ahead had me slowing the van. I passed by two police cars parked under the streetlights, one in front and one behind a vehicle, a black BMW with its trunk wide open. Blankets and jackets hung out the back. Gym bags, backpacks, tennis rackets, and shoes were strewn along the ground. I looked up in time to see my Heather leaning on one of the police cars with her hands in her pockets. I hit the brakes out of reflex but then drove into the parking lot of the Purple Lotus Day Spa across the street. With shaking hands, I backed into a parking spot in the building's shadow then watched the goings-on. There were two heads bobbing in the back of the second police car, and I had recognized Tucker's hair flip.

I so wanted to call Michael and ask if I should get involved now or wait? My gut sank at the realization I had always parented alone; Michael was just there as a sounding board, sort of a silent partner. Just knowing he would back me up used to give me the confidence to make parental decisions. What would he tell me to do right now? He'd say Heather was physically safe, so sit back and let the scene play out. It was not in me to sit back, but as the police officer spoke to Heather, and she nodded her head, seemingly listening, I did precisely that.

The second police officer pulled his head out of Tucker's car's passenger seat. Holding a small paper bag, he walked over, reached into the back of his own car, and pulled out a handcuffed Tucker. If my heart wasn't racing before, it was beating out of my chest now. This was serious. At least Heather wasn't handcuffed.

The other policeman left Heather's side, took the paper bag, and opened it. Tucker was shaking his head vehemently. I could imagine him saying, "It's not mine."

Heather dropped her face into the palms of her hands, and I wanted to go and comfort her. She had to be scared to death. The cop returned, and they exchanged a few words. He handed his cell phone to Heather, her thumbs went to work, then handed the phone back to the cop. I picked up my phone and waited for the text to arrive. Nothing. It hurt that she wasn't reaching out to me.

As one police officer reacquainted Tucker with the back seat of the cruiser, the other picked up the stuff off the ground and shoved it into the trunk of the BMW. The two officers spoke for a few minutes then went their separate ways. One drove away with Tucker and the other kid in the back seat. The other officer returned to Heather and leaned on the car next to her. I debated whether to get out of the car when a white Audi pulled up behind them.

Michael. Michael?

Michael jumped out of his car. Heather ran, arms reaching, and gave him a tight bear hug.

Heather had texted Michael. How could she call her father when he wasn't even living at home? I'd be damned if he played the good guy to my bad guy. I punched the steering wheel with my palm.

Michael greeted the cop with an extended hand. He sent Heather to his car and talked to the policeman for a few more minutes. I pulled the lever on the side of my seat and lay back, hoping Michael couldn't see me, but if there was one person on God's green earth who would recognize my van, even in the dark, it would be Michael. I stayed hidden-not-hidden until I heard both cars take off, then I raced home.

When Nicole asked, I let her believe I couldn't find Heather, knowing her father would bring her home. Nicole played with her bowl of ice-cream as she pleaded her case that this was an excellent reason why I should never take their phones away from them.

Heather entered the kitchen with Michael close behind. Nicole jumped out of her seat. "Why did you go with them? They were drunk. I told you it wasn't a good idea."

Heather didn't say anything. She walked through the kitchen then up the stairs. Nicole followed directly behind her.

I figured it was best to play dumb. "Where was she?"

"Well, she was headed to the county fair but didn't quite make it," Michael said, still standing only one step in with his hand on the door handle.

"I thought you told Tucker to stay away from her." Thinking I might have shown my hand but then remembered Nicole had told me Heather left with Tucker, I asked, "Is she drunk?"

"No. But the boys were. They were arrested. Luckily, the cop let Heather call someone to pick her up," Michael said.

"And she called you? I'm the one here at home, worrying about her," I said the words that had been on the tip of my tongue for almost an hour. "What did you discuss while you were over here earlier tonight? Did she tell you she was grounded and that she couldn't have her phone? You can't un-punish her."

"I didn't say she could go out. Get your guilt under control, Jules. She didn't want to call you. She called me because, according to her, quote, I'm the sane one of the two of us, unquote. What's going on with you two?" He looked at me accusingly.

I cringed at how easily Heather managed to turn the situation into something about me. Suddenly I saw how we played good cop, bad cop with the girls when they were little. Me being the disciplinarian, and my gratefulness for Michael's support was interpreted as me being the bad guy. Somehow, all these years, I went along with it and now I felt set up. Where the girls apparently saw control and injustice, I saw safety and discipline. And Michael just watched. Well, not anymore.

"Do you want some ice cream?" I asked, picking up Nicole's bowl of melted cream and placing it into the sink for Heather to wash in the morning.

"No thanks. I have to go," Michael said, stepping back from the door.

"Please stay. Let's talk," I said.

"I can't listen to you tell me I need to fix myself when you clearly have some fixing of your own to do," he said then closed the door behind him.

I cleaned the kitchen. I needed something to do, and Heather still had several more days of her punishment, and there would be lots more nights of dishes added after tonight's shenanigans. I didn't see the girls the rest of the night, but I strained to hear the tone of their murmurs.

When the twins were little and Curtis just a babe in arms, we were a tight unit. I was on top of everything, meals and naps, outdoor time for the girls, tummy time for baby Curtis. Dinner sharply at 5:30 p.m., then baths. Michael came home in time to read a couple of books to the twins, each insisting on choosing their own, and everyone was down for the night by 7:30 p.m. Even when the girls got older—in bed by 7:30 p.m. They couldn't talk, and they had to stay in bed, but they could read as long as they liked. Smooth as silk. Michael and I had time to watch a movie or a ball game together. We would have a glass of wine and talk about our day. Well, his day. Mine rarely changed. I couldn't have been a more consistent mom.

I poured a glass of wine and pondered over how I became so misunderstood. I loved my husband and adored my children. I feared for their safety and wished the best for them. But if three out of three thought I was the unstable one…how would I explain to him that we couldn't meet in the middle when we were all using different semantics?

It was after 11:30 p.m., but I needed to talk to someone. I called Pamela.

"What's up, girlfriend?" she answered.

"What's wrong with me?" I asked as I slid from the couch to the floor.

"Oh, Jules. I'll be right there."

A half a bottle of wine later, Pamela entered with a pizza. My girl really knew me.

I poured the rest of the bottle into a glass for Pamela and pushed the coffee table out of the way. Pamela joined me on the den carpet.

With the couch as our backrest, we ate pepperoni and mushroom with fresh garlic and basil slices over the pizza box. Roger sat next to us, anticipating any handouts. I told Pamela everything, less embarrassed about hiding in the Purple Lotus Day Spa parking lot than the fact that Heather called Michael.

"Oh, hun," Pamela said. "It's good that Heather feels comfortable enough to call her father."

"I know, but why does it have to be one or the other? He chose to leave. She should have called me."

"Is that what this pity party's all about? That Heather didn't call you? You sat and watched the whole thing. Why didn't you go over and help her?"

Leave it to Pamela to point out the obvious. Why didn't I help her? I certainly didn't enjoy watching her suffer.

"I was mush. I was glad I found her, but I was pissed that she was with that kid again. I was happy she was safe but angry that she left without asking. I was sad that I couldn't talk to Michael and felt guilty that she's been so lost."

"Okay. That's mush. Think of it this way. What if she did call you, and you stepped out of your van from across the street? Pretty sure that wouldn't have gone over well at all."

A silver lining. I leaned over in my slight daze and hugged Pamela. The pizza box slid off our laps, and Roger got away with a pizza bone—what the kids called the last of the crust with no sauce or cheese on it.

"How am I going to fix this?"

Chapter 24

The day of…
Nineteen months earlier, 6:20 p.m. to 7:15 p.m.

I rushed into the Wilmington Trauma Center and was directed to a private family waiting room. I pushed open the heavy windowless door and came face-to-face with Michael. He was paler than pale with red-rimmed eyes, and his hands curled into fists as I approached him. He did not reciprocate my hug.

"Where's Curtis? How is he? What happened?" I needed answers.

"He went to the school nurse with a severe headache. Then he began throwing up. That's when the nurse tried to get a hold of you. God, Julie. Where were you?"

I reached for his hand, and he pulled his arm and turned away from me when I didn't answer.

"He had a seizure in the ambulance," Michael continued with his back to me. "He was unconscious when he got here. They rushed him into surgery after a CT scan." Michael walked away as if he couldn't bear to be near me and backed into a chair. "He was bleeding in his brain. Jesus, Julie, where were you?"

"I don't understand. He was at school. A seizure? And now he's in surgery?" I cradled my face in my palms. This was my fault. God was punishing me. "Did he hit his head or have a fall?"

"By the way, Pamela is picking up the girls and bringing them here."

Shit. The girls. I was supposed to pick up the girls. How could I forget them? I slumped into the chair across from where Michael sat. "This is a great hospital. Curtis is in good hands."

"He better be," Michael said as if I caused Curtis's headache.

I stared at his back as he looked out the large window overlooking the parking lot. His solid, dark, silhouette was all I could see as if he

129

was purposely hiding from me. No matter what he said or did, Michael couldn't make me feel any worse than I felt right then.

"Mom. Dad." Heather and Nicole burst through the double doors with Pam following behind.

Both Michael and I rushed to greet them, each from our respective corners of the room. I slowed as to not compete with Michael for their hugs. Heather nodded her hello and headed away from me. Nicole hugged me and left her arm around my waist while Michael answered what questions he could.

"I just wish someone would come in and tell us he's okay," I said and buried my face into Nicole's shoulder, avoiding Pamela's interrogating eyes.

Nicole left me standing alone and joined Heather on the couch.

Michael offered to get drinks for everyone, undoubtedly grateful for something to do away from me. "Want to come?" he asked the girls.

I began to ask them to stay, but then my heart sunk lower than I thought possible when they both looked at Pamela, silently asking permission. With a nod of her chin, she sent them with Michael.

Once the girls left the room, Pamela patiently waited until I could no longer not look at her. I braced myself for her interrogation.

"Julie, where were you?"

"I needed some time alone." I couldn't look into Pamela's eyes. She was the one person in my life that knew me inside and out. I had to come up with something she couldn't see through, but I had no idea where a mom of three would go to be alone. "I went to a spa." I realized I should have come up with something better the second the words were out of my mouth.

"Without me? Never. Where were you?"

Chapter 25

Weeks passed since Heather's trouble with the police, and we fell into a muted routine. The girls had dinner with Michael after he picked them up from their activities three or four times a week. I got my wish. Michael was now more involved with the girls.

On the nights the girls were with me, I went overboard with cooking meals. I tried new recipes and even made desserts. This morning I had baked a quiche. Heather put her and Nicole's plates in the dishwasher even though she had been ungrounded for a few days now. Maybe three weeks really was long enough to form a habit.

"Mom, I can't find my shirt for work today after school."

"Did you look at the ironing pile?"

Her norm was to text me from school to have her shirt ready at pick up, but ironing had taken a back seat. I had been trying to prioritize my studio time so that I could deliver the paintings for Alicia's Bethany Beach client as soon as possible, for various reasons. Money for one and filling the space in my head for another. Michael and I had texted only a few times, but I knew he'd been in touch with the girls, which was more important anyway. With Michael not around, I raked the fallen leaves in the front and backyards and took out the garbage. I wanted everything just as it should be when he returned, as if we hadn't missed a beat.

I began to pour my diet cola for my morning school run when Heather returned with her shirt and handed it to me to iron. I was impressed she thought ahead yet stymied how she blatantly expected me to iron it for her.

"I'm not ironing until Saturday. I have to get changed." I handed the shirt back to her and pointed to the laundry room. In the time it would have taken me to iron the damn shirt, Heather struggled with opening the ironing board and asked me how much water to put in the little holey thing. She wondered which outlet I plugged the iron into and what temperature should be used for her shirt. Surely, I'd seen this child iron before. Hadn't I?

Her ploy, intentional or not, worked. I grabbed the shirt and ironed it, justifying my actions because at the rate Heather was dallying, the girls would be late for school.

"Don't go anywhere. This is the last thing I iron for you. Listen and learn. Then you can teach your sister."

As a mom, I was slightly embarrassed. Heather didn't know how to iron. The girls had done laundry before. I was pretty sure they'd done all different laundry tasks, like put it in the washer, switch to the dryer, etcetera. Well, from now on, they would be doing their own laundry: wash, dry, fold, iron, and put away. I'd let them each pick one day a week to get it done. Let's see how independent they wanted to be when I stopped doing things for them.

"What time do I need to pick you two up today?" I asked the girls, decibels higher than average to get past their earbuds as we rushed to the van.

"I have photography club 'til five," Nicole responded as she walked around to the far side of the van and slipped into the back seat.

I reached back and pulled an earbud out of Heather's ear.

"I can't wait 'til five. I have to work at four," she said, clearly proving she heard Nicole's response; therefore, my question the first time. "I'll just ride the bus home."

"That's silly," I said. "It'll take you another thirty minutes on the bus. I'll come pick you up at 2:20 then can take you to work, and then I'll go wait to pick up Nicole."

"Why do you even bother to ask?" Heather shoved her backpack into the seat next to Nicole. "Just tell me what you want me to do." She slammed the sliding door shut and inserted her earbuds.

I went completely still. Alicia told me to listen to myself when I talked to the girls, to listen to what they said, and maybe I would start understanding how they perceived me. Here I was, trying to be kind, helpful, and efficient. Heather saw my suggestion as a command. Now what?

I backed out of the driveway and noticed Mrs. Amberly sitting in her rocking chair on her porch. Again, it looked like she was talking to someone, but I didn't see anyone else around. As I shifted from reverse to forward in front of her house, Mrs. Amberly waved. In my rearview mirror, I caught Nicole waving back.

As the van made its way down the street to the stop sign, my mother had replaced Mrs. Amberly on that porch. How I missed when my mom lived only a few blocks away, in her own home. I wished I could drive past and wave to her, but she was cheated by cancer after finally living in a forever home. Since her death a few years after the twins were born, I often thought of her empty life after raising her children with no hobbies and even less ambition. I never missed her parenting advice. She had little to offer, but still, she was always pro Julie. It had been a long time since I'd felt like I had someone in my corner.

What would she think about what was going on in my family now? Would she blame me for not keeping my house and home in order? It was what she knew and what she cherished, so my guess was, she'd be devastated and ashamed of me.

As I remembered why I had started down the path of my mother, I asked Nicole, "Who was Mrs. Amberly talking to?"

"That lady's crazy," Heather said a little too loudly over the noise playing in her earphones.

"Shut up. You don't know her," Nicole said adamantly. "She talks to her son."

"Crazy, I tell you."

"I didn't know she had a son." I jumped in before Nicole got wrapped up in Heather's belligerence. "I've never seen anyone else on the porch."

"No, he died over fifty years ago." Nicole pulled an earbud out of her ear as she became invested in the conversation.

My heart pinched at the thought of me living with the memory of Curtis for the next fifty-plus years. "Oh, I didn't realize."

"That's because you've never taken the time to get to know her. I enjoy talking with her." Nicole sighed.

A new discovery every day. That's what it felt like when you're housing teenagers. I had seen Nicole come from across the street a couple of times, but when I asked, she said she had gone out for a walk. The thought that my daughter enjoyed talking to a stranger, when she used to speak to me, struck a chord deep inside.

"Mom, she's a sweet lady. She says talking to her son every day keeps him alive in her heart."

I understood exactly what she meant by that, and thoughts of Mrs. Amberly's son watching over my son warmed my heart. I dropped the girls at school and headed directly to Pamela's for Friday morning coffee with my friends.

"Jeff says he hasn't heard much from Michael lately," Pamela said over her coffee mug.

"Well, I haven't a clue what he's been up to," I said and meant it. "He drops the girls off but never comes in. I hope he's getting some help."

"That would be great," Alicia said. She put down the knife she used to slice the fresh-from-the-oven lemon poppyseed cake and served us each a piece.

"I've been informed by the twins that they are old enough to make plans with their own father without getting me involved."

"I suppose they're right," Alicia said, placing the remainder of the sweet-smelling bread in the center of the table.

"I still think this isn't far from normal," Pamela said. "I remember not wanting to talk to my mother in high school. And you, Julie, you were always pissed at your mom." Pamela set her coffee mug on the table. "Speaking of high school, I ran into Karen Westerfield at the grocery store the other day. Boy, she keeps a lot of trivia in that little blonde head of hers. Anyway, she said she and Marnie Price are working on our twentieth high school reunion already. And Mrs. Otterman, our tenth-grade algebra teacher, passed away last month. That woman must have been 120 years old. She also said she saw Chad Knight in town last year."

"Really?" Not prepared to hear Chad's name, I sputtered. I didn't know where to look, and it was apparent. "He's been away a long time." I hoped I sounded genuinely curious. "I'm surprised anyone recognized him."

Pamela's eyebrows raised as she cocked her head in confusion.

I avoided her eyes. My heart began to race, and I added, "Interesting."

Alicia volleyed between the two of us in silence. When nothing more was said, she took it upon herself to change the subject. "I asked Liz to come up with a guest list for the twins' birthday party." She scrolled through her phone for the email then slid it toward me.

I picked up the phone and read the list of nine names.

Only six girls and three boys. I probably should have asked the girls myself for some ideas, but when I happened to bring up the twins' upcoming birthday, Alicia said she'd have Liz get some ideas and find out the list of friends. "That's it?"

"Liz said these were the only kids at school they hung around with, mostly at lunch. These two are Nicole's photography friends," Alicia said, pointing out the names.

"Of course, we could invite Tucker and his friends," Pamela said.

"Not funny," I said and grabbed a pen and notebook out of Pamela's kitchen office cubby. "What does Liz think we should do? A cookout? A movie night?"

"They want a spa day," Alicia said.

I dropped my pen. "I really don't know my girls at all."

"I think you don't want to recognize your girls are growing up," said Pamela.

I could tell Pamela had not let our previous conversation go. "I can't afford to pay for a spa day for twelve kids. And what about the boys?" I couldn't wrap my head around the idea.

"First of all, boys like to get pampered as much as girls," said Pamela. "Second of all, you don't have to invite all of them. Why don't I call the club and get a price say for six girls? Heather, Nicole, and Liz, then we'll let them choose the three others to invite."

"Pfft." I resigned with a go-ahead flip of my wrist. My girls asking for a spa day was as foreign as them asking to go hike in the artic.

Alicia and I chatted about the possibility of other cheaper options. But I came up with nothing. I'd lived with the sisters their whole lives, and now I didn't even know them. How depressing. Where and when did I lose track?

"Okay. I got them down to $125.00, including use of the hot tub and sauna, a massage, mani-pedi, and hair." Pamela was clearly proud of her finagling.

"Oh, that's not bad," I said.

"A person," Pamela added with a seriously-you-thought-that look.

That would be over $700.00. There was no way I could afford that. Not even if it were just the two girls. No way Heather deserved it.

"All that stuff would normally be over $350.00 a person," Pamela said, as if getting a deal was the issue. "But there's a catch. We have to do it during a school day. They have an opening for six the Thursday after their actual birthday."

Sometimes I wondered how Pamela and I lived in the same world. "Let me think about it," I said, doodling on the notepad. Adding up not only the spa cost but also the cake and goodies overwhelmed me. I needed time to consider how to pay for my one and only option. Ugh.

I shook my head, knowing that somehow, I would put this spa birthday together for the girls. "Could I get an advance on the Bethany commissions? I have a couple of them completed?" I asked Alicia. I was getting through the paintings, one at a time, and Alicia had said her clients would like everything completed by the end of October. "That way, I won't have to involve Michael and justify such an expensive birthday."

"Don't worry about that," Pamela said as she collected our empty plates off the table. "It'll get charged to my account and won't need to be paid until the end of November. And something else…" She didn't continue speaking until she turned on the faucet and rinsed off the dishes in the sink. "Heather asked if, for their birthdays, I would take them to get their licenses."

My heart cracked from the betrayal. Alicia proved she already knew about the girls' request when she broke her stiff sitting posture and, as if on cue, quickly squatted beside me. This was an ambush. My two best friends were biding their time to tell me that, once again, my children chose not to talk to me or ask me for help.

"I'm asking you, not telling you," Pamela said as she pulled up a chair on the other side of me.

A pang of guilt hit with the relief that the girls didn't ask Michael to take them instead. And as much as I hated that the girls had grown closer and closer to Pamela since the one day she had picked them up from school, I was grateful she was in their lives. The girls always said they called her Aunt Pamela because "aunt" made her family. It really did take a village.

Chapter 26

Days passed quickly and quietly as I focused on the Bethany Beach paintings. Michael seemed to be more tolerant of me. We discussed the girls' schedules which allowed me time to finish up the five large canvases. I enjoyed having an excuse to lock myself away in my studio and delve in the zone. A few afternoons I got so carried away with a painting I forgot to cook dinner. If the girls happened to be home, they made themselves sandwiches. At least they were capable of not starving to death.

When the last of the paintings were complete, I returned to the historic Ranford garden for Pamela's fundraiser in November.

Coincidentally, but I thought maybe not, Alicia picked me up to deliver all the paintings for the Bethany Beach house on the same day Pamela planned to pick up the girls from school, get their driver's licenses, and take them out to dinner.

I resolved my feelings of betrayal by turning them into gratitude, per Alicia's encouragement. "Pamela didn't betray you. Be grateful the girls had someone to go to during their parents' crisis." And since Michael was okay with Pamela taking them for their licenses, probably okay with anyone but me taking them, it was more important that the girls were relaxed and happy while taking the test. I knew the chances of me creating stress, which would be Heather's take on anything that went wrong, would not help my cause of getting my family back together. In the big picture, I could let this one go.

What I did have a hard time resolving was that I agreed to this expensive birthday party. In normal circumstances, I would never have agreed to this extravagance, and neither would have Michael. I felt like the girls were taking advantage of our family situation. If I didn't give the girls the spa party they wanted, I'd be a terrible mother. And I didn't want them to have any more ammunition to take to their father and have him give them the birthday of their dreams. The kaleidoscope began to revolve, and I shook it off.

I had about $200.00 squirreled away, money I had pinched from the grocery budget, and a little left over from a previous commission after paying for the girls' activities. Maybe I'd ask Michael to pay for half the party. But then I'd have to justify the whole spa-day thing, admit that I stashed money and confess how much money I made on commissions. When did we get to the point where I kept secrets from my husband?

With the unusually warm October wind in my face, Alicia and I drove down the coast to Bethany Beach.

"The girls are excited about their birthday. I was shocked that the other parents would let their daughters skip school for a spa day," I said, unzipping my jacket and smelling the salt air as we neared the ocean.

Maybe I'd give up the family van once the girls left for college and get myself a convertible. I pictured myself delivering the paintings strapped down in the back seat then imagined the wind tearing them apart. Maybe not.

"I'm in trouble because now Liz wants a spa day for her seventeenth in a few months," said Alicia.

"It's a fancy party for sure, but at least they conceded to tacos at home afterwards. Pam's baking the cake, of course."

"And I'll help you cook, plus bring beverages. Colas and waters. And wine for us."

I gave Alicia a big thumbs-up. I removed my sunglasses and leaned back. With the sun on my face, a feeling of gratitude washed over me. Things had been calm. Michael and I had talked on the phone a few times about nothing remarkable, but we talked. The birthday party was a great excuse for us to touch base. He never questioned the concept, nor asked about the cost, and said he'd come by.

"I'll be serving tacos around five thirty," I informed him.

"I'll be there."

"Thank you," I said.

"Don't thank me. I'm their father."

"You know what I mean."

"Do I?"

"Michael. I mean, thank you for wanting to be involved."

There was silence for a few moments, but I didn't want to say anything more. I didn't want him to think I was being difficult.

"Julie, I miss the girls, and I do miss living at home. It's just… I'm not ready to have this conversation yet."

He didn't say he missed me. Was I the "it's just"?

I didn't want to push, but I didn't know how not to. I swallowed hard, prayed I wasn't being difficult, and said, "We'll talk when you're ready."

"Thank you," he said. "I'll see you tomorrow at five thirty." He didn't have to thank me. I was his wife.

I opened my eyes as the car slowed and turned into Alicia's client's neighborhood. A white van had parked in the driveway, and a man, tool belt on hips and a Home Depot bag in hand, stepped out and opened the back door of his van. All my paintings were neatly packed and wrapped in brown paper.

"Hi, Alejandro. Thanks for meeting me here. This is the artist, Julie Scott. You've hung some of her other paintings."

I shook his hand.

"Alejandro has been helping me with my installs for a while now." They exchanged words in Spanish, then Alicia said to me, "We'll go in. I'll show him what's what, then you and I can bring the rest of the paintings in to hang."

Alejandro pulled out the largest canvas and followed Alicia up the stairs. I let the two of them go ahead of me then walked behind with the next largest in my two hands. Why waste the trip? I had grabbed the canvas for one of the guest bedrooms, the painting of dunes in turquoise and greens mimicking the gentle movement of the tall grasses between the house and the beach. The second guest room's art was a triptych, three frames of a slightly modern take on a celestial landscape in amethyst ombre, and the third provided the warmth of a fading sunset in pinks and oranges that Paul Cezanne would have appreciated.

After the last perfectly suited picture hung on the ideal wall in each room, I waited in the car. Alicia took over ten minutes to say her thanks and goodbye to Alejandro.

As I sat in the car, waiting, I thought about Michael and realized sadly, at some point, I had stopped wishing for his return and found myself hoping things would get easier without him.

Alicia abruptly opened the car door and slid into the driver's seat, jolting me out my feelings of inadequacy.

"Let's eat an early dinner since Pamela's taking the girls out. Where do you want to go?" Alicia asked as we turned out of the neighborhood.

"Let's pick up some sandwiches and eat on the beach."

We pulled into one of the side streets leading to the beach after stopping at a local deli. Alicia dug a blanket and a couple of towels out of her trunk, and I carried the sandwiches, water, and boxed wine.

"Finish your water," I said, having gulped mine down. I set the boxed wine on my knees and filled my plastic bottle with wine. Alicia handed me her bottle. We ate in silence, except for shooing the seagulls.

I wondered how the girls were doing. Were they having trouble with the written part of the test? I could picture Heather being cocky and Nicole being a nervous wreck and hoped they could overcome. Glad I wasn't there to feed into either of their shortcomings.

"How are you doing?" Alicia asked. "I mean really doing?"

"Let's just say I'm on automatic."

Alicia flipped the cowl of her sweater up over her head, covering her ears.

"Do you ever wonder how different your life could be if you had altered just one choice along the way?" I wrapped my legs with a towel as the air was colder near the shore then made a pillow with the other and stretched out.

"I don't like to go backward. It wouldn't do any good."

"I don't mean anything specific. But like taking the left instead of that right, visiting one bar instead of the other that one night. What if my dad got transferred somewhere else my senior year?"

"You would have lived your life not much different than you are now," said Alicia.

"Really?" I sat up and folded my leg beneath me.

"Julie, you are who you are. If not Michael, then you would have found some other Steady Eddie. You would have found your forever home the first time you bought a house. You'd have kids, a dog, and that white picket fence."

I had heard those words before.

"I'd like to think I'd learn to play the guitar, move to New Zealand, and sing at a tiki bar overlooking the ocean. I'd stay up till two a.m. and roll out of bed after lunch in time for my yoga class." Knowing how tone-deaf I was, I giggled while Alicia laughed out loud but covered her mouth with her hand to keep in her wine.

"No," she managed to say while waving her hand to stop me from going on. "No, that would never, ever have happened. Don't feel like you are missing out on something."

"It could have." I put on a deep sad frown.

"Julie, you don't want to travel, and I'm not sure your singing would be appreciated down under. Plus, you can't keep your eyelids open past ten p.m."

"If I don't drink more than one glass of wine, I can," I said, stuffing the paper wrappers and napkins into the deli bag.

"Julie. You're an artist. You've always been a painter. You are who you are. Enjoy it."

But why did I feel unsettled? And had for a long while now. Since I was already up to throw away our garbage, I left my sneakers and socks on the blanket and walked toward the ocean. My toes stiffened when the ice-cold saltwater ran over them and took my breath away. I covered my mouth and nose with my hands and breathed in and out, willing the warm air to my toes, so they'd wiggle and warm up, just as my father taught me on one of our family daytrips to the beach.

I hadn't walked the shoreline alone since the day of Curtis's accident. But the last time I was at the beach with the whole family was over two summers ago. I could hear the kids' laughter and the splashing as they ran from the incoming waves. I could feel Michael's hand in mine. I didn't like walking the beach alone with only my shadow. I glanced back at Alicia, who was talking on the phone, her hands in the air expressively interpreting her conversation. I made a U-turn and headed back to our blanket.

"I'll let you know when and if it happens," she said then hung up her phone. "I ordered accessories for a job, and some might end up back-ordered."

"No use worrying about it now," I said. Look at me giving Alicia some of her own advice. I must be learning.

"I know. But if it happens, I will have a lot of explaining to do… I've made a mess of things. My client didn't want me to use this particular wholesaler, and I kind of did anyway." Alicia's water bottle crackled as she finished her wine.

"See, this is what I meant earlier. What if back then you had made one different choice…" I was wondering about her as much as myself.

"It makes me feel unprofessional. I should have listened." Alicia smiled to cover her guilt. "I feel like a fraud."

She was no more a fraud than me. "We all have our secrets."

"And sometimes the longer you keep them," she said, "the bigger they become."

Chapter 27

The day of…
Nineteen months earlier, 6:45 p.m. to 8:30 p.m.

Between Michael's accusing stares and my self-loathing, I couldn't sit comfortably in the trauma center's waiting room, so I meandered up and down the hallway, not wanting to go far in case the doctor came looking for me. I left the girls sitting thigh to thigh with their father. Pamela stood, staring out the window.

What was I thinking? Taking a few hours for myself? "Please, God, don't punish Curtis or the rest of my family for my selfishness. I didn't mean it when I said I was tired of being Mom or Mrs. I love my family. I am so grateful…"

"Mr. Scott," the doctor who must have met Michael before the surgery pushed the door open and called to him. I spun around, sloshing a stream of water from my paper cup onto the shiny hallway floor.

"Yes!" I answered as I raced up the hallway. "Yes. How's Curtis?"

"This is Julie, Curtis's mother," Michael said, holding the door open for both the doctor and me to enter.

"Dr. Kumar." The doctor shook my hand in greeting. "I'm the head of neurosurgery here at TCW. Come and sit down." He pointed to the circle of chairs. I gestured for the girls to join us.

Dr. Kumar explained that Curtis was in critical condition. "Your son sustained a severe brain injury. We call it an ABI, acquired brain injury. He had an aneurysm, a weakening of an artery wall. Rare in someone his age, but not unheard of. He was most likely born with it. He had yet to regain consciousness when he reached the surgical wing. That was not a good sign. We intubated him immediately to optimize his oxygenation and ordered a CT scan before we brought him into surgery. We repaired the bleed and removed a few blood clots. We also performed a ventriculostomy, a hole for drainage to control his ICP, his intracranial pressure."

I opened my mouth to ask a question, but nothing came out. I wasn't sure I wanted to hear the answers to the questions racing in my mind.

"Where is he now?" Michael filled the silence.

"My team had some difficulty controlling Curtis's blood pressure. We have him on medication for that, as well as an anticonvulsant to prevent any more seizures. We'll monitor him with EEGs. He's on other meds for pain and sedation. Also, he's on a ventilator so we can help him breathe."

"He's not breathing on his own?" I asked. My knees weakened.

"No, he's not, at least not well enough," the doctor replied.

"Can we see him? Is he awake?" I was desperate to hold my little boy. A sob from the girls drew my attention. How many times could my heart break?

"They're bringing him to ICU now. He's not awake, but I don't expect him to be. Give us about an hour. Then you can visit him two at a time. As I said, he's in critical condition. He has a lot of tubes and wires attached, so prepare yourselves. It will be touch and go for the next twenty-four hours or so."

"What does that mean? Touch and go?" Michael asked.

"We need to keep his vitals stable. If we can manage that for twenty-four hours, then we will reassess his situation." Dr. Kumar gave the twins a stiff nod and a warm smile then left the room.

What seemed like hours later, seeing Curtis for the first time was a punch in the gut. Tubes and wires, bursts of breaths and beeps, stale coffee, and rubbing alcohol invade my senses all at once. I stopped moving forward and closed my eyes in order to separate my son from the discordance. Michael stood at the foot of the bed, staring at the boy in the bed. He reached out and gently cupped Curtis's toes. I pulled a chair beside the bed and drew out Curtis's hand from underneath the blanket. It was warm and pink like it was supposed to be. But he didn't press back when I squeezed.

I swallowed hard as I allowed my eyes to trace up a bruised shoulder and over a soft neck brace. A bandage helmet surrounded Curtis's angelic face.

"No, no, no, no." I choked on my words. I kissed Curtis's open palm then met Michael's eyes. I wanted, no, I needed, him to comfort me. But there was no comfort in his eyes, only accusation.

Michael, trembling, rubbed the palms of his hands on his pants. Seeing the rejection in his eyes, I quelled the urge to reach out to him. Michael rocked side to side then mouthed the words, "I can't." When he backed out of the room, my chest ached for him, and I never felt so alone. Acting on the urge to run after him wasn't an option because I dared not let go of Curtis's hand.

I didn't know how long I sat, silently begging God and the universe to save my son. I was sick with sorrow, truly sorry if I had brought this on. Michael had no idea how his accusatory tone hit home. I was guilty not of causing Curtis's head injury but of voicing out loud that morning in my shower that I was tired of being Mom to the kids and Mrs. to Michael. I had wished for a change, not for an out.

A knock on the doorframe distracted me from my pleas. A nurse with a kind smile entered, taking the chart off the foot of the bed. She placed a thermometer in Curtis's ear, adjusted the white clip on his finger, then recorded the same numbers off the monitor she had written down fifteen minutes prior.

"Is he going to be okay?" I murmured.

"Time will tell. On the plus side, he's young and healthy. He needs rest to heal. I'll be right outside this door if you need anything." The nurse squeezed my shoulder.

"Julie?"

As helpless as a baby, I looked up at Pamela. She slid past the nurse and to my side.

"Pamela. He needs to be okay."

Pamela squatted next to my chair and placed a hand over mine and Curtis's. I leaned on her shoulder until my tears dried.

"Julie, whatever you're thinking, wherever you were, this is not your fault. It was totally unpredictable. It would have happened even if you were at home. Or if we really were at lunch."

"Not now, Pamela," I said with heavy guilt.

Pam raised both palms in surrender. "There's nothing we can do but hope and pray. The girls want to come in and visit. How do you feel about that?"

I lifted my eyebrows in response. I couldn't fathom the correct answer. I brought the back of Curtis's hand to my lips. Would seeing Curtis like this upset them too much?

Chapter 28

The girls' birthday spa day arrived on a sunny, crisp October day. They slept in, but I got up early to pick up balloons and donuts from the grocery store. When I returned, they were upstairs, giggling. I could feel their excitement through the ceiling.

I held out the van keys for whichever twin grabbed them first and said, "You can drive to Sarah's house, but then I have to drive since you can't drive with anyone in the car but direct family members."

Neither of the girls raced for the keys. "Mom," Heather said. "Aunt Pamela is going to drive us, and the other girls are meeting us there."

"We figured you'd want to stay home and set up our taco dinner," said Nicole.

"I'll take you," I said. I appreciated Pamela setting up their birthday at her spa and taking the girls for their licenses, but I couldn't let her be the buffer between my girls and me forever. I was their mom, and whether they liked it or not, these things were my responsibility. "I have to go to the grocery store anyway. I forgot the cheese." I hoped and prayed the girls hadn't been in the overflowing cheese drawer in the fridge. "Text Pamela. Have her meet us there."

Pamela stepped out of her car as we pulled into the parking lot, and then Alicia pulled in beside us as we climbed out of the van.

"Happy birthday, girls," Pamela said and pulled my twins in for a group hug. "Julie, I'll bring all of the girls home once they're relaxed and prettied up. Liz too." She addressed Alicia. "That way, you two can get the festivities set up. Grab the cake out of my car and take it with you now."

"Jeez, thanks. All I have to do is brown some beef," I said then quickly added, "and pick up some cheese."

Within five minutes, all six girls gathered around Pamela in the parking lot. "Have fun." I waved at the giggling gaggle of girls as they followed Pamela as if she were Mother Goose into the club's spa.

"I have to pick up some wine, then I'll be right over," Alicia said. "Do you want me to pick up the cheese since I have to stop anyway?"

I laughed. "I have plenty of cheese."

Alicia eyed me with suspicion. "Have you already had a drink?"

I shook my head and put my arm around her as we walked to our cars. I explained to her how I lied to my children so that I could drive them to their spa day birthday party.

After helping me add two leaves to the dining-room table, Alicia took over the browning of the ground beef and chorizo, which sizzled in a pan. While I sipped my wine, she enhanced the meat with onion, garlic, and herbs.

We took our time chatting and setting out bowls of shredded lettuce, chopped tomatoes, sliced scallions and olives, quartered limes, several flavors of shredded cheeses, jalapeños, salsa, and sour cream.

"We have to have guacamole too," Alicia said, digging through my fruit bowl for avocados.

I placed the two-tier cake on the far end of the table. The wide round bottom layer, Heather's favorite dark chocolate with chocolate chips, was frosted with vanilla buttercream and decorated with different-colored earbuds and pink ballet toe shoes. The top layer, a camera carved out of vanilla bean pound cake and covered with chocolate ganache, was filled with chocolate mousse for Nicole. Pamela also made sugar cookies in the shapes of fingernail polish bottles, lipstick, a blow-dryer, and a hand mirror. She had iced them to perfection and wrapped them in cellophane bags for the twins' guests to take home. I set the waters and colas in a large tin bucket filled with ice on a chair at the end of the table.

Knowing the girls wanted to have their birthday dinner here, in our home, had me figuring things were on an upswing. Things with Michael were going a bit slow, but they were moving forward. Hopefully, by the upcoming holidays, my family would be back together. We'd have a new normal, but we'd have each other under the same roof.

At ten past five, Michael walked through the front door. "Did I get here before the girls?" he asked. He seemed excited, and it had been a very long time since I'd seen a self-induced smile on his face.

Roger was certainly excited to see him. He paced in front of Michael, not letting him get too far into the house, demanding attention and a pat on the head.

"They should be here in about five or ten minutes," Alicia said, pouring a glass of wine for him.

"Thanks, but I'd rather have a beer," he said as he peeked out through the blinds in the living room, as if looking to see if someone was following him.

"I'll get you one," I said, hoping there were a few cans in the garage refrigerator left over from the cookout. I knew he liked beer with his pizza and tacos, and it bothered me that I didn't think to make sure I had some in the fridge for him.

Alicia must have been reading my thoughts. On my way into the garage, she said, "Oh, my bad. I was in charge of beverages. I should have thought to get some beer."

I returned with two cans of months-old beer. Hopefully, that would be enough, but if not, I'd run out and get a six-pack once the girls arrived.

Michael fidgeted with his car keys and peeked through the blinds again.

Confused, I said, "Michael, this isn't a surprise party. The girls know you'll be here."

"I know. But I brought them a surprise," he said, still peeking through the blinds.

I joined him, separated the blinds with my hands, and saw Michael's car in the driveway behind Alicia's. Mrs. Amberly stood, collecting her mail from her mailbox, taking her time reading the front of each piece, evidently trying to figure out why all the cars were in front of my house.

"What am I looking for?" I said, taking a step back.

"I bought the girls a car." Michael pulled his shoulders back, proud and happy. He wiggled the keys in front of me.

I saw red. How dare he take it upon himself to gift the girls a car. How dare he make such a large purchase without discussing it with me. The ringing in my ears silenced all other sounds as pressure resonated throughout my head and heart. How dare he take away my daughters' dependency on me.

The image of the key's jingling from Michael's fingers fractured into a million pieces and began to circle in front of my eyes.

"You won't have to drive them around," he said, his voice echoing in the tunnel of my hearing. "You'll have more time for yourself, and you won't have to share your van." In slow motion, he looked at Alicia for someone to agree with him. "You said you loved having the extra time to paint on the days I picked up the girls. I thought you'd be happy."

Alicia approached me as if a crack in the floor below would expand with one false move. From outside, several car doors slammed with nowhere for the echoes to go in my compressing mind. Michael rushed out the front door. I had yet to move, afraid if I did, I would throw up and implode right then and there.

Screams of delight bellowed from the front yard, breaking through the pulsing in my head as the girls were surely getting the good news of their sweet independence from me.

Pamela was the first to enter. She peered around the opened door. I stood in front of the living-room windows, afraid to take that first step, and Pamela knew it. She put an arm around my shoulders, holding me up as I tilted to the right. As I placed one foot in front of the other to move forward, I had to fight the rotation of the merry-go-round in my head.

"Get it out before the girls come in. They're ecstatic, and you will definitely be the bad guy if you say anything about that car right now," Pamela said.

Alicia handed me the box of tissues from the end table as I sat on the couch. I would never again have my alone time with the twins as a captured audience. I wouldn't get to hear about the goings-on while the girls talked to each other or their friends on the phone. I would never be privy to their activities or schedules because I wouldn't have the need to know.

"Did you know?" I asked.

"Absolutely not." Pamela vigorously shook her head. "I would have told you. I know it would be the last thing you'd want."

I looked at Alicia for her answer.

"I knew nothing, I swear," she said.

I nodded my head and blew my nose with shaking hands. I attempted to tuck away my anger and pain and prayed for some strength to get through dinner.

"Go on upstairs and wash your face. The girls are coming in now," Alicia said, helping me up. "We'll get them making tacos."

Ice-cold water shocked away the unwelcomed pressure in my head. As I dried my face, the happy chatter of six teenaged girls in the rooms below filled the space around me. Within the din, I could hear the click of Nicole's Canon as she snapped photos. I heard the murmur of Michael and Pamela and, occasionally, Alicia's high-pitched voice chiming in. I should go downstairs and join the party. But it was all going so smoothly without me, and the girls hadn't yet questioned my absence.

I retrieved the girls' gifts from my dresser drawer. The silver and gold boxes had been wrapped and ready to go for several months, but they certainly couldn't compete with a car. I hoped Michael had a plan to teach the girls about car maintenance and safety and the cost of gasoline and insurance. I didn't have the funds for any of that. He had better be planning on taking care of those things. How could he have done this without talking to me?

My chest tightened, and my right leg shook uncontrollably, preventing me from descending the stairs. Feeling dizzy, I crumbled and sat on the top step. The chatter from below cramped my brain. How long could one remain stunned?

Michael had achieved Best Parent of the World, which I thought I had won when they got their spa party. I now possessed the bottom of our family totem pole. I worked hard to be the one on top, the one moving forward, the one to pull the rest to standing. Where there once was five, then four, I was now a pillar of one. How would I deal with this new normal, or at best, my latest normal? Normal was a hypothetical—an aberration people strove for, not knowing that it didn't genuinely exist. Somehow, I knew there were several new, untried normals in my future.

Pamela appeared at the bottom of the stairs. She waved me down.

I shook my head. I couldn't do it. "Tell them I have a headache. And to have fun," I whispered and turned onto all fours, pushed to stand, and retreated to my bedroom.

I lay down with my legs out straight and crossed at the ankle, shoes and all. I released my breath once I realized Pamela hadn't followed me. The right thing to do would be to go downstairs and act as the hostess I knew I was expected to be. But I became content with listening to the laughter, including Julia Roberts's in *Pretty Woman* blasting from the TV, and imagined the girls sitting cross-legged on the floor in the den, eating their handheld tacos with bright, fancy manicures, sparkles in their updos, and prom-perfect makeup until I heard the rumble of Michael's voice. I guessed he was sitting in his old, ugly lounge chair, which I had moved to the corner of the room within a week of him moving out.

Dishes clanged as the table was cleared, and Pamela called out, "Cake time," so loud it was obviously meant for me.

Frustrated with myself for choosing to miss my daughters' only seventeenth birthday party, I got up determined to join the festivities. When I heard Heather say, "Wait," I held my breath, expecting at least one of the twins to appear outside my bedroom door. I stood with their gifts in hand, prepared to greet them.

"This is a good part," said Heather from somewhere down in the den.

"The whole thing's the good part," Nicole said as I took a step toward the party.

"Pause it and come grab your cake," Pamela said. "Then you can turn it back on."

They all began singing *Happy Birthday*. Without me. My legs dropped out from underneath me, and I fell back on the bed, crushed by my girls worrying more about missing out on Vivian and Edward at the polo match than the absence of their own mother at their birthday party.

Imagining Julia Roberts in her brown polka-dotted dress and big floppy hat, I hauled myself onto my feeble legs once again and convinced myself to descend the stairs.

"Michael? Would you like a piece to go?" Pamela asked as she entered the kitchen near the bottom of the steps.

I stopped on the third step and listened.

"Am I leaving?" Michael asked.

"Pretty sure it's as good a time as any," Pamela said.

The corners of my mouth curled, and my legs became more stable just knowing Michael would be leaving.

He called the girls into the kitchen. "Here. For gas money," he said. The girls thanked him profusely and said their goodbyes. He must have given them cash or gift cards. I wanted to dropkick him.

As I heard the front door close, my jaw unlocked with an audible exhale.

Pamela met me in the middle of the staircase and handed me a glass of wine. We both took a seat on the steps.

"What was he thinking?" I whispered, still not able to swallow Michael's surprise.

"I honestly think he's trying to help you out," said Alicia, who joined us in the middle of the staircase. She placed a finger over her lips and pointed toward the den. It must have been quite the sight to see the three of us, three grown women, huddled on the staircase as if hiding from the teens in the den.

"I think he was trying to win the girls over," Pamela whispered.

"I'm sick to my stomach just thinking about them out there, in their own vehicle," I said.

"They're good drivers. I promise you," Pamela said. "It's a natural progression. They start out gone for hours at a time before they're gone for good."

"Let's not go there," Alicia said. "Our job as moms is to prepare them while they're still in our nests. And that's what you've been doing. Maybe it's a sign he wants to come home?"

"I was so ready to do anything to get Michael back in the house. Now I don't know how I feel." The doorbell rang, preventing me from thinking deeper into my newfound feelings.

"I'll get it," said Alicia, closest to the bottom stair.

Pamela took my hand and led me down the steps. I slid my gifts on the console with the other ones. Susie's mom arrived to collect the extra three girls and take them home. "After all, it's a school night," she said.

"But we didn't open our gifts," Nicole said. She asked how I felt and if my headache was gone as she moved a couple of wrapped packages on to the dining-room table. The other girls joined her and brought over the rest of the gifts.

I nodded my head then shrugged my shoulders in question to the other mom. "Would you like a glass of wine?"

The adults joined the girls in the dining room and watched Nicole and Heather unwrap movie passes, hair-curling kits, and assorted nail polish from their friends. Liz and Alicia gave them monogrammed blankets, and Pamela gave them each a crisp fifty-dollar bill. The girls had saved my gifts for last.

As they lifted the top of the small white boxes, I held my breath. They each pulled out identical sterling chains with Curtis's March birthstone dangling from it. The aquamarine stone shone in its silver setting with Curtis's initials and birthdate engraved on the back.

Nicole jumped up and pulled me out of my chair for a hug. Heather placed her necklace back. Pamela pulled the box to herself, squinting a reprimand at Heather. "Beautiful," she said, and she emphasized for Heather's benefit, "Celebrating Curtis's birthday, instead of the day he died."

"I love it, Mom. Thank you," Nicole turned and handed me the necklace to place around her neck.

Heather pulled the box back from Pamela and squared up the lid. "Thank you," Heather said, clearly out of obligation; but the hitch in her voice betrayed her stoic profile.

Alicia grabbed a garbage bag and picked up the torn wrapping paper and neglected ribbon as Nicole and I handed out parting gifts of homemade cookies and walked our guests to the front door.

As soon as we said our last goodbyes, Heather asked, "Can I take our new car for a spin?"

And so it began.

"It's a school night," said Pamela. "And you can help us clean up from your party, which I most generously organized, Alicia most graciously cooked for, and your mom most obligingly paid for." Then she picked up the keys to the new car and handed them to me.

I dropped them on the counter as if their contact burned my palm. Embarrassed by my reaction, I hooked them on the leash hook by the garage door, proving to the girls, or maybe myself, they were there for the taking.

With the girls' reluctant help, we made short time of the cleanup. I sent them upstairs to bed with armfuls of gifts after an appreciative goodbye to Pamela and Alicia, who left only after I held out a steady hand to prove I was all right.

As I sat alone at the kitchen table, eating a piece of birthday cake, the girls, upstairs in the middle of a dispute, blaming each other for me not allowing them to take the car out.

I was so full of anger toward Michael. There was no room for his name to even flitter into my mind. Instead, I thought about how I was going to avoid the fight in the morning when the girls wanted to drive themselves to school. Better come up with my excuses now, or I'd never fall asleep. Thank God for Pamela when Heather asked to take the car out earlier. I was too stunned and pissed to remark.

I stared at the keys, again thinking about what to say in the morning. Would anyone suspect me if the car mysteriously went missing or caught on fire overnight?

I took my glass of wine and the keys from the hook and walked out the front door. The car had been pulled into the driveway. By whom? I couldn't say. But there it was in all its glory. A four-door, relatively new, grey sedan, much nicer than my van.

I sat in the driver's seat, trying to imagine my girls in it, wondering how they'd decide who'd drive and who wouldn't. That was not going to go over well. I shivered at the thought. My mental kaleidoscope was in full rotation now, spiraling thoughts. I tried to be helpful; they took it as controlling. Interest in their activities was me being nosy. 'Round and 'round. What to do? What to do? I laid the driver seat back and looked out of the moonroof. Every once in a while, I'd lift my head just enough to sip my wine.

When I woke up, my wineglass, luckily empty, lay on the passenger side floor. The pitter-patter of rain on the glass above splattered, blurring my vision. As the drops became heavier and heavier, I thanked the heavens above. The girls couldn't possibly drive themselves to school the first time ever in the pouring rain. They would have to wait for a nice, sunny, clear day.

I jumped out of the car and ran into the garage, looking forward to a good night's sleep.

Chapter 29

I slept well but woke up disappointed to see the bright October sunshine. I quickly dressed so I could be downstairs before the girls fought over the keys to their new car. I let Roger out the back door then noticed a note on the kitchen table held down by an empty wineglass.

"Mom, we got up early to go out for breakfast. Didn't want to wake you. Hope the wineglass wasn't planted in case we got pulled over. Thanks for the vote of confidence. H."

"Shit," I said and plopped into the closest chair. I couldn't believe I forgot the wineglass. Moreover, I couldn't believe Heather thought I would do it on purpose. "And crap." They knew I was in their car.

With the decision whether or not I would allow them to drive to school this morning made for me, I poured my daily canned caffeine and wallowed. What I really wanted to do was drive to the school, march up the steps, and call out the girls for taking the car without talking to me. But what would that accomplish? I couldn't win for losing.

I tapped a finger on the table and looked around. I hadn't woken up to an empty house in…well, ever. My mind was blank, my body numb. I purposefully tried to think. Could one even make themselves think? Breathe. Think.

My right leg began to shake, my chest tightened, and the pressure behind my eyes built. Conscious of my brain literally telling me to breathe, I ran up the stairs and directly into the shower. I turned the one big handle all the way around and sat as the water soaked into my pajamas until I began to feel again. Cold. Neutral. Warm. Hot. When the water borderlined scalding, I quickly backed onto the tiled bench.

I reached up and adjusted the water to a warm, relaxing temperature and stripped off my heavy, drenched flannels. I had the whole day to myself. Nobody needed me to do anything for them. I should take advantage of the extra me time this morning, but I wished someone had organized some options. I wasn't sure if I had a million things to do or nothing at all.

I could do the girls' laundry. They might like that. No, that's not for me. I could cook meals and freeze them, but that's not for me either. Actually, they were both ultimately for me because I was going to have to do those tasks eventually. I could call Michael. Ugh. I could visit Curtis's grave. Hmmm. The rabbit hole sucked me in.

I'd never had this much time to think, let alone do. I could paint, clean, sleep, drink wine. I could do absolutely anything guilt-free and without anyone interrupting. I remembered the days I dreamed of this, and now that I had it, I didn't know what to do with it.

The spray from the showerhead was cooling as the hot water tank emptied. I took laundry off my list, at least for the next few hours, and stepped out of the bathroom into my bedroom. Roger stared at me, waiting right outside the bathroom door, as if to remind me that I wasn't alone after all. I threw on a dry T-shirt and jeans and went downstairs to conquer my yet to be planned day.

I took myself out for a breakfast sandwich then strolled through the grocery store. I hit every aisle, whether I needed to or not, and planned three meals I could throw together and freeze. On my way home, I swung by the florist and picked up a few loose heirloom roses, stalks of pink delphinium, and several autumn greens to make myself a fresh floral arrangement for the kitchen table, a luxury I wished I could do weekly.

Once home, I arranged the flowers, which inspired the Suzy Homemaker in me. I placed a three-pound chicken stuffed with sliced oranges and rosemary into the lower oven to bake and salted a large pot of water set to boil. I squeezed and mixed dense raw hamburger, sausage, and eggs between my fingers. The firm yet not-resistant texture relaxed my mind. I then focused on rolling two-inch meatballs between my palms to within millimeters of each other. Continuing to keep my mind from wandering, I glanced at my flowers to remind me to enjoy my new life of leisure. I had spent enough time and energy letting Michael's gift of a car get me down. This was his doing, and I wasn't going to make it my problem.

Once the meatballs browned in a frying pan, I placed them on a cookie sheet, three rows of five, then placed them in the top oven. I blended canned Italian tomatoes with layer by layer of fresh herbs, enjoying the aromas. I made twice as much sauce as usual, some for baked ziti and some for meatballs.

I dumped two boxes of pasta into the pot of boiling water then pulled out my largest frying pan. I prepared equal portions of chopped onions, celery, and carrots and cooked them with garlic and parsley, rosemary, thyme, and cornstarch and chicken stock. Then I let the partially cooked ziti cool under cold water. I hunted down baking tins to freeze the baked ziti for another day and dug out my ceramic ramekins for individual potpies I'd put together once the chicken baked. It felt refreshing to have the time to cook plan-ahead meals, knowing I wouldn't have to scramble at the last minute for several meals in the future.

Once the pasta had cooked and everything else simmered and baked, I took Roger for a walk. It wasn't even noon yet, and the panic of not knowing what to do next began to rise. On my return, Mrs. Amberly, rocking on her front porch, bundled up in a not necessarily needed heavy, wool shawl, waved me over.

Oh, not now. I've got meatballs in the oven, and they needed to go into the sauce. Roger needed a drink after his long walk, and I really should get to my painting. All of a sudden, I could think of a million things I could be doing. But I went ahead and cut across her front yard.

"Hello, Mrs. Amberly."

"Have a seat." She offered the rocking chair next to her. "And it's Nora."

"Thanks, Nora. Beautiful day," I said, taking a step back. "I just wanted to say hi. I have meatballs in the oven and sauce on the stove."

"How have you been holding up?" the older lady asked me, her beautiful silver-grey bob curled at the nape of her neck, naturally framing her aging face.

160

"You know, I never thanked you properly for all you did after Curtis passed," I said.

"You sent me a perfectly appropriate thank-you note," she said and raised one eyebrow.

I couldn't stop my sheepish grin. "I should have thanked you in person. What you did for my family was above and beyond. Organizing meals with the neighbors and sending over your lawn guy to help us was very much appreciated."

The wind picked up and whistled through the oak trees. Through the dancing leaves, I saw my house across the street for the first time from this vantage point. It could use a paint job, and one of the shutters was off-kilter. The white picket fence was no longer white, and there were many broken or missing pickets begging for attention. The hydrangeas surrounding the front door with dried blooms needed pruning, and the one large oak tree in the front yard held nary a leaf yet still dwarfed our house. In the summer, our house must be all but hidden. But it looked well-loved and mostly cared for. In the silence, I took a seat.

"I know what it's like to lose a child..." Mrs. Amberly sounded as if she needed time to complete her sentence, but looking into her pained eyes, I realized she had finished her thought. The heaviness of loss still weighed her down after all the years. My chest filled with anguish for her heartache, as well as mine. Roger pulled away, and I knew he felt the drop of frequency in the energy around us.

After a few moments, Mrs. Amberly and I spoke at the same time.

"Nice talking to you," I said.

"You have a sweet girl in that daughter of yours," she said.

"Yes. Nicole's a sweet girl," I said. Nicole was too personal a subject to discuss with this stranger, yet I remember Nicole was perfectly content with Mrs. Amberly comforting her the night Heather took off with Tucker. Feeling as if Nicole might not like me talking to her newly found confidant, if that was what Mrs. Amberly was to her, I said, "I really do have to get back to my kitchen. Nice chatting with you."

161

How awkward it was, visiting for the first time with my neighbor of over sixteen years. We spent more time in a comfortable common silence than sharing words, so I could see how Nicole would want to be her friend.

With the aroma of red sauce and meatballs in the air, the chicken cooling on the counter, and the inside of my refrigerator cleaner than it had been since we bought the house, I picked up a novel—one I had started reading over a month ago. I sat up, feet flat on the floor, focusing on the words on the page determined to get through a chapter in one sitting.

With a yawn, I said out loud, "I, Julie Cahill Scott, can do whatever I want all day long from now on." I slid to the left and rested my head on a pillow. I had half an hour before the girls should be arriving home from school, so I stretched out on the couch. I could read or not read. I could do whatever I wanted.

The buzz from my phone on the coffee table woke me from my not-quite-asleep nap. I jolted up, dropped the book on the floor, and grabbed the phone. A text from Nicole: *Mom, can you come pick me up? I can't find Heather or our car.*

"Shit. First day out, and Heather pulls a stunt like this," I said as I texted Heather and told her to call me immediately.

I wish I had the guts not to pick Nicole up. To make her wait for Heather since she was part of the decision to take the car to school this morning without talking to me. I didn't want either of the girls to think I would drop everything and change my plans just because their particular plans didn't turn out. Wasn't that why Michael had bought them a car? I should tell Nicole to call him. They didn't want me involved in their lives, yet they wanted me to be there at their beck and call. The merry-go-round returned. Damned if I do, damned if I don't.

Nope. She's safe and I'm not going to jump. I texted Nicole I'd come get her after I finished up what I was doing, but to call me if Heather showed up.

I pulled apart the chicken and put together the chicken potpies. I covered them with piecrust and put them in the oven.

I sat down at the kitchen table with my purse and keys in hand. I stared at the clock on the stove and listened to my steady breathing. It had been twenty-five minutes, and I wanted to give Heather time to show up or at least make sure Nicole realized she was now on my schedule. I reluctantly turned off the stove.

When I pulled up in front of the school, Nicole and Liz ran down the steps and met me by the time I came to a full stop.

"Mom, I hate her," Nicole started as she slid into the back seat after Liz.

"Stop. You don't hate her. She's a jackass, but you don't hate her," I said.

"She wanted to drive to school this morning then said I could drive home, and then we'd switch tomorrow."

I was slightly impressed the two came up with a compromise but surprised that Nicole really thought Heather would hold up her end of the deal.

"She just wanted to show off," said Liz, another surprise because she usually didn't have any input. Then I wondered if they had planned on driving Liz home. I didn't ask. I didn't want to know.

"Well, don't worry because neither of you are going to drive to or from school tomorrow." In the rearview mirror, I saw Liz give Nicole the I-told-you-so look.

"I didn't do anything wrong," Nicole uncharacteristically punched the back of the passenger seat.

"Cool it," I said. Thanks, Michael. Thanks for dumping this on me. "I'm going to call your dad. This is not my problem. You can work it out with him." I really wished I had told her to text Michael to pick her up. Let him see how great his idea was to buy the girls a car.

Nicole and Liz hopped out as I put the car in park then let themselves into the house. I called Michael from the driver's seat and growled because I had to leave a message. Gone were the days he would pick up my calls on the first ring. I got my words together as I listened to his recorded spiel about how he was busy at the moment, to please leave a message, and he'd most likely get back to me by the end of the day. But if it's super important, I could call some other ten-digit number to speak to his assistant in person. At the end of his droning, I hung up.

"What I have to say is important, but I don't think your secretary can help."

Next, I texted Michael and asked him to call me. I sat in the car as the afternoon sun heated the interior. Fury built inside me. What if Michael didn't call me back? How could he take away my parental control by giving the twins a vehicle and he not be here to supervise them? Had he not been listening to me the last year? A car for them would be trouble. I was perfectly fine driving them around. We didn't need the extra insurance bill or gas costs. My hands were tied. If I took the keys away, I was the bad guy. If I let the girls fight over the car, I might as well just hand over the keys to Heather and tell Nicole sorry. And why hadn't Heather responded yet?

I decided to drive to Michael's work. We had to solve this before tomorrow morning. I put the van in reverse as Heather whipped the new car into the driveway behind me. I flew out of my van, met Heather as she opened her car door, and pulled her out by the collar.

Chapter 30

The day of…
Nineteen months earlier, 8:30 p.m. to 2:00 a.m.

*T*he twins, as desperately innocent as the day they were born, each held one of their father's hands as the three filed into Curtis's hospital room. Behind them, Pamela stood in the doorway and gave me a nod as if to say, "It'll be fine. They're ready to see Curtis."

"The nurse said we could all come in if we're quiet," Nicole explained to me before I could stop them. She released her father's hand and fell into my arms.

The four of us stared at the little boy lost in the chaos of tubes and bandages. I longed to hear his laughter and complain about him playing video games. I wanted to remind him to take Roger for a walk, to fill his water bowl.

I led Michael to my chair. In a stupor, he sat. I placed Curtis's frail hand into Michael's palm. Neither moved. "It's okay, Michael. You won't hurt him." Michael cringed and remembered he didn't want me near him. I backed away, knowing he preferred at the moment I didn't tell him what to do. I pulled up a second chair for the girls and signaled them over. Heather sat in Nicole's lap and leaned on her father's shoulder.

I took the moment to go in search of Pamela. "Can you go home and take care of Roger?"

"Sure, love. What can I bring back for you? I assume you'll spend the night?"

"Whatever you think I'll need." I left it at that.

She gathered the girls' book bags, and I handed her the heavy turquoise necklace choking me and weighing me down. Not wanting any further conversation, I excused myself to the restroom.

I returned to the empty family waiting room. How could this happen? Today of all days, the one time I ever shut off my phone. I berated myself further. I didn't just shut my phone off. I stuffed it in the glove *compartment, ensuring it didn't distract me. Curtis had to be okay. How could I forgive myself if he didn't come through this? How could Michael?*

I returned to Curtis's room and planned never to leave until he woke up. I prayed. I promised. I wept. My one job as a wife and mother was to keep my kids safe.

I hugged him just a little too long most mornings, knowing, at his age, hugs would soon become few and far between. He was already stepping away from me, brushing me off as his buddies approached before ball games. I could feel him slipping away, growing up. It was different for the girls. They moved away faster and louder, but they had each other, so it wasn't as heartbreaking. But knowing Curtis was my youngest and my last, I held on a little longer and a little harder each time I had the opportunity to hug him.

Logically, I knew I couldn't have foreseen nor prevented what happened to Curtis, but my heart kept reminding me I didn't kiss him goodbye. I let him run off this morning, assuming I'd see him after baseball when I'd kiss him good night and say, "See you in the morning, sunshine."

I squeezed his hand, and his lack of response tore at my heart.

Chapter 31

The fear in Heather's eyes as I grabbed her by the collar and pulled her out of her car forced me to check my anger, so I let go of her shirt. She fell back against the rear door. Still, rage coiled inside me growing like a runaway snowball. I had to remind myself this wasn't who I was.

"Where have you been?" I demanded and shuffled a couple of steps back so Heather could close the driver's door. Just then, Nicole came running out of the house and shoved Heather to the ground.

"Whoa, hold up." I grabbed Nicole by the arm and pulled her back toward me. I pictured Mrs. Amberly watching her barbaric neighbors and swallowed my next words. Yelling at my kids like a wild banshee in the middle of the driveway wasn't going to solve a thing.

"Girls, inside," I said calmly and held out a hand to help Heather off the ground. She ignored it, of course. I dug deep for what to say, and all I could think of was, where the hell was Michael?

The girls sat at the kitchen table, looking at anything but each other. As I bagged some of the meatballs into individual portions, wrapped the containers of baked ziti in tinfoil, ready to freeze, and sealed the six pot pie ramekins, I constantly peeked at my phone on the counter, hoping to see Michael's text pop up. I was so angry my face hurt from the tension in my jaw.

"For the life of me, I can't figure out why your father bought you two a car. You've only proven my point. It's brought out the worst in both of you. In one day, you've become irresponsible, self-centered, self-indulgent, inconsiderate…" The rest I said under my breath.

I called Michael again in front of the girls, hoping they realized the seriousness of the matter.

Nicole's eyes glinted accusingly at Heather. "See what you caused?"

Heather's eyes flew wide open, professing her innocence in the situation. I shook my head and returned to stirring the meatballs which I had left simmering in sauce for tonight's dinner.

"Michael, please call." I left yet another message. "This car idea of yours isn't going over very well." I hung up and placed the phone on the table in front of me. I lined it up perfectly square with the grain in the wood and drummed my fingers.

"Are we going to sit here until he calls you back?" Heather asked. She pulled her phone out of her bag. "He'll call me back if I text him."

That hurt, but she was probably right. "Go ahead," I said.

My gut wrenched when Michael immediately answered her call. Heather began, "Dad, Mom's here, flipping out over the car..."

I jumped up faster than a kangaroo sitting on a sharp pin and grabbed the phone away from her. "We have to talk. You need to come over."

"Now?" Michael asked. "I'm at work." Signaling my impatience, I exhaled noisily. His tentative voice cracked like he was talking down a crazy person. "Okay. Okay. Give me a few minutes to finish up here, and I'll be right over." When I handed Heather back her phone, I realized that the crazy person he sounded afraid of was me.

One moment I thought I had my world in my grasp. The next, my world sifted through my fingers. I buried my face in my hands with my elbows on the table, drained of energy. I wasn't sure why I even bothered. Michael would show up, agree with whatever solution I dished out, then leave, and nothing would change.

The girls got themselves bottled water, but I could feel the air move as they rolled their eyes behind my back. Nicole brought me a diet cola. I couldn't even lift my arm to take it from her. I thanked her with a thin smile as she put the can on the table. What I really wanted was a glass of wine, a whole bottle to be honest.

I put both palms around the cold can of cola. The crisp condensation cooled the bitterness throughout me. I rolled the can across my forehead in hopes of snapping out of my frustration. I had to get ready for battle. The girls' car had to go. If Michael didn't live under this roof, I was in charge of this house and these girls. He could take the car with him when he left, for all I cared. Feeling confident again, I took a sip of the cola as Michael entered with a pizza and two salads. The girls ran over to help him with his burden, their relief from his appearance would have been comical had we not been in the middle of our family's demise. I hid my relief by going to the garage fridge and digging out a beer from the new stock.

Jaws were tense as I listened to everyone bite into their pizza, everyone apparently wanting to keep their mouths full so we didn't have to talk. Nicole's knife screeched across her plate as she cut her lettuce and let it clang like an end-of-shift bell when she put it down. Heather gulped her water, with each gulp becoming louder from the force of the one behind it. The fizz from Michael's beer after he took a sip itched my brain. As the can met the table, the crash exploded in my mind. My kitchen had never been so silent yet so deafening. I grabbed my temples to stop the ruckus.

"Are you all right, Mom?" Nicole asked.

I plucked my fingers off my temples one at a time and took in a deep breath. "Actually, I'm not. We need to be talking, not eating."

"Julie, relax," Michael said, with pizza in his mouth.

Wrong thing to say, Michael. "You're telling me to relax when you keep waltzing in here, dropping bombs like pizza and cars?"

"That's a bit dramatic. It was almost dinnertime, and the girls needed a car," Michael said.

"What about me?" My brain was choking from the lack of air in the room.

"You have a car," Michael said, his humor not lost on the girls, although they stopped their giggling when I shoved my chair back and stood.

"Enough. Michael, you gave the girls a car without discussing it with me, and in less than twenty-four hours, it's been a disaster."

Roger paced in front of the back door, clearly uncomfortable with the tension in the room. I let him out, allowing me time to collect my thoughts. I didn't want to have this conversation in front of the girls. But they were the ones we were here to discuss. I had to calm down if I was going to get my message across clearly to all three of them. The car had to go. I poured myself a glass of wine before I went back to the table.

"Listen," I said to Michael and calmly sat again, "if we're going to discuss this as a family, then we need to be honest with each other about where each of us stands."

"Okay, you start," Michael said coolly, tipping his beer bottle, wringing it dry.

"You bought a car, gave it to two seventeen-year-olds to share, and left me to referee. Not fair."

"Well, I'm not here to referee," Michael said as if he tossed the ball into my court.

"Well, who's choice was that? I'm pretty sure I didn't pack your bags and help you out the door." There, ball back in his court.

"You weren't making it easy for me to stay."

"Easy? Who said life should be easy? We're all having a tough time, Michael. We..." I pointed around to the girls and me. "We three are doing our best to cope with Curtis's death, each in our own way. And now we have to deal with your absence too. In some ways, that's harder. Because you're not gone, Michael. You chose to leave."

"This is supposed to be about the car," Heather said, standing up. "If you two are going to hash out your personal shit, I'm out of here."

Michael grabbed her elbow. "Sit down, Heather." He handed Nicole a napkin in time to catch the first of her tears and slumped back into his chair.

"You're right. This is about the car. If you can't share, then you can't drive it," Michael said to the girls, then looked at me and said, "There. They have guidelines."

I guffawed. "Seriously, that's it? You think it's fixed?" I stared at the girls. How was it that at this moment, I couldn't think of the million things that could, and most likely would, go wrong? Where was all my ammunition I thought of on my way home from picking Nicole up?

I redirected the conversation to the girls. "How are you two going to fix this? You"—I said directly to Heather—"will take advantage of your sister like you always do. And you"—I said to Nicole—

"will never stick up for yourself and come crying to me. So how is sharing going to fit into this?" I could see the harshness of my statements in their eyes, but I felt empowered by letting the truth spew from my mouth. "Against every bone in my body and thought in my head, I spent hours trying to convince myself that damn car could be a plus for me." I glared at Heather. "Since, apparently, I had the whole day to myself, I planned my day accordingly, until I was interrupted and had to stop what I was doing to pick up your sister from school."

"I went back to pick her up, but you already did," Heather said as if there was fault to pass around.

I threw my hands into the air at Michael. "She left school early to drop off a friend, which by the way, is against the law, and still had not returned forty minutes later by the time I picked up Nicole."

"You could have told me you were leaving," Nicole spoke directly to Heather. "I would have called Mom earlier."

Feeling manic, I laughed again. "See, they don't get it." I glared at Michael.

"Okay. Okay. Calm down," Michael said.

"If you tell me to calm down one more time…" I said with such strain it hurt. I pushed off from the table to fetch more wine. But rage shot through me, and I picked up the pot of simmering meatballs and hauled it at the sink. "And here's the damn homemade meatballs I made you girls for dinner. Fricken' waste of my time."

Without looking back, I ran up the stairs and slammed my bedroom door. Michael was right, I had to calm down. But I'd be damned if I calmed down because he ordered me to. How was I supposed to get across to him that when he left this house, our home, we became parents who lost the respect of our children, especially me? When he left, we became parents the girls had to choose between, parents the girls could play off one another. And now, because of my behavior, I just handed him the keys to the castle. Well, he could have them.

The whispering and undertones of laughter from the kitchen below kindled my ire as I marched down the hall to the attic. With each step, I was more determined to leave the three of them to fend for themselves.

I stopped short at the office door when I saw the unmade bed. I stepped in and picked up a shirt from a pile of clothes on the floor. It was Heather's. When did she start sleeping in the office? How did I not know?

Shaking my head, tired of not understanding the goings-on in my own home, I continued to the attic and grabbed a suitcase, purposely ignoring Curtis's things. I couldn't have anything pulling at my heartstrings, reminding me of my dream to raise a family here in my forever home.

At the top of the stairs, before reentering my bedroom, I strained to hear what Heather was saying. Something about how she needed the car at night because she worked, and Nicole didn't. Good luck with that, Michael.

If we could afford for Michael to stay in a hotel and me at home, what's the difference if I stayed in the hotel and Michael stayed home? Then he could find out for himself just how fun it was to parent alone.

The suitcase bumped down each step as I dragged it down the stairs. Michael watched me with disbelief as I made it to the bottom step. A weekender bag of toiletries and reading materials slipped off my shoulder and hit the floor. I obviously wasn't trying to sneak out of the house, as Michael did in the middle of the day when no one was home, but I was definitely leaving.

"Where are you going?" Michael asked.

"I'm leaving."

"Mom. No," Nicole said, not quite as sincere as I would have hoped from her.

"Jules, this is silly. It's after eight p.m. Where are you going to go? You can't leave," Michael said, backstepping as I moved forward with my bags.

"Why? Why can't I leave? You up and left. You had no problem leaving me to deal by myself. Have at it, Michael. It's all yours." I yanked my suitcase into the garage.

"Jules, you don't want this," he said as he followed me, closing the door between the girls and us.

"You don't know what I want because you don't want to talk," I said and heaved my suitcase into the back of the van. I stomped past him, opened the door to the kitchen, and called for Roger. The girls hadn't moved an inch.

Roger responded with ears tucked and his tail between his legs. I opened the van's side door and motioned for him to jump in. At least someone did as I asked. I returned to the kitchen one more time and gathered Roger's leash, some food, and his water dish.

Nicole followed me with wide eyes. "Mom, please don't go," she pleaded and grabbed my arm with both hands anchoring me in the kitchen.

I kissed her on the forehead and shook her off. "I'll be in touch. I love you."

I reached for Heather, who stood behind Nicole and backed away.

"Heather, please," I said, not knowing what I meant by it.

How could they possibly understand what was going on? The crazy bus I chose to jump on was leaving. Heather grabbed Nicole's hand and pulled her away with her as she stepped back, establishing a united front. Her message was clear. They could let me leave, not caring if the door hit me on the way out.

Chapter 32

A s I drove toward the coast, hunched over the steering wheel and leaving my family behind, tears didn't come. I slammed on my brakes and swerved away from an ear-splitting honk, just missing a car as I drove straight through a stop sign.

"I'm sorry. I'm sorry," I called out to both Roger in the back seat and the taillights of the car I barely avoided. The near accident was the exclamation point at the end of my tumultuous day.

My stomach sank as I got to the dead end of a street and faced the Atlantic Ocean. I didn't recall any of the rest of the twenty-five-minute drive it took to get here. Not good. I leaned back and rested my head on Roger's, which appeared between the front seats as soon as I put the van in park. Did I think the girls would bar the door and not let me exit or throw themselves on the ground in fits of anguish over my leaving? Did I really believe Michael would stop me? I certainly didn't expect them to make it so easy for me to walk out the door.

I threw the van into gear and drove around with Roger panting in my right ear. What the hell was I supposed to do now? How deep the muck a mother could create when she was hopelessly wavering between family and self.

The neon lights of Jefferson Liquors caught my attention. I slowed and turned into the parking lot, noting they were still open.

"Be right back, Rog."

I ran in and searched through the mid-shelf wines. It wasn't a night for a top-shelf, and I never look at the bottom shelf. My phone dinged, and Pamela's face stared back at me. Not now. I had no answers to the questions she would ask. I stuffed the phone back into my pocket and grabbed a familiar red blend for $13.99. I set the bottle on the counter.

A dramatic exhale departed from the irritated twenty-something cashier with purple hair, pierced nose, and a full sleeve of tattoos standing behind the register. What would I have done if either of my girls came home looking like her? Distracted by the size of her stretched earlobe hole and whether the ring inside was plastic or metal, as if that mattered, I jumped when the clearly agitated girl squealed, "Ma'am?"

"Oh, sorry," I said and handed her a twenty-dollar bill from my pocket.

"Don't you have a credit card?" she asked, refusing to take the twenty-dollar bill from me as if it had cooties.

"Oh, sorry," I said again and rummaged through my pockets. "It's in the car." I pushed the twenty across the counter. Anyway, I didn't want to use my debit card. I didn't need Michael seeing every dime I spent. "Don't you accept cash?"

"Yes, but I already counted my drawer," she said.

"Just give me back a five. It'll be close enough." I cradled the bottle to my chest.

"It'll mess up my drawer."

Really? Wasn't it her job to take my money in exchange for a product she was selling? I stepped back with the bottle of wine, wanting to make a run for it.

"Anyway, we're closed," she said, glancing at the clock on the wall to my right. Two minutes after ten.

"You weren't closed when I walked in."

She pulled off her black Jefferson Liquor vest and grabbed her keys as if she were going to lead me out and lock the doors behind me. "If you want to get drunk, there's a bar around the corner."

"Ha," I laughed. As if I could get drunk off one bottle of wine. "It's not about getting drunk. Well, not always. Not tonight."

"Then go across to the gas station and get some water or a soda. They're open 24-7 and take cash."

"I don't want water." I could hear the pulse in my head, not a good sign for me lately. "I want wine. This wine." Even if, for some strange reason, she handed me a different, more expensive bottle of wine, for free, I wouldn't have left without this exact bottle.

Now the purple-headed autocrat backed up as if I were the crazy person. She's the one who wouldn't take my cash, a perfectly reasonable source of payment.

"Listen," I said. "Drinking wine isn't usually about getting drunk. It's about holding the glass, smelling its aroma, and relaxing."

"You don't drink it?" said the young girl, cocking her head in question with palms facing out as if to protect herself from me, say, if I jumped over the counter and strangled her.

"Of course, I drink it. But it's about that first sip. It changes everything. Just take the twenty. Keep it all, and ring it up in the morning. Please?" I gritted my teeth at the frustration of having to continually cover up my vinegar face with a honey smile.

The girl contemplated for a moment, seemingly weighing her odds. She dropped her hands. "I drink hard seltzers." As if that explained her whole being.

She took the twenty off the counter and held it up to the security camera behind her. "I'm putting this in my pocket for tomorrow," she said clearly and slowly. I waved to the camera and left with my bottle of wine.

With the heater on high, warming up the van, I dumped flat, warm diet cola from days ago out my window and wiped the lip of the plastic bottle with a crumbled-up, hopefully not used, napkin I found in the console between the seats. The glove compartment provided a wine opener. As I twisted the handle into the cork, I recalled the last time I drank that particular wine with Michael. My subconscious loved playing tricks. I half-filled the disposable bottle with the wine.

What I said to that poor, young, unapologetically expressive girl was true. Drinking wine was all about that first sip. The earthy tones brought me right to sitting with Michael, eating surf and turf in a dimly lit, practically empty seaside restaurant with Nora Jones singing overhead. When the DJ on my van radio finished talking, and the song which followed was anything but a Nora Jones tune, I sighed and turned to Roger.

"What have I done?"

I returned to the dead end I had found earlier, took my plastic bottle of wine, and hooked Roger to his leash. Grateful I wasn't totally alone, and not sure why no one had stopped me from taking him, I set aside thinking about accommodations for the both of us.

First, I needed to walk. I donned my windbreaker and kicked off my sneakers. With only the late October moonlight to guide us, I led Roger to the ocean's edge.

Torn between my heartbeat racing from fear of what I'd just done and the tingling excitement from being on my own for the very first time, I exhaled in small spurts. My steps began to gather speed as I inhaled and exhaled with purpose. I capped my bottle of wine and started to run, feet splashing through the receding waves with Roger's leash dragging in the water twenty feet ahead of me. I reveled in my blank thoughts and the view around me, my succor. The sound of waves crashing and rustling grasses on the dunes were the music of my heart.

The one constant of my father's Naval career was that he was always, without exception, stationed on or near water, the East Coast or the Gulf of Mexico. I was never far from the ocean, which still grounded me to this day. My breath caught up to my cadence, and I stopped abruptly. Head down, hands on my knees, I huffed like the untrained runner that I was. The Saint Sebastian charm tumbled from beneath my collar and tapped me on the lips. A kiss from Curtis. I crumbled to the sand and cried. I missed my boy. And I couldn't help but wonder if Curtis was still here if any of this would be happening. Roger licked my face and burrowed his nose under my chin as if to help lift me up. I stood by way of all fours and let Roger lead me back to the van.

As I opened the trunk, it dawned on me there'd be no towel there. In my haste to pack and get the hell out of Dodge, I didn't once consider where I'd go or what I might need. I packed a few outfits, my jacket, a toothbrush, and a few books. It was more than halfway through October, and I never dreamed of needing a beach towel. I pulled out an old packing blanket, which I kept in the back of the van for when I delivered paintings, and shook it out. I wrapped the blanket around my shoulders and, looking like a pretty pathetic homeless pair, sat in the van and blasted the heat.

I thought about Pamela waiting at home for a reply from me. I'd text her back as soon as I found a place to stay for the night. I was sure she'd say to come to her place, but I had to do this on my own. I needed time to myself, and the girls were safe with Michael at home. Scrolling through my phone, I looked up hotels and rentals near where we sat. Hotels with off-season prices of $199.00 or more per night were tempting, but I had no idea how long I would need a roof over my head. Anyway, half of those places didn't take dogs. I looked into cottage rentals, but most were offering monthly deals, and I was sure no one would answer my request after business hours. The sky darkened as clouds covered the moon. I wrapped the blanket tighter around my shoulders.

With Roger in the passenger seat beside me, I drove to the closest hotel I could find with a vacancy and which accepted dogs. I got a $69.00 room for one night, two blocks in from the beach.

A dry, warm heat and damp, musty smell greeted us as I opened our door with a real metal key. Roger didn't follow me. I held the door open for him, but he sat in the hallway in protest of something he didn't like emanating from the room. Shivering in my damp clothes, I pulled him in by the collar, wondering what he knew that I didn't. He immediately jumped up on the queen-sized bed, rolled, and wiggled, drying himself off on the crisp, overbleached bedding.

"Great," I said through chattering teeth.

I turned on the TV for company and stripped out of my wet clothing. The shower knob screeched as I turned it on. Water little more than dripped out of the showerhead. I leaned in and pushed down the valve handle on the bathtub faucet. When nothing changed, I yanked on the handle, and the shower dumped a torrent of water on my back. At least it was warm, and it served to inform me that I'd rather have a nice, long, hot bath.

Unable to avoid focusing on Michael and the girls any longer now that Roger and I had a roof over our heads, and glad I was smart enough to have stopped for a bottle of wine, I slid under the near-scalding water until it reached my collarbones. My bent legs, crossed at the ankles with my knees peaking just above the waterline, relaxed in the steaming heat. I kept the hot on trickle so the heat could sink to my bones as the water cooled. I wanted to stay there until the hotel ran out of hot water.

As the shivering tension left my body, regrettable thoughts entered. I went back and forth between needing to be home and letting Michael deal on his own. Since I surprised myself by leaving, I wasn't even sure where to begin.

I wanted to call Pamela or Alicia. But then again, I didn't. Pamela would say to stop being a drama queen and worrying the girls were sitting at home, suffering without me, because most likely, they were watching a movie and eating ice cream. Alicia would say that if things were bad enough for me to leave my house, my forever home, then things were terrible, and we needed to talk it through.

I didn't want to talk to anyone. I didn't want to leave the warmth of the tub nor have to explain my actions to anyone. I slid forward, and my head sank under the water. I held my breath until I couldn't hold it a second longer.

"Argh," I screamed as I emerged, splashing water over the side of the tub. What the hell was I doing? And where would I go from here?

With a too-small towel wrapped around my body and another around my head, I stepped into the room only to find Roger, standing on the bed, wagging his tail. I stepped on my tiptoes. It dawned on me then that my splashing scream didn't even tempt him to jump off the bed. Roger refused to walk on the rug, not even to save or protect me; whatever that was all about was legit enough for me. I immediately dropped my towels in front of me and jumped like hopscotch onto the bed beside him.

"Okay, buddy. I hope I packed some socks."

I poured more wine into one of the plastic-wrapped paper cups supplied by the hotel and fluffed up the pillows behind my back. Overfatigued tears came, and I allowed myself to miss my family and my home. That was the truth of it. I messed up. Guilt infiltrated my anxiety. The memory of the morning I didn't want to be Mom or Mrs. for just one day reverberated in my mind. The accusatory karmic energy weighed down my shoulders, and a little voice inside me told me I got what I deserved. I was no longer Mom or Mrs. I no longer had my dream home and ideal family. I'd lost my son to God and my girls to my husband. Why couldn't I have been content with what I had? Why did I feel like I needed something more? More was now so much less.

My phone rang. I was ready to apologize, say, and do anything Michael or the girls needed me to. But when Pamela's face once again appeared on my screen, I pressed the red decline button. I didn't want to talk to her. Actually, I didn't want to hear what she had to say.

So she wouldn't continue to text all night, I let her know I was okay and that I'd call her in the morning. She responded with three red hearts and a glass of wine emoji. I assumed that she had talked to the girls and probably already got their versions of what happened tonight.

I closed my eyes, and again my mind operated as a kaleidoscope, each piece of a broken image justifying itself in a certain position, making a beautiful symmetrical abstract yet no sense at all.

My life was a paradox. I wanted to confront my family, and yet I needed them to come to the table on their own. And I needed space to see where I fit in, where my perception of me lined up with others' opinions of me. With that courageous yet scary thought, I clicked off the television and slid under the covers. Whether I fell asleep or not, there was nothing I could accomplish at the moment.

Chapter 33

*H*eather and Nicole took turns keeping Curtis and me company in the cavernous hospital room, lit only by the lights of his monitors. I could feel Michael standing in the doorway behind me when he'd come to check in. Once I turned to offer him a seat, but as soon as our eyes met, he looked away and disappeared.

At 2:00 a.m., Nicole sat with her legs stretched out over my lap, dozing off, when an alarm went off above Curtis's head. Several nurses rushed in, and one of them asked us to wait in the hallway. We exited, and Nicole ran to the waiting room. Two doctors hastened in and closed the door, leaving me on the other side, looking through a small rectangular window.

"What's going on?" Michael asked as he came up the hallway.

I reached out a hand which, with eyes wide open in panic, he took in both of his.

"I'm not sure. All of a sudden, alarms went off."

I backed away from the door, allowing Michael to peek through the window, but he shook his head. He didn't need to see. It had seemed like forever ago, but I looked at my watch, and the alarms had gone off less than two minutes before.

When the door finally opened, a nurse said, "Please go wait in the family waiting room. The doctor will speak to you shortly."

Nicole and Heather, both of whom I had no idea were right behind us, turned and led the way.

"But why? What happened? What's wrong?" I needed to know.

"Please," the nurse said as she corralled Michael and me with her arms, directing us toward the waiting room.

I looked over my shoulder before we turned the corner and saw several nurses wheel Curtis's bed out of his room.

I turned to run to him. "Where are they taking him?"

Michael grabbed me by my trembling shoulders and led me to the waiting room. Twenty minutes later, the nurse that directed us out of Curtis's room returned with sorrow in her eyes. I unfolded myself from the couch.

"I'm sorry we had to rush you out. Curtis had a stroke," she said, professionally and motherly.

"Doctor Kumar says things need to go well for the first twenty-four hours, so what does this mean?" Michael asked with a hitch in his voice.

"The clock starts over," the nurse said. "I'll come and get you once Curtis is back settled in his room."

I turned to the girls and reached for Michael's hand. This time, he did not respond in kind. Nicole's eyes were knowing. She reached out and took her father's hand, then one of mine. Heather grabbed her father's other hand but refused mine. I wanted to believe she left space for Curtis to hold hands between us. But I knew in my heart, her lack of completing the circle had less to do with Curtis and more to do with me. My family was broken.

Chapter 34

T he early morning sun crept in through the side cracks of the too-small hotel window shade. I rubbed my eyes and stifled a yawn as I uncurled my legs from around a still sleeping Roger and sat on the edge of the bed after tossing and turning all night. I leaned over to grab my phone, making sure my toes didn't touch the floor, and searched for texts or phone calls which surely came in throughout the night. But there were none. I could be on the side of the road, dying. I bet they thought I'd be home any minute or that they'd wake up and find me downstairs, sleeping on the couch Michael used to occupy. I'm sure they thought I could never last out here alone. Well, I'd show them.

In need of a large diet cola and breakfast, I grabbed the towels from last night and hobbled over to where I had left my shoes. Then I packed my few belongings.

"Come on, Roger," I said, calling him toward me as I held the door wide open. "Come on, boy." He stayed on the bed, tail wagging.

I retraced my steps, lifted him with both arms, and carried him out to the hallway. "Tonight I'm going to make sure you'll enter the room before I pay for it," I said as he happily trotted down the hallway. I looked back into the room, cringing at what could have repelled Roger.

Sitting with Roger under my feet in the barely heated, plastic enclosed patio of a breakfast and burger dive down the road, the morning air quickly cooled my scrambled eggs and bacon as I texted the girls to check in, in case they cared. The aroma of fried bacon, baked bread, and brewed coffee drifting from the open kitchen windows magnified my appetite. Yet I had a hard time swallowing. There had to be a next step, and I needed it to be the right one.

I glanced at the time on my phone and rubbed the back of my neck. Anticipation was eating at me. I wanted to go home, but a little voice inside prodded me to take some time for myself, just the weekend, and figure out what I wanted. I only needed one thing, but I couldn't bring Curtis back. Maybe without the girls around, I could sort out what I truly wanted. We couldn't continue the way things were. Something had to give, and it had to give in me.

With pseudo confidence, I scrolled for a place to stay tonight, and maybe tomorrow night, then when I went home Monday, the girls would be at school and Michael at work. I'd have time to settle back into my studio and my kitchen and set a schedule that would serve me before anyone else. I could think that way because the girls had that damned car.

I wanted to have a firm plan for the weekend before I called anyone so that no one, meaning Pam nor Alicia—I didn't see my family knocking down any doors—could talk me out of my decision to stay away for the weekend. I found vacancies in hotels, motels, and a few cottages. But most of them were costly, even off-season, and only a few of them accepted pets.

A slim, young blonde entered the diner patio, head down, phone in hand, just like one of my twins. Future generations would soon develop a set of eyes on top of their heads so they could see where they were going while on their phones. She ordered large fries, grabbed a bottle of ketchup off the counter, and slid into a booth. A theme song from a familiar TV show signaled a phone call. She chatted amicably with her caller and pulled her fingers through her hair as her fries were delivered. She talked and laughed, dipped her fries in ketchup, and chewed all at the same time. Her smile never left her face. Her nonchalance was what broke me. I feared I had taken that away from my girls.

Just about the time a little voice in my head convinced me to just go on home, a charming little white beach cottage caught my attention as I scrolled. The notes said it was only half a block off the beach and $155 a week until they began renovations in the spring. I figured neither the house nor I were ready to make a commitment, so I might as well drive by and take a look.

I sat in my van outside a semi-dilapidated, wind-worn, white picket fence as a cool, damp ocean breeze rolled in one window and out the other. Across the street, an inviting wooden pathway led to the horizon between two small cottages. It called my name, but I wondered whether I should continue on this trial quest for self-discovery. My quandary came in the irony of me supposedly holding my poor girls back from their independence as I sat here contemplating mine.

If I didn't go right home, would that be a good decision or a bad decision? For my family or me? Wouldn't me being away from them be a win-win? Geez, I wanted to call Michael and ask. How silly was that? I rubbed the St. Sebastian charm between my fingers, a habit as calming as a child's thumb sucking, and prayed for a sign.

A sweater-vested, gray-haired, grandfatherly type opened the screen door and waved. I almost hit the gas and took off, but instead, I waved back. The elderly gentleman began to cross the overgrown front lawn with a friendly smile.

Roger and I met him at the white picket gate and greeted him. "Hi, I saw your listing online. Your home is adorable," I said.

"Wow, I just posted it this morning. Hi, I'm George, George Paquin. It's time to rent her out, but she needs a lot of work," he said, his sentiment clear in his words and tone. "Come on in and check her out. We were planning to renovate last year when my wife, Helen, got sick. She passed last spring. I couldn't bring myself to come back here until just recently."

My heart skipped a beat. His wife and Curtis have undoubtedly met. I sent up a thank-you.

Leaving Roger within the perimeter of the white-picket front yard, George and I walked around the four-room, one-bath cottage and out to the sizable, fenced-in backyard.

"Can I have a dog here?" I bit my bottom lip and crossed my fingers behind my back.

"Sure. We've had several over the years. Let him in and see how he likes it." He walked to the front door and let Roger in.

I prayed Roger wouldn't embarrass me with his snobby, finicky behavior of last night. But he leapt into the living room, and after a quick tour with his nose low to the ground and tail waving high in the air, he met us at the back door.

The sun-faded wicker furniture on the back porch instantly offered evenings of wine in hand as the sun set behind the trees at the far end of the yard, and the sound of waves crashing on the shore circulated from the front of the cottage. It was all I needed. "Does it come furnished?"

"If that's what you want to call it, it's all included," he said. His hand slid across the back of the lounge chair.

"George, it's adorable. But…" How on earth could I explain I was living day to day, let alone minute to minute? "I'm looking for something just for the weekend, just a day or two." My phone rang. Fear caused a second's hesitation in wanting to know who it was, or who it wasn't, so I peeked. It was Nicole. I excused myself and took a seat on the deck.

"Hi, honey. Is everything okay?"

Roger ran from corner to corner of the backyard, comfortable with the lay of the land.

"Hi, Mom. I miss you. When are you coming back?" Nicole's voice evaporated all my self-doubt. Someone did care. I was going home.

Yet as I looked back through the screen door into the cute retro kitchen, something in my head clicked. I fought the grind of the kaleidoscope gears revving, and newfound courage snuck up on me.

"I'm not sure. Is everything good there?"

"Yes, except Dad can't cook. He burnt the pancakes this morning, and Heather's—well, Heather."

I suddenly realized today was Saturday, and I didn't cook a single pancake. It never even crossed my mind. Was that a good thing or a bad thing? I was a bit tickled Michael attempted to stay true to our Saturday morning tradition. Maybe he wanted me back home too.

Nicole continued, "We have a Halloween party this weekend, and I need help with my costume, and Aunt Pamela wants some of my photographs for her auction, plus…"

My heart grew three sizes, knowing I was needed, but my logical brain held back my excitement. The emotional me wanted to ask lots of questions, make plans, and give suggestions, which always led me down the wrong path.

"Okay, okay, slow down." I couldn't let a Halloween costume be the line I drew. "I'll be happy to help you with your costume this week, and you know I'd be glad to help you with the photos for the auction." I steadied my breath. Roger chased a squirrel across the yard then ran in a circle and leapt up onto the chair next to me. He liked it here. I nodded my head, ruffled Roger's ears, and eked out, "I just can't come home right now."

"I get it, Mom."

Nicole's voice brought tears to my eyes, inspired by her vote of confidence. If that's what it was—what exactly did she get?

I wasn't sure if I was prepared for Heather's grilling, but I asked, "Can I speak with Heather?"

My fingers-crossed tone was quite evident, and I was relieved when Nicole said, "She's at work."

"We'll talk soon and make a plan. I love you," I said.

"Okay, but where are you staying?"

"I'm not sure. But when I am, I'll text you the address."

I didn't know where else I would go, but renting the cottage, even just for the weekend if that was even an option, wasn't a decision I was ready to make. I sat for a moment, out on the back deck, in the fresh air, noting, with Halloween approaching, how time crawled as it flew by.

I found George in the living room, opening windows. "Gotta air the place out. If you want it, I'll have it cleaned up in a couple of days. Then you can have it as long as you like," he said with a wink.

He must have heard enough of my conversation with Nicole to figure out what was going on. I hoped the heat traveling up my face wasn't glowing red.

"Why don't you go for a walk on the beach and think about it. Just find the wooden path across the street. You'll hit sand in less than a minute."

Perfect idea. "Yes. Thank you. That's exactly what I'll go do." Roger followed me out the door and to the van to get his leash.

Somehow, centered, I crossed the street with a newly unearthed calm. In the distance, the aquamarine ocean met the clear blue sky, and my cadence sped up automatically. I kicked off my shoes as we met sand, and not seeing another soul in sight, I let Roger off his leash. He dashed directly toward the water, and so did I.

The vastness of my view opened up space within me. Like Julie Andrews, I spread my arms wide and spun around. Space. That was what I needed, space. My own space. I turned until I fell to the sand. In all my dreams of the perfect family home, I'd always shared what was mine. I never committed anything to me, myself. Even my art studio was only temporarily mine, anticipating the day when one of the girls would want their own room.

As I stood and brushed off the sand, Roger halfway down the beach, dodging waves, I recognized this feeling from my youth. My rooms weren't my own. I knew I would be giving them up soon enough when we moved, so I never committed to any of them. I never taped posters to the walls, no matter how much I loved Michael J. Fox in *Family Ties*. I never committed to friends. I could never have a pet, not even a goldfish, because "how on earth would we move that?"

Everything I couldn't commit to in my childhood, I made sure my children could. I wanted them to claim lifelong friends, rooms, and memories. All these years, other than my family, I hadn't committed to anything but diet cola and cabernet sauvignon.

Knowing it sounded like I felt myself a martyr, which I knew I was not, was I even capable of committing to myself, to the exclusion of everyone else? And why did I feel I had to boycott my family to find myself? I whistled for Roger then plopped on the sand. He turned on a dime and came charging at me.

By never putting my wants ahead of the others, I'd never come up with what I needed to make me my best. If I had to make a list...

I jumped up right before Roger pounced on me and ran away as he shook and took chase. I threw a piece of driftwood, and he picked it up between his teeth and ran in the opposite direction. He looked back as a dare to follow. I ran after him faster and freer than a cheetah in the Safari.

The space around me fed my soul. Breathing the ocean air focused me as I had never focused before. I slowed my run and pulled out my phone to open my notes app and began journaling.

Julie's wants: Be home with my family. Michael and I all fixed. Nope, wrong. The deal was in exclusion of all others. I knew what I didn't want. I didn't want to be alone. I didn't want my girls to hate me. I didn't want to stay in this limbo. I picked up my shoes, knowing until I had a list of my wants, I couldn't go home.

George placed a box of books into his trunk as Roger ran past him through the open gate and sat on the front stoop like he was home.

"Beautiful, huh?" he said and invited me in through the gate before he closed it behind us, like the proper gentleman he was. "I have spent over fifty years walking that beach."

"I think..." Even if I just stay a couple of nights, it would be cheaper than a hotel. "I'll take it for a week. But I sort of need it, like today."

"I don't have cleaners coming until Monday..."

"If I can have it today, I'll clean it up for you. It would be therapeutic," I said, trying not to sound too desperate, just helpful. "Just for a week."

He stuck out his hand, and we shook on it.

He showed me the list on the inside of a cabinet door with all the house maintenance phone numbers he assumed were still current. He exchanged the check I handed him with a handwritten schedule for the week. He crossed off the housecleaners and left the rest of the list: garbage day Tuesday, lawn care Friday, and the bug guy was scheduled for Wednesday, but I'd have to let him inside. I'd let George know later that I wasn't going to be here past Monday, so I wasn't concerned in the least.

Guilt from putting my family second and pride from putting myself first battled within. A buzz of optimism crept into my fingertips, and I rubbed my hands together in excitement. I made a commitment to me, even if it was to clean somebody else's house.

As I lumbered toward the empty cottage after walking George to his car and grabbing my suitcase out of mine, the hypocrisy of what I had done slapped me in the face. Throughout all the years, I hated how family members had left me one at a time—my brothers and sister, my father, my mother, Curtis, and then Michael—yet I had never, not for one day, lived alone.

Chapter 35

George had left a bucket of cleaning items under the kitchen sink, and I went to work on the cottage. Scrubbing the bathtub was as cathartic as a massage, but my empty list of wants weighed heavily on me. Roger stayed by my side for every step of dusting, sweeping, and scrubbing. The girls would love this place, and I envisioned how fun it would be to vacation here as a family.

Michael, especially, would love being able to walk the half-block east to the beach and the one block west to the center of town, which included a four-building intersection providing a small grocery and liquor store, a pharmacy with a diner counter in the center, an Ace hardware store slash gift shop—must be a husband-and-wife team—and Todd's Garage with a restaurant and bar on the floor above advertising live music on the balcony every Friday night. Pretty much all a guy would need.

Thoughts of Michael brought me to wondering how he was handling his mess of buying a car for the girls. Would he understand the predicament he put me in? Would he call me and beg me to come home and deal with it together like we used to deal with every other family drama? If he did, could I wait a day or two and not jump at his beck and call? Who was I fooling? He'd never admit that car was a mistake.

As the cottage took on its new sparkle, my confidence grew accordingly. It reminded me how I conquered that fresh-start feeling I got every time I had moved into a new home as a kid. It was a familiar yet unsettling feeling, and I was surprised I welcomed it. My justification for being here, for deserving time to myself—albeit with my phone by my side—overpowered the guilt of not being home with my family. After two hours of nonstop cleaning, I craved a diet cola.

"Crap. I have to go to the grocery store." I rummaged around in the cabinets and found a box of teabags. "Tea can't go bad."

Wrong. The teabags had been visited by tiny critters. They were definitely bad.

"I'll be right back, Rog," I said, remembering I needed more dog food too.

I found a pen and paper in a junk drawer to the left of the fridge and wrote my shopping list—harder to do for a party of one than I thought.

I drove the one block to the grocery store, knowing I would have wine bottles to carry home. Shopping for one after shopping and cooking for a family turned out to be hugely depressing. I traveled up and down the four aisles several times, choosing my wines, before I could decide on what to eat. Deli sandwich items and fresh veggie salads seemed the most logical, plus frozen potpies and pizzas. I grabbed a dozen eggs from the dairy fridge, and as I turned the corner, a flyer pinned to a corkboard in the restroom hallway caught my attention. "Yoga classes held in the conference room in the back of the hardware store, every morning at 7:00 a.m." I took one of the several copies off the board and stuffed it into the pocket of my jacket.

Fifty minutes later and with a frozen chicken potpie in the oven, I sat in the antique wicker chair on the back deck, wine in hand, as the sun set behind the trees. I wondered if making the homemade potpies, meatballs, and ziti just two days ago was a harbinger to what had followed. There was comfort in knowing I had left several frozen meals for my family to eat.

I put away my What Does Julie Want list as streaks of purple and orange shifted in the sky with the not-so-distant rhythm of the breaking waves. It was as I pictured. The longer I listened to the hypnotic crashing and ebbing of the tide making its way from the front of the house, the kaleidoscope slowed, almost but not quite coming to a halt. Maybe once it stopped, I could sort out the image. Before I could get ahead of my circling thoughts, my phone buzzed me out of my optimism.

"Hi, girlfriend. Where are you?" Pamela asked, always straight to the point and reminding me to send Nicole my address.

The contrary part of me wanted to say I was sitting in self-induced loneliness, dodging every thought that came into my head, trying to dump everything out so I could start from scratch, but I said, "What are you doing right now?"

"Not much. Jeff's out of town. Are you going to tell me where you are?" Pamela said.

I scrolled through my texts. "It's not like you've texted me."

"I wanted to give you time. And it's more like you haven't texted me. But Heather did."

"Oh shit." I knew it. "Let me tell you my version. I'm sure it'll be different."

"You better. I'll get Alicia and meet you. Where are you again?"

She made it sound like I was never going to tell her and that it was a secret, which led me to wonder if it should be. But that was silly. I couldn't do this totally alone. I gave her my address and put two more frozen chicken potpies into the oven.

Waiting in the almost dark, after turning on the one lamp in each room of the unfamiliar house, the confidence and determination I garnered throughout the day had waned. The kaleidoscope reappeared, and panic loomed with each cracked and splintered shape. What was I doing? Who did I think I was, living in a beach cottage, alone, away from my family as if on vacation? It went against everything I'd always fought for. How were things going to change if I weren't at home with the girls? Yet—and here's where the kaleidoscope made sense—even if I were home, would anyone be interested in making a change? Would Heather or Nicole or Michael respond calmly to what I had to say and discuss options or even ask questions? Ha. I learned long ago, nobody asked questions because then they'd be held responsible for hearing my answers. But how could I fix anything if I wasn't there?

The front door opened and shut down the scrambling in my head. The kaleidoscope jolted to a stop, and I jumped up to greet my friends.

"Saw your van outside. What an adorable cottage," Alicia said as she entered with two bottles of wine.

"And such a great location," Pamela agreed, walking straight to the kitchen as if she had been there before and dropped a vegetable tray on the table.

"I lucked out finding it. I think George, the owner, felt sorry for me and thought I was homeless," I said with a smirk and winced, acknowledging he wasn't too far off.

"George?" Pamela smirked and raised her eyebrows.

"Oh my god, Pamela. The man's over eighty years old." I pulled the chicken potpies out of the oven and placed them on hot pads on the old laminate table for four.

"Straight from a sixties diner," Alicia said, running her hands over the smooth Formica. "I love it."

Breaking into our potpies to let the steam out, we took time to enjoy our wine and the veggies and dip. Pamela went straight in for the kill. "So, I got the rundown from Heather—you got mad because you had to pick Nicole up from school."

Wine spewed from my mouth. "Excuse me?" I laughed at the audacity of my impolitic child. "Is that really all she said?"

"I figured you'd tell me something different," Pamela sat back in her chair and tipped her glass toward me, giving me the go-ahead to share.

I recapped what happened the day after Michael delivered that car emphasizing how hard it was for me to accept my newfound freedom and fulfill my day.

"And that's the irony of all this," said Pamela. "You left the forever home you had to have to get over your childhood of moving every two years, and what? Rented a space to live in all by yourself? I don't know if I'm really proud of you or ready to pull out the straitjacket."

"Perfectly put," I said. "Have you ever been inside a kaleidoscope?"

"What?" Pamela stammered.

"Never mind," I said. "I'm totally confused, as well as angry, guilty, and sad." I flipped my potpie over, needing it to cool off faster so I could soak up the wine I was gulping.

"A kaleidoscope creates an optical illusion with a mirror system," Alicia said. "Mirrors," she emphasized.

I blinked, now sensing the persistence of my visiting kaleidoscope. She understood, and now I did too.

"We're getting way off track here," Pamela said.

"Not really. You feel fractured. Let's take care of each shard one at a time," said Alicia, addressing my obviously building anxiety. "I get the angry and the sad. Michael dropped a big one. But I believe he was trying to…"

"We're not here to defend him," Pamela said. She sat up straight and raised her eyebrows in a challenge to Alicia.

"Hold up here. You two don't need to get physical," I said with both hands out, as if breaking up a boxing match. I said to Pamela, "Thanks for sticking up for me, but I need to hear the truth. I can't seem to sort that out anymore. Apparently, my perception of things is a bit splintered."

Apologizing to Alicia because she had to hear it all again, I told Pamela about overhearing the twins talk a while back, not wanting to tell Pamela before assuming she would just defend Heather.

"Okay, I get it. They think you're a control freak. But honestly, Julie, that's nothing new." Pamela lowered her shoulders. "And I kind of agree with Alicia. I don't think Michael purposely upended things. I think he was honestly trying to help free up some time for you."

I feared Pamela's sister-brother act was angling for me and Michael right now, but I needed Pamela to be pro just me. "He should have talked to me before he bought that car. I was perfectly fine driving them around."

"You mean, driving them around was a perfect excuse to fill up your schedule, so there was no time for you to do something for yourself." Pamela's bird's-eye view.

"That wasn't my intention." My scalp prickled, having to defend my actions. "I'm their mother. It's my job to drive them around. And be available when they need me. I screwed that up big-time once, remember."

"Julie," Alicia said, "your job as a mother is to support your children in becoming good, healthy adults and allow space and time for them to fail and discover new skills and…"

"I know all that." I stood up and dumped the rest of my potpie into the sink with a loud bang. "The problem is, I don't know how to support without them viewing it as control. I don't know how to allow them to fail when I can so easily prevent their fall."

Alicia came up behind me and placed her hands on my shoulders. I instantly broke down and turned to cry on hers. After blubbering my way through the logistics of my fallibilities, I knew my friends were right. I had kept blinders on when it came to fixing my family.

Pamela looked at me straight in my eyes. "The lies we tell ourselves are the ones that hurt us in the long run."

"Geez, when you put it that way…" I huffed and signaled my two very best friends to follow me into the tiny living room. Pam sat on the frayed, floral-patterned, blue couch next to me, and Alicia folded one leg under her as she dropped into the faded denim sofa chair across from us. Roger circled between us before settling down.

"So what's your plan now?" Pamela asked.

"You don't need a plan," Alicia said in response to the panic on my face. "You only need the next step."

"Truth?" I said, pulling a comfortably worn quilt over my legs. "There's a part of me dying to get home and straighten everything out, get things back to normal. But that's just it. I've done that. We don't have a normal. Things have been up in the air for almost two years. What would you do?"

"I'm not touching that with a ten-foot pole," Pamela said as she stuck her palm in my face.

"Thanks," I said with pouty lips.

"Seriously," Pamela said. "You have to figure this out on your own. If you go back, will Michael stay or go back to the hotel?"

I hadn't even considered what Michael would do if I returned. Had he even checked out of the hotel he had been living in, or was he still holding on to it thinking I'd be home soon?

"You've only been away one night. How much time do you need?" Alicia asked.

How much is enough? I scraped my hand through my hair and shook my head. "I don't know. I don't know. I don't know."

"Can I throw something out there?" Alicia said, scooting to the front of her seat.

"Sure, why not?" I said, a little leery of Alicia's tone of voice. She was always thoughtful with her advice, but something in the pause before she continued warned I might not want to hear what she had to say.

"Maybe it's not in you to stay in the same four walls you've fought so hard to maintain for you and your family. It's in your blood to move around, experience different people, different things. That's what your upbringing taught you. Maybe you've been fighting the wrong battle. Maybe if you embrace some instability and unknowing, as you had to as a child, you wouldn't be restless in your perfect, static, forever life."

Mind blown. Never in a million years had I considered how growing up moving around was part of me, but I knew I was always fighting something deep inside. It was what I was used to, and all I knew. My tight grip on my home was actually meant to keep me in one place, and I forced it onto my family. If holding time and space in place for my family was counterproductive, then I was to blame, and it was up to me to change.

We sat in silence, allowing me time to think. If I went home now, what would be different? Would we all fall right back into our abnormalcy? Did the girls need more time with me or without me? Did I need more time without them? Would our separation be the great equalizer? Surely, time apart would allow all of us to determine what we were missing, if anything, and what we needed from each other. I needed time to think about what Alicia said. What if I genuinely had been fighting the wrong battle since the beginning?

"And what about your painting?" Alicia sat back in her usual calm style, not quite finished dropping her two cents worth.

"My painting?" See, this was my problem. At no time, staring at my empty What Julie Wants list, had I considered my artwork, the very thing that had soothed my soul since my early years when sketchpads and art supplies traveled with me from house to house and kept me from feeling totally desolate. I couldn't get past Michael and the twins' happiness to see my own.

I got up, threw the quilt over Pamela's lap, and walked into the front guest bedroom. Twin beds flanked the east-facing window, and I imagined my easel fitting snugly between the two with morning sunlight coming in, warming up the space and illuminating the room while I painted. I held on to one of the headrails and looked out the window into the dark and could imagine the beach between the two houses across the street. As I turned to leave, peg holes on the posts of the bed got my attention. These were bunk beds. If I put one on top of the other, I'd have more than enough room to paint and definitely would have space for the girls, should they ever want to visit.

I walked back past my friends chatting in the living room and through the kitchen into the master bedroom with Roger at my heals. I considered the room, then wandered through the only bathroom in the house, then out its second door back into the kitchen. Roger headed to the kitchen sliders, and we went out onto the back deck.

I looked up at the dark sky dotted with stars winking at me and rubbed my St. Sebastian charm. I asked the universe if I could really live here, alone, at least for a little while. Roger jumped up into an old wicker chair and stretched to meet me at eye level, as if wanting to answer me.

"Roger, get down," I said.

He had never jumped on furniture at home. It was not allowed. He raised his eyes and wagged his tail, knowing he was getting away with something. He liked it here and was telling me to stay awhile. Maybe Alicia was right. Maybe I had the feeling of not wanting to be Mom or Mrs. not because I didn't want to be Mom or Mrs. but because I had an itch for something new, to change, to grow.

I entered the living room, interrupted Alicia's and Pamela's conversation, and announced, "I'm staying."

Alicia's mouth dropped open, clearly not expecting my news. Pamela, on the other hand, pumped her fist in the air.

"For the whole week," I clarified. I could commit to that much.

I stayed up a few hours after Pamela and Alicia left, washing dishes and the sheets from the main bedroom, which I should have thought about earlier. Tomorrow I'd buy new ones so I'd have two sets. I texted Michael, Heather, and Nicole with my address and explained I'd be by in the morning to pick up a few things.

"There, let them stew on that," I said as my gut tightened. I wanted to shut off my phone but dared not.

Exhausted, I climbed under the fresh sheets and lay in the dark, staring at the paneled wall through the streaks of moonlight. It was too quiet. I couldn't remember what I was used to hearing, but this wasn't it. I cracked open a window to hear the roar of the surf and snuggled under the covers to hide from the cool breeze I'd let in. Now if I could just get the scenarios of how tomorrow would go out of my head so I could sleep.

Chapter 36

The day of...
Nineteen months earlier, 3:00 a.m. to 6:45 a.m.

*A*s I fretted while Curtis endured his second surgery of the night, the girls, in an unrestful sleep, slumped on the couch in the family waiting room. Nicole's legs rested on the coffee table, her lap a pillow for Heather. Michael slept slouched in a chair, his legs extended straight in front of him and crossed at the ankles. A soft snore wheezed out from under the baseball cap covering his face. They were blessed if they could fall asleep here, on this furniture, in this room, guilt-free, with Curtis down the hall, fighting for his life.

I paced back and forth in front of the window at the end of the room. A hard rain fell, hypnotizing me. Little droplets slid and slithered on the glass until the next one interrupted its path, splitting it in two until it ran out of the liquid that they were.

"What is taking so long?" I desperately wanted to be with Curtis. I twisted a tissue so tightly little pieces floated down to the floor like snowflakes. "Let him be okay, God. Please just let him be okay."

The pink glow at the beginning of the sunrise challenged me to have faith. My father used to always say, "With each new day comes hope." Exhausted and transfixed, I stared as bright orange pushed its way out of the horizon.

"Excuse me, Mrs. Scott," Dr. Kumar whispered from the doorway and waved me to him.

"Dr. Kumar," I greeted him in a whisper from across the room. On my way to the door, I tapped Michael on the shoulder, and together we faced the doctor.

"Of course, we can tell more as time goes by, but right now, things do not look good. I need you to be strong for your daughters."

Michael and I looked at each other, neither wanting to show each other their fear. Except the color in Michael's face had drained. "What exactly are you saying?"

"Mr. Scott," Dr. Kumar said, looking directly into Michael's eyes. "Your son is not responding well. He is not breathing on his own, and we cannot regulate his blood pressure. Pupillary reactions and motor response to painful stimulation are absent. We will continue to monitor the EEG for a while longer, but I think you need to prepare for the worst."

My mouth fell open. With fingers over my lips, I asked, "Are you saying my baby could die?"

"Is there anyone else you'd like to call? Grandparents? Close family members?" Dr. Kumar asked.

"But he just had a headache." My voice shook and raised in pitch. I pulled Michael's arm over my shoulder and held on tight, inhibiting the mania bubbling inside. I looked up into his eyes, and I could tell he could hardly contain his own.

"There is very little we can do at this point but hope and pray, but understand, I do not expect any improvement." Dr. Kumar gave my hand a tiny, unhopeful squeeze.

"Can we see him?" Michael asked.

"Yes. Get your girls and visit Curtis as long as you'd like."

Chapter 37

Before opening my eyes in a semi-dream state, the roar of the ocean brought me back to summer vacations at the beach; only this trip there was no Curtis. I woke in a panic, recognizing the strange bedroom with reluctance. Once orientated, my whys and wherefores aligned.

I sat on the back deck, wrapped in a warm woven blanket, planning my visit home. I would arrive with goodies in hand, an antic I learned from Michael, and tell everyone I needed time on my own. I wouldn't give any explanation or excuse so that I couldn't betray the anxiety over my decision. I prayed no one would bring up when I last had acted upon the need for time to myself, which my own heart had yet to forgive.

I'd ask my girls and Michael if they needed anything from me while I was there—I couldn't help myself—then gather my art supplies and a few more changes of clothes, towels, and sheets. I'd make a plan with Nicole to help her with her costume and, of course, ask Heather if she needed help, assuming she was going to the same party as her sister. Then I would return to the beach cottage and paint and paint and paint. Simple as that.

My nerves took over, and my early morning confidence receded quickly when I stopped by our neighborhood donut shop for a diet cola and a box of half a dozen vanilla-frosted donuts and two coffee rolls.

I pulled into the driveway and paused. Which door should I use? The front door or the side door? Should I knock or just walk in? Great. I had managed to displace myself from my own home. Had Michael felt that way? Had he knocked when he brought in the pizzas? No, he had walked in through the garage then straight into the kitchen.

This was silly. This was my house as much as theirs. Since the garage was closed, I went in through the gate and used the side door into the kitchen, like our family always did. I wished I had brought Roger. That would be a reason to be in the backyard, but I had left him back at the cottage, not wanting to chance the girls talking me into leaving him here at the house.

I knocked on the side door then turned the handle. Locked. I dug out my keys and looked around as if I were breaking in and didn't want any neighbors to see.

I unlocked the door and stepped into the kitchen, feeling as if I were stepping into a pressure cooker.

"Hello," I called out and placed the pastries on the table.

"Hello?" I peeked into the garage and saw the girl's car parked in my space—made sense for early morning weekend—but Michael's car was not home. I didn't trust my memory and looked out the living-room window to see if his car was in the driveway or on the street.

Tiptoeing upstairs, assuming the girls were asleep because they both couldn't have fit in Michael's two-seater Audi, I pushed open the slightly ajar door and found two empty unmade beds then remembered Heather had been sleeping in the office. Nope, the office was spotless and totally vacant. But I did note a new printer on the desk. I wandered back into the girls' room, stood in the middle, and soaked up their atmosphere. Heather's side of the room had clothes piled on the floor, writing journals and an assemblage of pens and markers on her desk with piles of books on the dresser. Nicole's ballet bag hung on the back of her desk chair. Photos and sketches patchworked the wall over her bed. Her side of the room, desk included, was Marie Kondo tidy—the total opposite of Heather's side. I had been in this room a million times. How had I never noticed these nuances of my children?

I shook my head in self-reproach for not knowing the habits of my daughters and what went on in my own home. Yet when closing the door behind me, I couldn't deny the fact that I might not have been paying attention.

"Hello?" I called out again.

I had texted I'd be by in the morning. Did they leave the house, avoiding me on purpose? With pressure building in my gut, heat inched up my cheeks due to anger or embarrassment. I wasn't sure which. I ran into the bathroom, splashed water on my face, and released the pent-up tension with a groan.

As quickly as I could, I packed a small suitcase with necessities, grabbed the pillows off my bed, and threw them into the van. I subdued feelings of gathering all my personal belongings, needing them to be with me, not wanting to leave anything behind. But that was silly. I'd be home soon enough. I gathered necessary paint sets and my easel. I placed them into the back of the van, then working up a sweat, I again ran up the stairs to get the canvases I was working on.

"Mom?"

"Julie?" Michael and Heather called up the stairs. I froze as if I was caught stealing.

I exhaled and called out, "Up here." I grabbed the smaller of the two canvases I was working on from my studio and met Michael in the hallway.

"Hi," he said awkwardly, and the twins' bedroom door closed. I felt a slam in my heart.

"Hi."

"Do you need any help?" Michael asked.

Wrong, Michael. Do I need help? How about, are you back for good? Or I missed you?

I turned sideways past him, down the stairs, and out to the van. I sat on the rear bumper, arms crossed, under the opened hatch, not wanting to go back inside for the other canvas and face either Michael or Heather.

I simmered, convincing myself to allow Michael the opportunity to do something, anything right, and not to be so trigger happy. Expect nothing, then I wouldn't be disappointed. Pep talk over, I swung my legs to gain momentum to hop off the rear of the van when Michael appeared with my large canvas, the one for the fundraiser.

"Thanks," I said behind gritted teeth, instantly triggered once again. Guess he couldn't get rid of me fast enough. I grabbed two edges and slid the canvas in the van at an angle.

"Want to come in?" Michael asked.

Not knowing if he meant it or was backtracking trying to be polite, I wondered if this was a trap.

So I shot back my own question, "Are you ready to talk?"

I could see in his eyes he wasn't, so I climbed in the driver's seat without waiting for his answer.

He held my door open, and I could tell he wanted to say something. I started the van but then dropped my hands into my lap in a gesture of submission.

After a moment, I met his pleading eyes, but words didn't come out of his mouth. I reached for the door and pulled it shut. He stood in the garage as I backed out of the driveway.

I drove straight to the cottage and took Roger out for a walk. The beach was quiet. Only one other person walked in solitude with their unleashed black Labrador sideswiping the surf. Roger took off down the shoreline in pursuit of a playmate. I half-jogged after him, summoning him to turn around, not in the mood to be polite to a stranger.

As I approached the dogs prancing in the cold waves, I acknowledged the other dog owner with a half-wave. The woman, who appeared close to my age and wrapped tightly in a plaid wool blanket, nodded her head but didn't approach. Good. She wasn't in the mood to chat with a stranger either.

In the silence of the crashing surf, the two of us stood, a hundred feet apart, and watched the dogs chase and paw at each other. Like summer beach buddies, they pushed each other and raced in and out of the waves. I popped my collar up around my neck and pulled the zipper under my chin. It was a beautiful October day. The sun was bright and warm, not a cloud in the sky, but the ocean breeze left a chill.

Eventually, the dogs tired, not of each other but from rabble-rousing in the waves. The lab darted over to his owner and shook the saltwater from his coat. Roger, stunned his playmate had left him in the surf, looked at me then back at the black lab. As the woman walked away with her dog by her side, Roger finally gave up and trudged over the sand to me.

"Oh, no, you don't," I said, running backward, away from my shaking dog. He shook, and I backed up until I landed on my rear end with Roger peering over me, licking my face.

"Okay. Okay," I said, pushing him away. I stood up and brushed off the damp sand. I looked around at the now totally empty coastline, and my heart filled with gratitude, blessed I could walk half a block to the beach, let Roger run free, and head back to a quiet home to paint with no one expecting anything from me. A smidgeon of guilt crept in. I mourned my lack of being needed. Let. It. Go. I shook my head, flinging away thoughts as Roger flung saltwater. Everyone knew where I was, and no one had begged me to stay home. Could one be sad and grateful at the same time?

The morning sun was still bright in the front room as it approached 11:00 a.m. I set up the easel, hoping for a few more hours of decent light. I found four wooden pegs in the top drawer of the dresser in the second bedroom. The next person to enter this house was going to be summoned to help put the bunks on top of one another, making ample room for my easel and painting supplies.

I reacquainted myself with the large canvas for Pamela's fundraiser and reviewed my sketch of the south side of the red-bricked Ranford house, which took up the left third of the landscape. Looking forward to bringing the painting to life with magnificent colors of a summer garden, I gathered the pictures of gardens I had printed from the Ranford house website and had blown up to eight by tens. Soon sketched hydrangeas, hibiscus, and Stella d'Oro daylilies, were surrounded by coneflowers, zinnias, and sea holly.

As the canvas filled in with penciled floral outlines, I dreamt of the perfection of my mother's colorful summer gardens in my early years. From when I could first remember, our homes were surrounded by color three seasons out of the year; and depending on which state we lived in, the winter season was somehow just as festive. What struck me years later, when planning my own gardens, was that my mother had only planted annuals. It seemed it would have been too hard to leave perennials behind. By the time I was in middle school, my mother's incredible garden skills were reduced to two or three potted arrangements on the front porch steps. "Gardening was too much work to leave behind for somebody else to enjoy," my mother said of her gardening days. She planted gardens that could travel just as efficiently as her children.

My phone rang, and someone might as well have thrown a hand grenade into the room. I jumped at the intrusion, my pencil flying. Because of the limited space, I knocked into the canvas, which fell onto the bed to my left, taking the easel with it. By the time I regrouped, the phone had stopped ringing.

Let them leave a message. If it was essential, they'd call right back. Who was I kiddng? I walked across the room and picked up the phone. There was no way I could let a phone call go without at least knowing who it was. Nicole's pretty face instantly cheered me up, and I called her back immediately.

"Hi, honey. What's up?" I said, sitting on the twin bed next to the fallen easel.

"I spent the night with Liz. By the way, Alicia says hi, and we're meeting Thursday night at her house to make our Halloween costumes." Nicole's ease drove me nuts. She hadn't asked me how I was or what I was up to. Was she not worried? Did she even care? And... why was I making this about me? Nicole called. I should be grateful. "Can we make my costume on Thursday night? It's the only time I have before this weekend," she sounded as if I was sitting with her at our kitchen table at home.

"Sure. I missed you this morning." I didn't want her to think I didn't care or didn't notice. Damned if I do... "No one was home when I got there."

"Nobody thought you'd be here that early. Dad and Heather went out for breakfast. I came home about fifteen minutes after you left. Sorry I missed you too."

There it was, the hitch in Nicole's breath. The telltale sign she was holding back tears. As sad as it was to say, it thrilled me.

"I think I already told you, but Pamela suggested I take some photos and frame them for the auction," Nicole said. "What do you think?"

God as my witness, my daughter asked for my opinion. I buzzed with excitement, which caused me to deviate from the details. "What do I think about what?" Now she was going to think I wasn't listening. Ugh.

"Do you think I should frame some pics for the auction? What if no one wants to bid on them?" Nicole didn't usually fish for compliments, so I instantly began to analyze why she could possibly be losing confidence in her photography.

"Honey, of course, people will bid on them. You're a great photographer. I'd buy your close-up photos of common items. They're beautiful and creative. I think you should do a set of three or four, in black and white…" Oh no, was I telling her what to do? Darn. I wanted to support, not direct. Why was this so hard? It took so much energy to parent with thought. I didn't use to have to think about it. I just parented by the seat of my pants. Wasn't that what all parents did?

"I was thinking the same thing," she said. "Maybe two sets of three abstract photos."

"Great minds…" Phew. Relief had me feeling as if I'd cut a corner in a road race and got away with it.

"When will you be home? Can we go shopping for frames?"

Her enthusiasm broke my heart. "Honey, I'm not sure when I'll be home, but we can get the frames whenever you'd like."

"You're going to live there forever?" Nicole let the words out with a long breath.

"For now, honey. But it doesn't mean you can't visit."

"Are you and Dad getting a divorce?" Nicole stuttered.

"You're never coming home?" Heather's voice blasted through the phone. In the background, Nicole yelled for Heather to give back her phone.

"Why don't you two come on over, and we'll walk Roger on the beach and talk," I said and crossed my fingers.

"Can't this week," Heather said.

"Maybe the week after?" I asked, realizing only then I subconsciously planned to be in the cottage longer than I first had thought.

By the thud hailing from the speaker, Heather must have thrown the phone back to Nicole. "You didn't answer my question," she said softly into the phone.

I didn't have answers because I hadn't talked with Michael, and I didn't want to talk to Michael until I had time to figure out my What Julie Wants list.

"We'll talk tomorrow after school. But I'll see you Thursday night for sure, with Alicia and Liz, right?"

Chapter 38

I was nervous to see the girls at Alicia's house by the time Thursday rolled around. A bit of October Indian summer had made the week of Halloween a great week to paint outdoors. I had gotten away with shorts and a sweatshirt, and this morning's sunlight in the front of the cottage couldn't have been more inspiring or encouraging.

I was well into the depths of the Ranford house garden, but by noon I couldn't focus anymore on which red color, candy apple or crimson, would make the best geranium. The afternoon seemed to go on forever. My unripe freedom created a sort of struggle within— guilt versus the bliss of taking care of only myself. I'd get back to my shards when I had some answers. Unable to stay focused, I invited Roger to walk on the beach with me.

Roger and I had settled nicely into a routine. Twice a day, first thing in the morning, and the last thing before dark, we walked along the seashore, allowing me to dig deep within myself as if I couldn't hide my truth from the salt air. Even he enjoyed his newfound freedom. He'd wait at the front door, anticipating his romp on the beach, which unfortunately, would only last until Memorial Day in May, not that we'd be here when leash season came around. But until I moved home, we planned on enjoying our leash-less beach jaunts.

I showered and dried my hair, not air-dried but with an actual blow-dryer, in hopes it showed I could take care of me with more time on my hands. Dawdling in the kitchen, I rearranged items in the refrigerator impatiently, waiting for 6:00 p.m. I fed Roger and jumped into the van before 4:00 p.m.

I got to Alicia's early even though I had picked up wine, a pizza, and some delicious tiramisu on my way over. Excited when I saw the twins' car in the driveway, I chided myself as my hands shook as I reached for the pizza. The girls and I had only texted a few times over the last couple of days. Nicole would chat. Heather would respond.

Time and distance had abated some of the tension, but our conversations were far from the ones we should have been having.

I hit the doorbell with my elbow, balancing everything on the pizza box. "Pizza delivery," I said as Alicia opened the door.

"Hi, honey. Come on in." She stepped back for me to enter.

Something was off. Usually, Alicia was all kissy-kissy and, "Here, let me help you." I followed her into the kitchen with my hands still full.

My delight in being there fizzled when I saw Heather. She averted her eyes as Liz looked at me, wide-eyed with trepidation. Nicole, her back to me, stood. As she turned, a black-eye and raw gash down her left cheek sent a shudder down my spine. Alicia caught the wine and tiramisu just before the pizza box hit the floor at my feet.

"What the hell…" I leaped over our dinner and took the hand Nicole held out for me. I looked straight at Alicia. "Did you know about this?"

"Not until she got here," Alicia said.

"I'm fine. The doctor said I don't need stitches, and I don't have a concussion," Nicole assured me.

"The doctor…" My mind spun. Why didn't someone call me? Why didn't Michael call me? "When…" Nicole pulled on my arm and sat me down.

"It was my fault," Heather started.

My anger rocketed. Of course, why wouldn't it be Heather's fault? "A car accident?"

"No, Mom. It had nothing to do with the car." Nicole took a sip of her water.

I looked around at the faces staring at me. "Well, what the hell happened?" The pop from Alicia opening the wine bottle did little to ease my nerves.

"Last night, Heather and I went to the mall. She was in Victoria's Secret, and I left to go to the bathrooms in the food court across the way." Nicole reached out for Heather's hand. "And I saw Tucker sitting on the fountain wall."

"Tucker was with another girl," Heather interjected, struggling with the pace of Nicole's storytelling, and for once, I agreed with her.

"They were kissing. Nicole interrupted them and told the girl to get her hands off her sister's boyfriend. I heard the commotion and ran out just as Tucker stood up, and Nicole shoved him. That's when the girl got really angry. You should have seen Nicole scrapping with her."

"You hit a girl?" I couldn't hide the shock from my face. Not my Nicole. Heather, maybe. But not Nicole.

"She shoved me first. I really wanted to hit Tucker, but that chickenshit ran away." Nicole winced when she attempted a smile and covered her cheek with her hand.

"You should see the other girl. Nicole tore her shirt to shreds." Heather sounded proud of her sister, but I still couldn't wrap my head around my daughter's damaged face.

Alicia handed me a glass of wine and put plates of pizza slices out on the table. The girls all grabbed one—none of this affecting their appetites.

Questions wanting out of my head jammed in my throat. After a couple of sips of wine oiled and loosened my jaw, I couldn't stop the words from spilling out. "Why didn't you call me? Does your father know? Did you go straight to the emergency room? Do you need some ice for your cheek?" Tears fell during my retching of words.

"Mom. I'm okay. The police showed up. They called an ambulance, and Heather called Dad."

"Are you in trouble?" I had to remind myself we were talking about Nicole.

"With Dad?"

"No, with the police."

"No. Not me. Since Tucker wasn't there to defend himself, the crowd of people told the police that the other girl smacked me first." Nicole could hardly chew her pizza without wincing in pain. Her pain was my pain.

"She's the best sister ever," Heather said and hugged Nicole from behind. "Who would have thought that little ol' Nicole would have stuck up for me?"

Nicole brushed Heather off and shook her head. "You've defended Tucker's behavior a million times, and look what he goes and does. I should knock you silly too." Nicole held up a fist.

"Oh, you don't have to worry about him anymore." Heather returned to her seat and took a bite of her pizza. "I'm done with him. We're going to just be friends from now on," Heather said and cocked an eyebrow with the tilt of her head, warning me off any further discussion.

Oh Heather, being "just friends" usually didn't work out. But I kept my mouth shut, thinking she could figure that out on her own.

It was then I noticed Heather's phone wasn't in her hand nor even on the table. Hmmm. Glad to know there was a silver lining in all this. My guts quivered each time I looked at Nicole's face, but to see my two daughters laughing and teasing each other while fighting over the one piece of pizza with the bubble in the crust warmed my heart.

"Okay, girls. Let's work on the costumes," Alicia said as the last of the pizza disappeared.

"What or who are you three going to be? And tell me about this party you are going to." I needed to get my hands busy before I picked up my phone to call Michael. Why did he let the girls go to the mall on a school night? Where was he? Why didn't he call me after the incident?

"We're going as the three witches from *Hocus Pocus*," Heather said.

"The Sanderson sisters. We'll be Mary and Sarah," Nicole said and put her arm around Heather. I was not used to these two acting all buddy-buddy, and it was hard for me to trust what I was seeing. I anticipated a punch line.

"And I'll be Winnie," Liz said and puckered her lips around her two front teeth like a fish and opened her eyes as wide as she could.

As Heather curled the long messy tresses of the blonde wig and I braided the brunette wig around a coat hanger so the hair could stand up and point to the ceiling, Nicole iced her cheek. Liz and Alicia cut out and sewed three hooded capes.

The twins sat side by side on the kitchen bench, drew plans for the three character's makeup, and made a shopping list. Every time Heather made Nicole laugh, Nicole winced and shoulder bumped Heather, saying, "Don't make me laugh."

Heather shoulder bumped her back, making Nicole laugh even louder. It was a sound I thought I'd never hear again. At least, not like this and certainly not with Heather as the instigator.

"Remember last year, Halloween?" Heather said.

Everyone silenced in contemplation.

"We didn't do Halloween last year," Nicole said, reminding us we didn't celebrate any holiday last year.

"I meant the year before."

"Scooby-dooby-doo," Nicole called out. "With Dad as Fred and Curtis as Shaggy."

"He complained about that scratchy wig and fake whiskers the whole night."

The more they laughed, the happier I became. To hear the girls recall the three of them as Shaggy, Velma, and Daphne and, of course, Roger as a long-haired Scooby-Doo, hinted at times when I stayed back at the house to hand out candy, still feeling part of the team, and the four of them drummed up their own adventures.

Logic overtook my worry. I no longer felt the need to be angry with Michael. But I wished he had called me or someone had called me when the fight happened. I tried to stay away from feeling they didn't call me on purpose. Payback? But each time Heather caught me watching them, her smile faded the littlest bit, like she just remembered to not be happy around me.

A thought flittered across my mind. What if the girls were this happy because I wasn't living under the same roof as them? My heart couldn't go there. I stood up and plopped the red wig on Liz's head and arranged the many braids into circles as a crown atop her head.

"So where is this party again?" I asked.

"At Tucker's," Heather said, as if going to her ex-boyfriend's a few days after her sister fought with his new girlfriend was the most natural thing in the world.

Chapter 39

The day of…
Nineteen months earlier, 6:45 a.m. to 10:03 a.m.

*T*he walls in the family waiting room at the Wilmington Trauma Center closed in on us. The twins sat on the edge of the couch, hip to hip, hand in hand. Their silent tears confirmed they had overheard the doctor tell us that there was little hope for Curtis. Not wanting to say the words, I just held out my arms.

Michael grabbed Heather's wrist as she darted off the couch and attempted to run out of the room. He pulled her into his chest, hugged her tightly, and said, "Let's all sit with Curtis." She melted at his feet, sobbing. I lifted her from her knees and pulled her into my arms with Nicole.

The Scott family stayed a few more minutes in the waiting room. We collected ourselves and gathered our courage then walked down the hallway as one unit. When we passed the nurses' station, I couldn't look. I didn't want to see the telling in their eyes.

Three hours later, Curtis took his last breath. Michael left the hospital by himself, no "goodbye," no "meet you at home," no hug for me nor the girls.

The nurses let me hold Curtis's hand as they unhooked all the wires and tubes, and the orderlies rolled out the monitors. When the room became too silent to bear, I tucked Curtis's arm by his side, pulled the sheet and blanket up over his chest, and kissed the back of his hand for the last time.

Chapter 40

S till on a high from the girls' new togetherness and our frequent conversations in a group text for the last three days, the first thing I thought about on Saturday morning was to whip up pancake batter even if it were just for myself. The second thing was that my girls were going to a Halloween party at Tucker's tonight. I called them a couple of times, in between paint strokes, just to be reassured their costumes were coming together and their night would go well.

Throughout the day, I threw myself into final details, adding light and shadow in and around the flowers of the Ranford house garden. It was one of my best paintings yet. I was proud to donate the piece to Pamela's fundraiser. As the sun set, I poured myself a glass of wine and sat in anticipation of the text the girls promised to send me when they arrived home from the party. Once settled, I picked up my latest novel—the third I'd read since I'd been in the cottage.

I found myself drifting from the words on the page to memories of the girls happily together. I hoped the twins were getting along at home, sharing that damned car, and doing some household chores. Images of piled-up dirty dishes, loads of unwashed laundry, and dust-covered furniture turned my stomach. As I imagined the conditions of the bathrooms, I cringed and almost jumped off the couch and made a beeline to the house. But instead, I took another sip of wine. Not my issue at the moment. But I would have liked to talk to Michael and see how he was doing. Not as far as the girls went but he himself. I hoped he was healing.

The time on my phone on the old water-stained coffee table read 7:00 p.m. The girls would be at the party, and he was probably sitting in his chair with a beer, watching hockey. I needed to let him have his space. The last time we spoke to each other, I had left the ball in his court. Since Nicole was fine, I had never called him about her escapade, figuring if he wanted me involved, he would have called me. I tried to negate the feelings that they didn't need me. I put the phone down and poured another glass of wine. Only three more hours, and the girls would be home. I quieted the flutter in my stomach by telling myself everything would be fine.

Out on the back deck, with a blanket around my shoulders as Roger attended to his business, the moon shone bright and just past full. The stars veiled the sky, but only when I looked at the moon. When I looked directly at the stars, they disappeared. I had to look askew to see their brightness. Like my daughters, when I directed my attention to them, they disappeared. Maybe with my love coming from a distance and a little to the left, they would accept it.

Just as I settled back onto the couch with my novel and wine, and a bowl of chips by my side, the glass in the front door rattled. I wasn't sure there was a knock, except Roger's ears went up at the same time. I peeked through my fish-eye view. Michael stood on the stoop with his hands in his pockets and his shoulders up to his earlobes. What's he doing here? How did he know where... Of course. I had texted the girls my address. It wasn't a secret.

I unhooked the chain lock and turned the knob then stepped back as the door opened to make room for Roger. Roger couldn't have been happier to see Michael and vice versa. He squatted down, and Roger wrapped him with fur and licks.

"I dropped the girls off at Tucker's, so I..." Michael said as he rose. Roger still pawed and begged him for attention.

I reached for his elbow and pulled Michael in. "Come on in. It's a bit chilly." I led him into the kitchen. With him behind me, I took the time to catch my breath. Grasping the chair stopped my trembling hand as I pulled it out for him to sit.

"Would you like a glass of wine?" I asked, wishing I had a Malbec and dying to know why he had dropped the girls off at the party instead of them driving themselves. Had he blessedly taken that car away from them?

He nodded his head as he looked around. "Cute little cottage."

"I love it. Actually, you and the girls would love it here too. The beach is literally across the street," I said, then whipped around to point out the back of the house, "and the little downtown is only a block that way and has everything you'd ever want."

"So you're staying?" he asked as he walked around the kitchen then stopped to stare out the back window. I poured his wine and put it on the table.

With a little courage because I couldn't see his face, I said, "It's what I need at the moment."

I wouldn't start our much-needed conversation, and I nodded my head in support of myself. If he wanted to get the conversation going, that was one thing. When he turned, I saw no emotion on his face. But as he got closer, I saw understanding in his eyes. As he sat again at the kitchen table, Roger settled under the table between us, as if not to choose sides.

"So I was saying," Michael began.

I held up a hand, signaling to hold there, and got my wine from the living room. It would have been challenging to sit there without it. He waited for me to have a couple of sips, just like he used to. He knew me well, and it felt good to fall back into our routine.

"So I was saying," Michael repeated and winked, "I dropped the girls off at the Halloween party so I have a couple of hours before I have to go pick them up."

I got stuck on the "couple of hours" part. Did he plan to spend those with me? My nerves buzzed, and the urge to jump up and busy myself brewed. "So you're picking up the girls after the party? They didn't drive themselves?" Sip.

His stare and silence led me to believe he wanted to say something. But instead, he got up to look out the back door again.

Did he not want to bring up the girls' car? Did he feel I had little confidence in his parenting skills? Speaking again somehow felt like a trap. I clenched my jaw between sips of wine.

He came back to the table and sat. "That was our deal. If they wanted to go to this party, then I was driving them back and forth, and I had to meet Tucker's parents before I left them there."

Imagine that. Michael, the responsible parent. "And the girls agreed? Good for you." Echoes of the many lead balloons from when I'd suggest anything similar rattled my brain.

"And you met his parents?" Too nervous to sit and chat, I rummaged through the fridge and pulled a block of white cheddar and a wedge of parmesan cheese.

"Yeah, they seemed nice enough. I just wanted to make sure they were really there."

"Of course." I arranged different cheeses on a tray with pepperoni slices and baby dill pickles. I dug out an unopened box of Triscuits. As I loudly ripped open the bag and dumped them out on the tray, I asked, "So how's it been going?"

Michael leaned back in his chair as I delivered our snacks to the table. With a slight grin, he said, "Are you done being busy now and making noise?"

I rolled my eyes and pulled my chair opposite him. We sat face-to-face, hoping I portrayed equality, yet the way I slinked into the chair didn't make me much of an adversary. "Things have been okay? At home?"

"Sure. Thank God you left all those frozen meals in the freezer."

I thought about the busy day I had to myself before all hell broke loose. Maybe I was preparing to run away all along and didn't know it.

"I don't know where to start," Michael said. He cleared his voice and straightened up in his seat. His eyes watered. "First, I need to tell you I am seeing someone…"

My breath stuck, and my glass tipped in my hand as he continued. In all the months we haven't been eye to eye, I never thought once that he would be having an affair.

"A therapist—Dr. Mahoney."

I put my glass down and let my breath out in spurts. Relieved and wanting to say something, I sat and listened.

"I'm sorry I left you and the girls alone. It wasn't a great move on my part, but once I did, I didn't know what to do about it. I had added the loss of you and the girls to my own grief. That's when I knew I couldn't fix me without help."

I stacked slices of cheese, pepperoni, and pickles on crackers, carefully placing each item on top of one another. He was talking, and I physically had to stop myself from interrupting him.

Michael fidgeted with his napkin, clearly uncomfortable with what he had to say. "Now that I'm beginning to understand my actions, I can empathize with yours."

I looked up, prepared to defend my actions, then quickly stuffed a cracker into my mouth so I couldn't respond. I needed to hear him say he missed me, he still loved me, or he needed me to move back without me prompting him.

He continued, "I couldn't do it your way, move on, accept the pain. All that positive thinking and planning ahead bullshit. I felt so guilty. A healthy twelve-year-old boy doesn't have an aneurysm. It should have been me." He shook his head while he talked. "I felt you were in denial by needing to get back to normal, by forcing us to move on. I thought you were running away, trying to get it all behind you. You couldn't see it, and I got angry and tried to ignore you."

"Are you saying I handled it wrong?" My silence couldn't hold out. I was listening, but I was most certainly not going to let him blame anything on me. "I went to therapy. I worked through things so I could survive and still be there for my other two children."

"No. No. I didn't mean it like that. You were on such a roll. I just felt you weren't sensitive to my needs. I know, I know. I'm an adult, and you needed to care for the twins. But I needed you too. I just wasn't going to be bulldozed into doing it your way. Hell, I didn't even have a different option. Just couldn't do it your way."

Without getting up, I reached behind me for another bottle of wine and slid the wine opener off the counter. Michael held out his hands, offering to open the bottle for me. Another familiar move. I held on to the bottle with a four-year-old's fervor. I wasn't a damsel in distress. I was perfectly capable of opening a bottle of wine by myself. Michael looked at me with a crooked smirk and raised eyebrows, indicating my ridiculousness. And he was right.

As he twisted and pulled at the cork, he continued, "I know I'm not good at expressing my feelings. It was easier to internalize and avoid everything. I distracted myself with work and refused to accept your actions as support. But now that I've spent some time away, time apart…"

I held my breath. I imagined covering my ears with my hands and mumbling, "Na, na, na, na, na, na." I wasn't ready to hear him say how good it was for us to be apart and maybe we should keep it that way.

He handed me the opened bottle of wine. "It wasn't good for my recovery to be alone."

I lifted my wine to my lips, as did he to his, and we stared at each other over the rims of our glasses. Was he saying that I shouldn't be alone? Or he didn't want to be alone? Did he want me to return home? Did he miss me? I needed to hear the words.

He grinned at me, and the stillness splintered. "It must be killing you not to talk. I can see words pass behind your eyes and play with the corners of your mouth."

I laughed like I used to always laugh with Michael, and it felt good to do so now. He settled back in his chair. Roger unraveled from below the table as if the tension had kept him down.

"Your turn," Michael said, handing me my glass.

I let Roger out the back door then turned and leaned on the door frame. "I don't know what to say. This is about you, isn't it?" This had to be about him. He was the one who needed space and left.

"But you're the one not at home." His expression told me nothing.

That wasn't a request to return. It wasn't an "I miss you."

"I don't know, Michael. Me being here, in this cottage, has very little to do with why you left the house."

Actually, being alone didn't bother me. I had made the choice to be here at the cottage by myself, and there was a part of me that loved the solitude. I just now understood that. Back then, Michael and I were on automatic, and not in a good way. We lived parallel lives, much like my parents, and that's what had to change first.

"Do you really believe that? That you being here has nothing to do with me?"

Again, I couldn't read his eyes. I turned around to let Roger in and mulled over Michael's rhetorical question. After giving Roger a snack, I took my wine into the living room. I purposefully snuggled with a blanket in the oversized chair so Michael had to sit across from me on the couch.

"Things seem to be going so smoothly. I'm not sure if you guys even want me back." There, I said it. I didn't want to. I wasn't going to. But what if he never said it?

"Of course, we want you back." Michael sat at the edge of the couch and put his wine down on the worn coffee table.

"Not 'of course,' Michael." But weren't those the words I wanted to hear? "'Of course,'" I said with quote fingers, "means I should assume you all want me back. But there's no one asking me to come back. Even Nicole tells me she misses me but doesn't ask me to come back. She wants to know when, but not asking me to." I couldn't stop the tears. "And now, I don't even know if I..."

"Wait," Michael stood up, took his wineglass, and placed it in the sink as I stewed in my truth. He came back out of the kitchen. "Are you telling me you don't want to come home?" he asked as he walked up behind my chair. I was grateful I didn't have to see his eyes.

"I didn't say that." I took a moment. This was not how I thought our first talk would be. I had no thought about my plans. "Sit down, Michael. Let me try to explain."

As I spoke, I chose my words carefully, trying to describe how I felt on the day that Michael didn't help clear out Curtis's room, and the time I overheard the girls talk so severely about me, and how I felt watching him socialize outside the house when he didn't say two words within. I did my best to make it about me and not him.

"Like when Heather texted you the day she and the boys got pulled over. It hurt that she didn't text me."

"That had nothing to do with you. I had met the cop, Greg Sloane, at a golf event last year. We ended up being partners because of our handicaps, and we've played together several times since. When he figured out Heather was my daughter, he told Heather to text me."

I felt like an idiot. It never dawned on me there was a logical reason for Heather to contact Michael instead of me. Perspective.

"And buying the car?" I could tell he was ready for this.

"I'll be honest. Your reaction surprised the shit out of me. It was my way of fixing everything. A peace offering. I thought you'd be so grateful you'd beg me to come home."

I was dumbfounded. He thought the car would fix us?

"I'll be honest with you," I said. "I'm not following your logic."

"Yes, I thought you'd be happy and appreciate having more time on your hands to paint. I never thought it would send you over the edge."

I nodded and slightly laughed. Looking from the outside, my reaction was entirely disproportionate to his actions.

"I'm sorry. You had moved out. We didn't make the decision together. And I felt you were taking the girls away from me. But now I can sort of, and I mean sort of, see that it was a nice gesture. But we've always made big-ticket item decisions together, and I felt you deciding on a car for the girls by yourself was the end of our partnership."

I gathered up the pieces of the napkin I had shredded during the clarification of my actions. "I saw a commercial the other day, don't even remember what it was for, but the father said, 'Ain't nobody happy if Mama's not happy.'" I looked at him. "I don't want that responsibility."

He crouched beside my chair.

I turned and looked him straight in the eyes. "I can't be responsible for yours or the girls' happiness, and you can't be accountable for mine." I turned away from his gape. "It's too great a responsibility, and I don't have that kind of energy anymore."

A soft buzzer went off. Michael stood and shut off the alarm on his watch. "I have to go pick up the girls."

I reached out and took his hand. "All I'm saying Michael is that I need time to figure out what makes me happy."

He pulled on the hand I held him with and helped me out of my seat. We walked to the door, and I looked at the blue Keds on my feet. Michael released my hand and lifted my chin with his fingers.

"We'll fix this," he said.

As I watched his taillights fade away, my gut fluttered—not from the inkling of hope he had left with me but from guilty nerves because my last thought was certain.

"I do want to stay here and fix me first."

Chapter 41

Michael and I texted over the next week or so. He kept me up to date on the girls' busy schedules, and I dropped hints in the form of questions like, "Are the girls helping with the dishes?" and "How's Heather doing ironing her work clothes?"

I told him I was ready to speak with the girls about what was really going on with me. We made arrangements for them to come over in a couple of nights, giving me the chance to meet a deadline on other commissions requested from Alicia. I had a new appreciation for my work—it paid my rent.

I made sure the cottage sparkled for the girls' first visit to the beach house, and by the time Nicole and Heather arrived, I was quite nervous. As 6:00 p.m. neared, I peeked out the dry-rot drapes covering the front window, and they ripped. When the girls arrived, Nicole jumped out first and ran through the gate. Heather stayed behind, taking in the surroundings.

I opened the door, and Nicole ran straight into my open arms. Roger greeted her with paws on her hips. Over her shoulder, I watched Heather walk to the wooden path across the street and stare down to the beach. I hoped she liked what she saw.

The breeze picked up, and I pulled Nicole into the cottage. I waved to Heather, not knowing if she saw me, and Roger ran out to greet her at the gate. I left the door open just a crack.

"This is so cute," Nicole said and gave herself a tour. "I can't believe you live at the beach."

I peeked out the front window. Roger chased Heather in circles, and their laughter and bark mixed with the roar of the ocean. Nothing sounded more pleasing. Heather ran into the cottage with Roger at her heels.

"Where's Rog's leash? Can I take him for a walk on the beach?"

"On the chest by the couch," I said. "Zip up your jacket and pull your hoodie on. It's pretty chilly today."

Heather left with the leash in hand and her jacket flopping in the breeze.

I shook my head. I couldn't help myself. If I didn't say anything and she got sick, I'd feel awful. But then again, if I didn't say anything, I wouldn't set myself up for disappointment. When was I going to learn?

"Don't worry, Mom. She'll zip up when the cold gets to her bones." As she laid her jacket onto the couch, Curtis's birthstone necklace swung out from her shirt collar. I tapped my St. Sebastian through my shirt, signaling for Curtis to pay attention.

Nicole rubbed the charm as if she had a message for Curtis also. "I wear it every day, Mom. I love it."

I hooked my arm in hers and led her to the kitchen. "I'm so happy to see both of you. How's it going? Are you eating?"

Nicole chuckled. "Of course, we're eating. Nothing's changed at home, except you're not there."

I was now officially confused. Things should be very different without me there, shouldn't they? "Is your father cooking? Did you work out a solution with the car? How's dance? Do you need any help with your homework?"

"Mom, it's all fine." She put her arm around me and led me to the kitchen table. "Dad's been grilling meat, hamburgers, pork chops, stuff like that. I make the salad or whatever. It's been fine. He's been to the grocery store, like, every day because he always forgets something. It's kinda funny."

I tried to keep a straight face, a little happy that things weren't going too smoothly for him. "What about the car? I've been worried sick about you two driving."

"Mom, we've got this. I get the car Monday, Wednesday, and Friday, and I have to drive Heather to school and dance and work. She has to drive me around on Tuesday and Thursday and Saturday. Sunday we have to figure it out on our own without fighting, or neither one of us gets to drive it."

"And how's that working for you?" I anticipated hearing how Heather wasn't going along with the deal.

"So far, so good."

"And Heather?" With her seemingly not wanting to be in the house with Nicole and I, I wondered if I'd lost what advances I'd made with her since the day we made costumes for the Halloween party.

"She's been fine. It bugs her a little if I have to drop her off at work. But then she has to drop me off at my Saturday photography club. Dad has to pick me up because Heather works at noon on Saturday."

I blinked away the green creeping into my brain. Michael got to drive the girls, and I was sitting here alone. I opened a bag of chips and mixed some dried French onion soup with sour cream for dipping. I wished the sun had warmed the air so we could sit on the back deck, but the cottage itself offered comfort and coziness.

"What about homework? Are you caught up?" Silly question on my part because both my girls were A students and enjoyed school, but I wanted to keep the conversation on her and not me.

"Nothing's too difficult at the moment. I have a research paper about some of the first famous female photographers like Anna Atkins and Julia Margaret Cameron. Dad helped Google some things last night and..."

Heather and Roger burst in the front door with the cold air instantly filling the small cottage. I was pleased to see her coat zippered up and her hoodie covering her ears. I called Roger through the kitchen and over to the back door. I rubbed him down with an old towel hanging over the back of a chair. I took my time wiping his golden knotted fur and soaked up Heather's excitement as she told Nicole about the beach, and Nicole gave her a quick tour of the tiny house.

Heather suppressed her enthusiasm when she saw me, as was her habit. It must take so much energy to remember to be angry with me.

"So what do you think?" I asked Heather about the cottage.

"It's cute, I guess. Love walking to the beach, but it took us forty-five minutes to drive here," she said and stuffed a chip into her mouth. Her tone had relaxed, which in turn relaxed me.

"So your father helped you with your report?" I asked Nicole, not wanting to give the floor to Heather just yet.

"Yes, well, he printed things off for me up in his office. That way, I could highlight info easier."

"His office at work?"

Nicole fidgeted, searching for words emphasized her uncomfortableness. She glanced at Heather, as if asking for help.

"No, there's a printer in his office at home," Heather said. "He works from home now."

"Every day?" I scratched my forehead to cover up the quick rise in my eyebrows. I wondered if Michael always had the choice to work from home or just made it happen since I was out of the house. "Well, it's nice he's able to help."

"He's always helped with things like that," Heather said. "He's the one that taught us how to count."

Not wanting to correct her or seem like I wanted to pick a fight, I kept the memories of me sitting with the girls at the kitchen table, counting beads and filling out preschool workbooks to myself.

"He would put M&Ms or Skittles on the table, and we had to count them. We got to eat them if we got the right number."

"And he got to eat them if we got it wrong." Heather smiled at the memory. "He certainly motivated us to learn how to count. I think we could add and subtract numbers up to twenty by the end of pre-K because of those M&Ms."

Again, dumbfounded, I never knew the girls and Michael shared memories like this. Were there more I wasn't aware of?

"How about loaded baked potatoes for dinner?" I asked, hoping the unconventional meal proved I had loosened up a bit.

"Really?" asked Heather.

"Sure, and a mixed green salad." I couldn't go too unconventional.

"Sure," the girls said together, and Nicole got up to start the salad. I scrubbed three large russet potatoes, rolled them in a little olive oil and sea salt, stabbed them with a fork, then placed them in the preheated toaster oven.

"So tell me more things you did with your dad when you were little," I said.

"Why?" Heather asked. "You going to compare then and now? You and him?"

"No, Heather. No." Had I given her reason to think that? "The M&M story was sweet, and so like your dad. It's comforting to know you three are getting along."

"We three have always gotten along," Heather said, still sitting at the table but slicing whatever vegetable Nicole brought to the cutting board in front of her.

"I didn't mean that. I just meant..."

"We've never had a problem with Dad," Nicole said, setting her knife onto the counter as if she didn't want it in her hand as she spoke. "We just missed him, and now he's back. He talks and jokes, and the other night we watched a movie together—like the old times."

Not like the old times. In the old times, I was laughing at his jokes and watching movies with them. I was torn between being happy for my children because they had their father back and sad because I wasn't part of their current picture. I caught on that I was the common denominator in all that made us unhappy.

"Mom, you said we could talk about what's going on when you're ready," Nicole said. "You must be ready 'cuz you invited us here." She turned back to finish cutting the cucumber for the salad. "And we have a few questions."

"I'll try to answer what I can, but honestly..."

"See, I told you she'd find a way to avoid our questions," Heather snarked.

I had just about enough of Heather's remarks. Where was the progress we had made? "Can I ask you a question?"

Heather nodded her head, crossed her arms, and leaned back in her chair as if nothing I asked her could affect her.

"Why are you so angry with me?"

She looked at Nicole and said, "See, she's deflecting. Now it's about me and not her."

"Stop," Nicole shouted. "Answer Mom's questions, then she'll answer ours." She looked at me to ensure that I would agree.

I nodded.

"Why are you always angry at Mom?" she asked Heather.

Heather squirmed in her seat until her feet flattened on the floor with her back erect. "I'm angry because you always want everything good and positive. And I'm sick of it."

That's it? I wanted everyone happy, so she was pissed at me? I needed to take her seriously and respond in kind, but what could I say to that? I looked back and forth between Nicole and Heather with my eyes bugging out of my head.

All I could say was "Really?"

Nicole's lips cocked on the right side, which made me smile, which in turn made Nicole laugh. Then I laughed, and finally, Heather laughed.

But the sentiment reminded me of what Michael had said. He couldn't stand the positive thinking, the planning ahead, and doing it my way, which was to accept and move on. Like father, like daughter.

"Okay, that was stupid," Heather said. "But geez, Mom, everything doesn't always have to be peaches and cream. I wish you'd just let me be sad when I wanted to be, or angry, or whatever. But you always need to see the bright side. Sometimes there just isn't one. It's like you put a fake positive spin on things…"

"It's not fake. It's how I feel, and yes, how I want you to feel. I don't like to see my children sad." I got up and knelt next to Heather. "I hear what you're saying, but why fight everything? I just want to help."

Nicole stood at the counter, crying, and it broke my heart.

"Do you feel the same way?" I asked.

"We didn't know it till you left," Heather answered for her. "Since you've been gone, I've been able to breathe. But the minute I see you…"

In the lull, I stood and broke our eye contact. I checked the potatoes, and they were almost ready. I stood with my back to the girls a few moments then put three plates on the table and put the salad between us.

My shallow breaths didn't help the anguished thoughts of my daughters' lack of ability to breathe around me. Was I that stifling?

For the first time since moving out, I was 100% happy to be living in the cottage. It was the best choice for all.

We ate our salads in silence. I'd look up every once in a while and catch the girls staring at each other. When the buzzer went off for the potatoes, I brought them over on a tray with butter, sour cream, shredded cheddar, bacon bits, and chopped scallions.

Before I sat, I put both my arms out and signaled for a hug like I had been doing since the day they took their first steps. They both succumbed, and I kissed them on the top of their heads.

"I'm not sure what to say to you girls, or if I should say anything at all, except I love you, and if you need me, I'm here for you."

"Will you answer one question?" Heather stepped back but kept an arm around my waist.

"I'll try," I said, leading the girls back to their chairs.

"Are you and Dad getting a divorce?" Heather stiffened, waiting for my answer.

"Have you asked him that question?" I asked, regretting it as soon as it came out.

"Actually, we did. He said we had to talk to you," Nicole answered.

I call chickenshit. Did Michael think I wanted a divorce? Did I think I wanted a divorce?

"Honey." I took Heather's hand. "It's all going to be fine. We'll figure it out."

"That's a non-answer. No positive spin, Mom."

I looked at my two beautiful—practically adult—daughters and sat down with one leg under me.

"Your father and I are not planning on a divorce. In fact, neither one of us has ever brought it up. But I can't work on us until I figure out me."

The girls' faces changed from indifference to comprehension as if now that I admitted I was partially at fault, they could relax. As Heather pulled off her sweater over her head, Curtis's birthstone necklace fell into place below her throat. For the first time in a long time, I felt I had done something right.

Nicole wrapped her arms around me, and Heather slowly joined us in another three-way hug.

"What can we do to help?" Nicole asked.

Chapter 42

The morning of Pamela's fundraiser came too soon. I had spent the last week helping her create signs and tags for each auction item and determined the floor plan for the event. It felt good to focus on such a meaningful project, especially when I knew the girls were in a happy place.

The girls and I spoke every day after school, sometimes for only a minute to say hi and bye, but there were a few Facetime calls regarding Nicole's framed photos she put together for the auction. We settled on six eight-by-ten color photos of close-ups of everyday items, like a melting ice cube on a granite surface, and a close-up of a lit matchstick, with its blue-to-yellow flame.

"You and Heather can meet us Saturday morning at ten a.m.… if you'd like to help set up." I had wanted to include the girls, not demand their help.

"Are we going to have time to come home and shower and change before the event starts?" Heather's face had popped into my screen.

"We should be done setting up by two or three. Then you can go home and get ready and meet back at six p.m. Tell your father to come then, too." I wanted the girls to know he was definitely invited.

And now here it was, Saturday morning, and Pamela and I were implementing the plan we had created for a festive event. Six-foot banquet tables covered with cream lace over white tablecloths lined the club's main dining room. Each table held at least five items alongside their descriptions, a bid sheet, and a Buy Now card—a card that allowed a patron to tear up the bid sheet and purchase the item for an outrageous price. It was a fundraiser after all.

Nicole arrived with her framed photos and found they belonged on the center table all to themselves. It warmed my heart when I saw her pick up one of the bid sheets from the table and pretended to swoon and fall into Heather's arms. We had set up each photo's bid sheet with a starting bid of $150.00, and someone could use the Buy Now card to purchase the entire set for $1,000.00.

I ran over to the girls, tags and tape in my hand, and gave them each a hug. "Well, what do you think?"

"No one's going to buy my pictures for $150.00. No way." Nicole's chagrin took me aback. Her usual confidence in her work had disappeared.

"If you get these prices here, I think you and I need to set up an Etsy shop," Heather said.

"Would you feel better if they sold for $25.00?" Pamela said as she snuck through the group with a basket full of wine and wine-glasses for the next display table. "Let's get to work, girls."

Over the next three hours, we, along with several club staff members, set out the items for the silent auction, decorated the ball-room for the live band and dancing, and helped the florist arrange small centerpieces on the dining tables and tall floral displays on the serving tables.

By 2:15 p.m., we were ready to go home and dress for the party.

"Wait," Nicole said as we donned our coats. "I need to take a picture of my photos on the table for my portfolio." The two girls ran to the center table.

"Does anyone have time for a quick bite to eat?" Pamela asked loud enough for the girls to hear.

"I'm starving. I could most certainly eat something," I said.

The girls agreed from across the room, and we followed Pamela to the bar for a sandwich or salad. After ordering drinks, two wines and two virgin strawberry daiquiris, Pamela asked the girls what they were wearing for the event.

"How fancy do we have to be?" Heather asked. "I was going to wear black dress pants and a simple black top."

"I have that blue dress from my last gallery show. The crocheted one with the bell sleeves," Nicole said. "Will that be dressy enough?"

"I think both would be fine," Pamela answered after a glance toward me.

In my silence, I felt horrible. I had never given one thought to what the girls would wear to the fundraiser. I thought of only myself, but only because Pamela took me shopping under duress, and I bought a beautiful, sleeveless, wine-colored cocktail dress with a cowl neck. My guilt subsided when I decided I had made progress putting myself first on this one.

"I'll tell you what," Pamela said, pulling the wrist of both girls on either side of her. "Why don't you follow me home, and I'll add a few accessories to your attire. Like a pearl necklace," she said, looking at Nicole. She turned to Heather and said, "How about a rose-gold belt and a chunky necklace with your black outfit?"

I couldn't thank Pamela enough. In my current state of parenting limbo, she managed to fill in the spaces I created with my fear of setting the girls off and losing our forward motion. We rushed through lunch with the girls excited to get ready.

"What's your father wearing?" I asked.

The twins looked at each other, each nudging the other with their chins.

Finally, Heather said, "He might be late."

Pamela took more offense than I did. "But he's still coming, right?" She waved over the waitress and asked for the bill to sign then excused herself to make a phone call.

"He comes every year," I said as I finished my wine and feigned calmness. "Is it that he's going to be late or not coming at all?"

"All he said was he'd meet us here because he would be running late," Nicole said.

"Well, tell him we'll save his spot at our table. We'll all hang out together, and I'll apologize later if I cramp your style." I smiled, making a joke for the girls' sake.

The girls' faces lit up.

"We'll make sure he comes," Heather said. "He just needs to wear a suit, right?"

I nodded. "Of course." I didn't want the girls to feel bad if their efforts didn't work. "If he really doesn't want to come…"

"He wants to come. He just needs to know that you want him to come," Nicole said.

I sighed in response. What more could I say? "Of course, I want him to come." I laughed at my usage of "of course." Michael always attended Pamela's events. But whether or not I wanted him to be at the event wasn't relative. I needed him to want to be here for us girls. "But tell him to come only if it makes him happy."

Pamela appeared and ushered the girls out of the bar. "We'll see you in a few hours!"

I said my goodbyes as the girls followed Pamela out of the parking lot.

After a hottish shower—hot water was not one of the cottage's strong suits—twenty minutes of blow-drying and curling my hair, and an attempt at false eyelashes, I was ready for the fundraiser event of the year.

When I pulled into the club's entrance, a man directed me to drive under the portico at the front. A valet opened the door and handed me a ticket. Getting out of the driver's door seemed far less elegant and made me far too lonely than getting out of the passenger door when the valet helped me out and would hand me off to my husband.

After I placed my purse on our table, I milled around with a glass of wine, inspecting the various auction items.

"Boo," Heather raided me from behind. Startled, I turned and hugged her and looked right into Michael's eyes.

"Oh, hi. Glad you could make it," I said and kissed him on the cheek.

He smiled, and Heather grabbed his hands. "Nicole's at her display table. Come look."

"Hold on," he said and let go of her hands. "I need to talk to your mother." He removed two glasses of champagne off a tray as the waitress passed by. He handed me one of the drinks.

"What are we celebrating?" I asked placing my nearly empty wine glass on the nearest table.

He then reached into his inside breast pocket and pulled out an envelope.

"For me?" I asked, looking at both sides for a sign as to what was inside. I slid the folded papers out to read. "You bought the beach cottage?"

"Not really. But if you want to purchase the beach house, all you have to do is sign on the dotted line." Michael shone with his Superman smile, which stated, "Here I am to save the day." All he had to do was throw his cape over his shoulders and stand with both hands on his hips.

"Awesome, Mom," Heather said. "We're going to have a beach house."

My legs weakened, and I grabbed the back of the nearest bar stool. This was what he did. He threw money at an issue, thinking it would either go away or make me happy, hopefully both. No matter how much I loved the cottage and Michael, Michael did what Michael did to fix a problem. Like that damned car. And all I wanted was for him to want to hold my hand again.

Michael's delight faded when I didn't respond. He just didn't get it.

"But the money?" I stared down at the papers.

"Not a problem. We've been saving for something like this. And he's giving us, you, a great price since he doesn't have to remodel to sell it."

Nicole ran over. "Did you tell her?" She sported a huge smile.

Seeing how excited she was, images of family beach days and Michael and mine's retirement flooded my thoughts. But I also didn't want to give up my space.

I smiled and put my arms around his neck and whispered, "Now all I need is time."

He kissed me on the forehead and released me to Nicole and Heather as they pulled on my arms.

"Come on, Mom," Nicole begged. "Come look at my table."

The girls had never looked prettier, older, or sexier. Nicole had on her blue crocheted dress with bell sleeves with a beautiful set of 10 mm pearls hanging from her neck and wrist. Two matching pearls dropped from her earlobes by gold chains.

"You two look beautiful," I said and kissed Nicole on the cheek.

Heather turned around like a model in her black bolero pants, black silk tank top, and a sparkling gold belt. With a sweep of a large square, smoky quartz ring adorning her hand, she directed our attention to her large David Yurman gold-and-silver hoop earrings. I'd have to be sure to give Pamela an extra hug for making the girls feel so special.

"Let's go look at the stuff," Nicole said. She led us toward her photos.

As a lady returned the framed image of a close-up of a gnarly, twisted piece of driftwood to the tabletop and moved on to the next display table, Nicole peeked at her bid sheets.

People had begun bidding on her photos, and two of them were up to $190.00.

"I'm so nervous and excited for you," Heather whispered to Nicole.

"Hello, Nicole. Julie," said the woman from the next table. It was Mrs. Amberly, our neighbor. "I see these are your photos, Nicole. They're beautiful."

"Hi, Nora," I said with a genuine smile.

Nicole side-hugged Mrs. Amberly, and they kept their arms around each other's waist.

"The Scott family is truly out to support the Wilmington Children's Cancer Center," Mrs. Amberly said. "We really appreciate your donations."

"We?" I asked, a little worried she was including her precious son.

"I'm on the board of the center. Have been since my son's death. It's my personal mission to make the center the best children's cancer institution in the world," she said and let go of Nicole after a little squeeze. "We'll talk later. By the way, Julie, I adore your Ranford garden painting. Thank you for donating it. The textures in your sunflowers remind me of Van Gogh's. Such emotions in each stroke. In fact, the whole garden reminds me of Van Gogh's Roses and Sunflowers."

Bubbles rose from my toes. I couldn't have received a greater compliment. The impasto style of my flowers in the painting, especially the sunflowers, was actually pilfered from Van Gogh's thick application of paint. I thanked her as she headed to greet other patrons.

Nicole didn't seem surprised our neighbor was here. "Isn't she sweet?" Nicole asked, rearranging her framed photos.

"Did you know Mrs. Amberly would be here?" I corralled my family with wide arms to back them away so others approaching could bid on Nicole's photos.

"Yes. She told me. In fact, the picture of the feather was from her backyard," Nicole said.

Heather and Michael broke ranks and followed the crowd heading for their tables. At the table, I ordered another wine, my last one for the night because I didn't want to pay for an Uber to drive me home to the beach cottage.

Pamela stood at the podium and welcomed the guests. She spoke about the Wilmington Children's Cancer Center and its needs and desires, including their new affiliation with a large collegiate research and development team. Finally, she introduced the auctioneer, a famous local news anchor. As dinner was served, the news anchor began announcing the items up for the live auction. She modeled a set of pearl necklaces of different lengths, one twenty-four inches and one eighteen inches. She offered a trip for two to Napa and a year's membership to the country club's exclusive gym, including a trainer for three months.

By the time dessert arrived, the fifth and final item was up for sale. The opening bid for my Ranford gardens painting of $2,000 got swallowed up by the second and third. Before my brain caught up, I heard the auctioneer say, "Going once. Going twice. Sold to Mr. Silberstein at table number three for $22,000."

I couldn't believe my ears. I looked at Michael, and his face appeared closer and closer. The next thing I knew, I woke up with my head in Michael's lap and the girls tugging on my arms.

Several strangers stood around us. "Lay her on the ground."

"Mom?"

"Here's a cold, wet cloth for her forehead," a voice called out.

"Should we call 911?" someone else asked.

"Julie?" Michael said.

"I'm fine," I said. Blinking my eyes to focus, I pushed myself up to sit. "Really, I'm fine."

Michael kept his arm around my chair and thanked the people who rushed to my aid. "Sit down, girls. Mom's fine." Michael whispered into my left my ear. "Are you really okay?"

A giggle erupted, and I put my hand on his right thigh and leaned in. "The price my painting went for…"

Michael nodded and joined in my giggling. His comforting hold brought me back to when we were inspired by each other, proud of each other's accomplishments. I could tell how impressed and pleased he was by the softness and sincerity in his eyes. A moment of hope. As our giggling dissipated and the moment became awkward, I asked if one of the girls wanted to walk to the restroom with me. Surprisingly, and with pride in her eyes, Heather volunteered.

I stood on wobbly legs, but by the time I reached the restroom, the congratulations and compliments people lauded along the way gave strength to my spine and legs. I did that. I sold a painting for $22,000.

"Go ahead, Heather. I'm perfectly fine now," I said and sat in the lounge section of the fancy restroom, needing a moment to myself, my right hand still raw from resting on Michael's thigh.

As Heather exited, she held the door open as Nora Amberly entered. "That was exciting," she said.

Her encouraging words added to my growing self-confidence. "It shocked me. I'm thrilled the children's center will benefit from the proceeds." I got up and took a small sparkling water from the mini-fridge. "Would you like one?"

"No, thanks. I've had my limit of bubbles for the evening." She settled back into a chair across from me. "Julie, I haven't seen your van at the house lately."

I sipped on my bubbly water and took measure. Friend or foe? Ridiculous. Why on earth would she be a foe? "Just trying to work a few things out."

We sized each other up is silence.

"I've been impressed with your work for a while now," Nora said. "The Dune painting in the club. Plus, my friend Gert Masters' interior designer installed several of your paintings in her Rehoboth Beach home—all beautiful."

"Thank you," I said. "It's nice to know there are people out there who enjoy my work." I swirled my sparkling water, hoping to get some of the bubbles out. Maybe it was the time of night, but too many bubbles were a real thing.

"Julie, I'd like you to consider sharing a little bit of your time and a lot of your talent to teach an art class for the kids at the center. Just once a week. We need a volunteer."

My first thought was, I couldn't possibly add another thing to my plate. But then I remembered there was nothing on my plate but me and my painting.

"You'll have a small budget for supplies," Nora continued to entice me. "And maybe Nicole would like to teach a photography class."

Now she was getting into bribery. But the idea did appeal to me. "How would it work?"

"There's an empty conference room on the third floor of the center. You could even paint a mural on the walls. We've been considering it for an activity room for the children. Art is a great activity to participate in during and in between treatments. It's something that siblings could participate in also."

"I'm intrigued," I said and stood. "Let me think about it, and I'll get back to you soon. And Nora, thank you for thinking of me."

Nora scooted to the edge of her seat and said, "Your art speaks for itself."

I heard the squeal as I exited the restroom and saw Nicole running toward me. My pulse raced as I glanced around for Heather. She was standing near the center display table with Michael.

"Mom. Mom," Nicole called, waving a piece of paper. She handed me the paper and caught her breath.

A Buy Now card, signed by Anonymous, stated that the signee would guarantee the purchase price of $2,000.00 for the entire set of six framed photos, the collection Profundity by Nicole Marie Scott.

Heather came up behind Nicole and grabbed her hand. "Let's take a picture of you behind the table before Mr. Anonymous picks up the photos."

I was beyond proud of my girls. Not only Nicole's success but Heather's support for her sister. No more Tom and Jerry. More like Pooh and Piglet. My heart warmed.

"Come on, Mom. I'll take a picture of you next to your painting before it disappears."

I stood and smiled with Vanna-hands presenting the painting.

Pamela neared, saying, "Give me the camera. I'll take a pic of the whole family."

We stood together, our family of four, with arms around waists and smiles as broad and bright as the crescent harvest moon.

Chapter 43

Having the four members of the Scott family together at the fundraiser for a whole evening tickled my heart, and I woke up with a joy hangover. Nonetheless, sitting here, drinking my diet cola alone on the back deck, comforted me with the feeling of belonging. I liked it here, on my own, knowing my family was happy in our forever home. The contradiction of it all baffled me. I picked up the papers to the cottage, still not sure how I felt about it.

My phone rang. The blanket slid off my shoulders as I shuffled in my slippers to hunt it down.

"Good happy morning," I answered.

"You're chipper," Pamela said. "Thanks again for your donated painting. Twenty-two thousand dollars sure made my fundraiser a huge success."

"Glad that amount of money is going to a good cause," I said, totally impressed with myself. "I'm still energized from last night, and Nicole's success too."

"I've got a few things to wrap up, and then I'm going to get on to our next event."

"Our next event?" I hadn't a clue. What was Pamela going to suck me into now?

"Yes, ding-dong. Thanksgiving is only ten days away."

Ugh. Really? I had been sure I'd have my issues sorted out well before the holidays and be back into the house by then. I turned on the shower.

"Pamela, I'm not ready."

"Of course, you are. Thanksgiving is Thanksgiving. I gave you a pass last year. But after last night, the Scott family will be back together under the same roof in no time."

I saw then how Pamela had orchestrated the whole thing. She invited Nicole and her photos. Michael had to come and see his daughter's display. I leaned on the bathroom counter, allowing the steam from the shower to fill the room.

"Things aren't the same anymore. But I'll talk to the girls."

"And Michael."

"Yes, and Michael. We have not discussed it, so I'll have to see what they want to do." Part of me wanted to plan nothing and see what the others would come up with. And see if their plans would include me. I could be setting myself up for disappointment, but I would not make a plan unless, of course, they asked me to. "I don't know, Pamela. I'm thinking we need to do something different this year. Start a new tradition or something. Maybe I'll wait and see what Michael and the girls come up with."

"You guys can come to the club with us. We can invite Alicia and Liz too. We'll have a Friendsgiving."

"I don't know. We'll see." I wanted the conversation to end. Thinking about the holidays now dissipated my euphoria from last night. Could I have my family here at the beach house? My safe spot? When George allowed me to pay my rent weekly, I could stay noncommitted about returning home. But now that I could possibly own the cottage, a selfish feeling of not wanting to share took over. Deep inside, I wanted Michael and the girls to drag me home, and it just wasn't going to happen. Was organizing the purchase of the cottage his not-so-subtle way of telling me not to come home?

Tired of fretting, I asked, "Come on over?"

"Let me wrap up this paperwork," Pamela said.

"I'm going to take a hot shower and relax for the day. I'll fix something for lunch. Give Alicia a call."

"Okay. And we're going to talk, Julie. Really talk."

Talk? I wouldn't let her talk me into Thanksgiving at the club. I needed the girls to figure out Thanksgiving and Christmas this year. I would do whatever they suggested. I couldn't be the planner. I couldn't risk choking my girls again. The warm shower suppressed my anxiety, but I wished it quelled my dread of the upcoming holidays.

I didn't mind doing something new and different this year. Last Thanksgiving was a non-Thanksgiving. Without Curtis, nobody wanted it. But the Thanksgiving before last still haunted me. I recalled how that last Thanksgiving had brought a new reality with it. By the end of that day, I had felt the beginning of my itch—the first inklings of not wanting to be Mom or Mrs. That was my beginning of needing a break.

I had planned that Thanksgiving like I prepared everything else, as if I were a military commander. Every little thing had a place and position, and every person had marching orders in each phase of the battle.

My guest list and menu were confirmed a month prior. Food that could be prepared and frozen was cooked and wrapped in foil the previous week. The day before, I had completely set the table, except for the plates which I piled on the buffet. The centerpiece had been picked up fresh from the florist that morning. All serving dishes had been set out with their corresponding serving utensil and a square yellow sticky note labeling which food belonged in which vessel just as I had done every year before, like my mother.

I had gone through the motions, though my heart wasn't in it. I wasn't sure why, but something just nagged at me. Since the only thing on TV during Thanksgiving Day was football, Curtis and I had always set up a card table for the annual puzzle in the living room. It gave the kids their own space and something to do. That year, I had ordered a thousand-piece puzzle of a family picture we took in front of the Governor's Palace from that year's summer trip to Williamsburg, Virginia.

I had prepared the turkey, stuffing it with sautéed onions, carrots, and celery, large slices of oranges, and whole twigs of rosemary, and I struggled with the dichotomy of it all. As tired as I was of the same old, same old, I relied on the predictability and constancy of the traditions I had curated over the previous sixteen years. They were exactly what I always dreamed of. Yet somewhere along the line, I had become disenchanted and bored. So I had invited friends and extended family in hopes it would add some excitement, something new to mix things up, but instead, it added more stress.

My brother and his family hadn't planned to arrive until 3:00 p.m., and he had to be on the road by 6:00 p.m. Didn't leave much room for error. I had begun to dread all I had to do to make everything go off like clockwork. The next day, Thanksgiving arrived. My brother and his family arrived late and packed up to leave even earlier than they originally planned. Curtis and I had carried out two of the warm, just-out-of-the-oven pies and placed them into his trunk. No thanks, and no apology.

Shaking off the distress and dismay from my past memories, I promised myself not to repeat them. This year, I hoped I could be patient enough to allow the time for someone, anyone—Michael, Heather, or Nicole—to come up with a plan. A new tradition.

Pamela and Alicia arrived three hours later. I had kept my mind busy with light housecleaning and grilling chicken for our fig and arugula salad.

"Want to take a walk on the beach before we eat?" I suggested and opened the bottles of white and red wine Alicia had brought.

"Sure. It'll only get colder as the afternoon goes on, so let's go now. I brought an Icelandic poncho," Alicia said and pulled a tan, grey, and cream, very warm-looking wool poncho out of a large shopping bag.

"I need one of these," I said, taking the soft cape out of her hands and sliding it over my head.

"It's yours," Alicia said and pulled two more similar, but not identical, ponchos out of the bag and tossed one to Pamela. "Surprise."

I unfolded and pulled the mock turtleneck up over my nose. "This poncho will be perfect for walking the winter beach as it gets colder in the coming months."

"So you do plan on staying here the whole winter?" Pamela asked.

I glared at Pamela for her translation of my statement but then checked myself. She had innocently exposed a truth I had yet to say out loud. I did want a future here in this tiny cottage.

"Pamela, not now," Alicia said, shuffling her feet. She put her arm around my shoulder. "We're here to celebrate last night's success for both of you."

"Not now what?" I asked. I removed the poncho and tossed it onto a kitchen chair. I didn't feel like a walk anymore. "Is this another ambush?"

"We've never ambushed you," Pamela grabbed her wine and the bag of avocado chips and brought them into the living room.

"If I follow her in there, this might not be pretty," I said to Alicia. "Is this an intervention?"

Alicia shrugged and set her puppy dog eyes on me and said, "Come on. Let's see what's up."

I grabbed my wineglass and the bottle of cabernet and sat down beside Pamela on the couch. No way was I sitting across from her, letting her be the one with the gavel behind the desk. Alicia took the seat across from us.

Pamela took both my hands in hers and said, "You can't hang here in limbo and wait for someone else to make the first move."

"Why not?" I honestly wanted to know.

Chapter 44

"Why not?" Pamela asked me as we sat on either end of the couch. "It's so unlike you to sit back and let someone else make a plan."

"That's not the point," I said. "If I made a plan and the others didn't agree, then I'm the only one disappointed." I didn't want anger to rule my thoughts. "They're doing perfectly fine without me. If they wanted me home, they would have told me last night, don't you think?"

"You can't have it both ways," Alicia said, scooting to the edge of her seat. "You've asked them to give you time to figure things out. Where does that leave them?"

"You've put them in an impossible position if they do want to ask you to come home," Pamela pointed out.

"Ugh," I said, falling into the back of the couch and pulling a blanket over my head. I realized the kaleidoscope didn't appear. It hadn't since I sorted out it was all about the mirrors. She was right. By asking the girls to give me time to figure myself out, I had taken away the option for them to ask me to return.

Pamela pulled the blanket off my face, and Alicia shook her head.

"How can we help you? Do you want to stay here at the beach house?"

"Or do you want to move back home?" Pamela asked, handing over a bag of chips as if we were having a normal conversation talking about the books we'd recently read for book club.

I ran into my bedroom and got the papers to the cottage. "Read this," I said, handing the papers to Pamela.

"He bought the cottage?" Pamela's mouth dropped open.

It was not very often that I had the chance to shock Pamela.

"Well, not really. He arranged the option for me to buy the cottage.

Having to see for herself, Alicia jumped up and plucked the papers out of Pamela's hands. "How romantic," Alicia squealed.

Pamela started chuckling. She fell back on the couch, laughing so hard her laugh went silent. I knew then that she understood how I felt, and I sunk into the couch next to her, in hysterics myself.

"What's so funny?" Baffled, Alicia backed up and sat in her seat.

Once Pamela caught her breath, she explained. "All Julie wants is for Michael to ask her to come back home. Instead, he says, stay here in the cottage." She started her belly laugh all over.

"You guys are mean." Alicia tossed the deed on the coffee table. "It's a wonderful gesture. He's trying to do something nice for you."

"Just like buying the girls' car," Pamela could hardly get the words out though her tittering.

"I know, and you're right. He means well." I sat for a minute, letting my abdominal muscles relax. "I do love it here. I have never once felt uncomfortable. Isn't that weird? Here I am, all alone, no family, and not in my forever home, and yet I am perfectly comfortable."

"Are you comfortable?" Pamela asked. "Or are you hiding?"

That plucked a heartstring. Was I hiding? From my family? I shook my head. "I'm not hiding. I talk to the girls every day and Michael a couple of times a week. You can't call that hiding."

"Okay." Pamela nodded her head in thought. "Okay. What or who are you avoiding?"

That struck a nerve. In defense, I blurted out, "I'm not afraid to parent my girls anymore. I've never fallen out of love with Michael. I've had lots of practice prioritizing myself and my work now. I've found value in painting again. I'm not afraid to be alone. In fact, I revel in it."

"So what is the problem?"

"Can I make a suggestion?" Alicia asked. "I think you need to go to your What Does Julie Want list. Go get it."

I didn't move, thinking Alicia was joking. That list was not meant for anyone's eyes but my own. Every time I'd cross an item off as achieved, I'd add two more wants. Plus, there were truths written down nobody needed to see, not even my very best friends.

Pamela rotated her wrist in the air. "Seriously, go get it. Let's see what living here alone has accomplished for you."

"That's mean," Alicia said to Pamela. "Julie, you are here in the beach house to work on you. We want to help. If you feel good about yourself and your goals, shouldn't it be time to go home or at least determine what you haven't accomplished here?"

"Or is something still nagging at you?" Pam asked. "What are you afraid of?"

The old me would have teared up during the interrogation, but I wasn't so much overwhelmed as I was genuinely curious myself. I looked at Alicia and asked myself, "What is keeping me here in this cottage?"

"What's keeping you from going home?" she rephrased my question.

"Same thing," I mumbled.

"Is it?" Pamela asked.

"I don't deserve them," I said into my fists. On the day Curtis died, I was tired of being Mom and Mrs. So what did I do? I hid my phone and disappeared. Because I was tired? Bored? "I just don't deserve them," I said out loud. I didn't merit the twins or even Michael.

"What did you just say?" Pamela stood up and faced me. "You don't deserve them? You don't deserve to go home? You are crazy, girlfriend. Where did that come from?"

Alicia held a hand up then motioned Pamela to take a seat. "Let's try to dig a little deeper," Alicia said in her most comforting voice. "Let's talk about Curtis."

"This doesn't have anything to do with Curtis. I went to a therapist. I understand my grief and its phases. I couldn't have prevented Curtis's headache, and my mind tells me it wasn't my fault. I loved him with all my heart and couldn't miss him more."

Pamela's eyebrows rose, and she looked at Alicia.

"What?" I asked.

Pamela sat up straighter as if what she was going to say needed careful attention in the telling. "You said your mind tells you…"

"I meant, logically, I know I wasn't responsible," I clarified.

Alicia sat in front of me on the coffee table. "What is your heart telling you?"

Impatiently, Pamela asked, "Where were you between noon and five on the day of Curtis's incident?"

As soon as I heard the question, the floodgates opened. I didn't want to go there. I was well over it. Wasn't I? And then I thought of my What Does Julie Want list and the words I traced over several times in several different-colored ink pens.

"Karma sucks."

It was time to say the words out loud, even the ones I had been avoiding thinking about. My fear in putting my story into audible words was that they would transmute into further bad karma. All my actions over the years as a mother and wife seemed to have come across so opposite of my intentions I didn't know how to function. But looking into the encouraging eyes of my two dear friends, a little courage sizzled in my veins, enough to want to take control of my future.

"I had been feeling down for a while before Curtis's incident. I felt invisible, taken for granted, disrespected. I wanted to get away, but I didn't really. I just wanted to feel appreciated. I'm sorry I bailed on you that day, Pamela. But when I had gotten out of the shower, I had three messages from Chad."

"I knew it," Pamela shoved a fist into her palm and explained to Alicia. "Chad Knight, her high school boyfriend. Part of our foursome, including Michael." Pamela opened the front door, and I thought she was going to leave. But she just stood in the doorframe and stared out. "I knew he had something to do with this."

As she cooled off the interior of the cottage, I didn't know what she was thinking, but she wasn't happy. And my stomach began to ripple as the words I said out loud would now have to be explained.

"Go on," Alicia said and took Pamela's place beside me on the couch.

I sipped my wine, thinking that it all seemed so silly now. But I started at the beginning and told them everything from the minute I received the first message from Chad.

Message number 1 from Chad Knight: Hi! Thank God for Facebook. I found you. I'm in town for the day.

Message number 2 from Chad Knight: Jules?

Message number 3 from Chad Knight: I'll be at Harvey's Diner for lunch a little after noon. Meet me?

My text was to Pamela: Sorry, have to skip lunch today.

"I thought it was a sign—an opportunity to do something for myself, by myself, without having to ask permission or rearrange anyone else's schedule. I was going to lunch with a friend, no different than if I were going with you, Pamela. I ran upstairs, applied some mascara, and put on my chunky turquoise necklace." My hands shook in my lap, just as they did when I applied my makeup that day. "I was excited, a bit nervous, doing something so out of character. I checked myself in the mirror then shut down my phone and tucked it into the glove compartment. For one day, I was not Mom. I was not Mrs."

"Why didn't you tell me? I would have gone with you," Pamela asked, closed the front door, and remained on that side of the room.

"Exactly. That's why I didn't tell you. And that's why I had thrown my phone in the glove compartment. I didn't want you or anyone else to talk me out of it. For months, I had been feeling down. I was lost in being a mother of three and Michael's wife. I didn't have my own identity. I didn't know who I was. I thought, just this once, I'd do something spontaneous. I wanted to be Julie Cahill, not Mom or Mrs. Michael Scott."

The excitement I felt that morning couldn't surpass the guilt I'd been living with since. "I was so nervous I could hardly put on my lip gloss. I couldn't believe I was really going to have lunch with Chad. To be honest with you, I never thought about my cell phone again."

"At least you applied lip gloss," Pamela joked, but not without a glare from Alicia.

"When was the last time you saw him?" Alicia asked, clearly bothering Pamela as she harrumphed at the question.

"I hadn't seen nor heard from Chad since he left for boot camp, the week after high school graduation, almost twenty years ago. He broke my heart when he told me he had joined the military. We had talked about marriage and kids after college. After I got over him…"

"Which took more than a year," Pamela said.

"Yeah, but I hadn't even thought about him since then. There was no way I would have married into the military, move my children every two years, and become my mother, subservient and under-appreciated in her own home."

"Yet here we are." Pamela threw her hands in the air.

I threw a pillow at her, but her statement wasn't misguided. "I knew it was silly to meet him. At one point, I had put the keys back in the ignition and revved the engine to leave. But at the thought of going home, that stale feeling took over, the weariness of being the perfect mother, the perfect wife. I was tired of keeping the picket fence perfectly white. My heart raced at the thought of doing something so off the cuff, something no one would ever dream I'd ever do. I hadn't felt that…alive in a while."

As I spoke, Pamela drew closer and sat on the corner of the coffee table.

"I jumped out of the van before I could change my mind again and walked the two blocks toward the boardwalk. I didn't want Chad to see my beat-up old family van with the 'Mom, Dad, twin girls, one son, one dog' stick figures on the back windshield, let alone the new dent in the rear fender from when I backed out of the driveway and into the mailbox." A confession to lighten the tension in the room. "It was cold. I remember the salty breeze blew strong in my face as I turned north onto the boardwalk. It felt so good, so refreshing. Then I thought that maybe all I needed was a long walk on the beach, and that would get me out of the ridiculous funk I was in. The salt air always fixed things when I was a kid. I stopped in front of the ice cream shop next to Harvey's Diner, thinking of turning around. The reflection of my turquoise beads caught my attention in the shop's window. I felt surrounded with their protective and positive energy. False courage. I stepped closer to the glass and focused on my face. Was I really going to do this? My gut protested, but I was determined to do something self-serving. I wasn't doing anything wrong. We were meeting for lunch, not in a hotel."

Alicia and Pamela sat attentively as I rehashed that moment for the millionth time, but the words exiting my mouth were harsh on my ears, and I stalled.

"It's okay," Alicia said and reached out for my wrist at the same time Pamela rolled her hand to move me along.

"I went ahead and entered Harvey's. I expected to see a crowd but only saw two couples seated at tables. A man rose from the back booth, and it was him. Chad. I waited for my heart to skip a beat."

"And did it?" Pamela asked.

Chapter 45

The day of…
Nineteen months earlier, 12:00 p.m. to 5:00 p.m.

A s I walked toward the back of the diner, Chad took my hand and pulled me into his chest for a familiar bear hug.
"Jules," he said.

He bent to kiss me, and I quickly offered a cheek. Still holding my hand, he led me to my side of the booth. He helped me take off my coat. I leaned over and placed my purse and coat along the bench and slid in, perched on the edge of the seat, leaving no room for him to sit next to me. A glass of cabernet waited for me.

He sat facing me, reached out and took my hand in his, and lifted his draft beer, "Cheers. I took the liberty of a fine cab. You talk about wine a lot on Facebook."

We took a moment to assess each other. His voice was gruffer than I had remembered, and the fully grown beard on his still baby face struck me as comical. He said it took about twelve years to fill in. He was chubby for Chad, his athletic physique always so important to him as a youth. There were hints of high school Chad, still good-looking with piercing blue eyes, even though his golden curls were dull and graying. He seemed familiar yet strange.

As he held my hand from across the table, he rubbed his thumb over my knuckles—an opiate for my nerves. I hoped he could find something in me to remind him of my youth, but his silence wasn't convincing. I saw myself through his eyes—thirty pounds overweight, long brown hair that hadn't been professionally tended to for over half a year, and a forehead obviously in need of Botox. I sat on my one free hand so I wouldn't grab my coat and purse and run out of there.

"How are you?" he asked, leaning back against the red pleather booth.

"Great" was my automatic answer. Uncomfortable with his attention on me, I said, "Tell me what you've been up to."

We ordered fried clams and shrimp po'boys in homage to our high school days, and he finally released my hand, uncoupling the energy between us. Flustered, I pressed into the seatback to gain distance. He didn't seem to notice as he told me about his worldwide adventures covering seven countries over the last twenty years. He had been married twice. He and his second wife, a girl from Thailand, had one child. They now lived in Germany, where his fourteen-year-old son attended school. He made it all sound so exciting, and I began to feel like I had missed out on something.

"And you?" Chad said, changing the subject. "I see you married Michael and have three children."

"Damn that Facebook," I said jokingly.

"No, really, tell me about you."

I told him about the twins and what a talented photographer Nicole was and how serious Heather was with her job and how they were both tremendous ballet dancers and students. I boasted about how athletic Curtis was and what a great man he was going to grow up to be because of his wonderful relationship with his father. He asked about Michael. I mentioned what a great father and coach he was and how his career was reaching new heights. I even admitted to having the best dog in the world.

He listened patiently then asked, "Now tell me about you?"

I thought I just had. He reached an open hand across the table. I stared at it then took it.

"You don't paint anymore?"

"Oh, yes, of course. Of course, I do. I paint commission work for an interior designer, my friend Alicia."

"So you have a friend too?" Chad raised his hand for the waitress to bring two more drinks.

"Ha. Ha," I said. "Yes, I have a friend, and we hang out with Pamela."

"Our Pamela? How is good old Pammie?"

"She met her goals. She married a wealthy businessman, joined a wealthy country club, and is the hostess with the most-ess."

"That's good to know. And Michael? You said he was a good father and coach. What about husband?"

Did I not mention what a great husband Michael was?

"Well, I'm glad you have three great kids and a dog to match."

I slumped in my seat and dabbed at the tears sliding down my cheeks with my crushed napkin. Chad slid beside me in the booth, and I scooted over, crushing my coat. He put an arm around me.

"I didn't mean to make you cry."

Deflated, I leaned into his shoulder. He lifted my chin and kissed me ever so gently. And it was nice. I turned my body toward him and sank into the familiarity of him. Twenty-two years disappeared, and I was sixteen again in the arms of my first love, still innocent of where kissing could lead yet filled with desire. Wanting more from him, I reached up and stroked his cheek. His beard, foreign to my touch, set off alarms in my head. I pushed him away with both arms, almost knocking him off the bench.

"I'm sorry," he stammered. *"I didn't mean to…"*

"It's okay," I interrupted him. But it wasn't. I grabbed my purse and coat. I ran out of the diner and straight to the ocean's edge.

I sank onto my knees and into the sand and let my shame seep down my face. I couldn't wipe from my mind the guilt of knowing there was a split second when I wanted things between Chad and I to go further. How could I let that kiss go as far as it did? How could I have chanced losing everything?

I walked the beach and let the sun warm my soul through the cold January breeze. My pace picked up as my shame turned into anger at my stupidity. I let him believe I was unhappy in my marriage. If I was restless and bored, that was on me; but I loved Michael, my three children, our dog, and that damned white picket fence. And I wouldn't have or want any of it without Michael.

As I retraced my steps, all I could think about was to return home and take Michael, Heather, Nicole, and Curtis into my arms and let them know how much I cherished them. Life with them would be short enough as it was, and I didn't want to waste or take for granted another moment with them.

Chapter 46

Ashamed of my actions, I looked away from Pamela as she dabbed at her own tears. "Chad grew a beard?" Pamela laughed with a sniffle.

I couldn't keep the corners of my lips from lifting at her remark, but I turned my face, not wanting to meet Pamela's eyes. "And then I found out about Curtis," I said.

Pamela squeezed onto the couch with Alicia and me. And she handed me the tissue box from the end table.

"Karma's a bitch." I sniffled. I shrugged then stood, needing to escape the pity coming at me from my girlfriends. "I had been with Chad for less than an hour. The rest of the day I spent walking up and down the beach, berating myself."

"Nothing happened, so why didn't you tell us long ago?" Pamela asked.

"Because I've just now admitted even to myself that I let Chad believe that there was a rift between me and Michael, and then when I kissed him, there was a long moment when I had given myself over to Chad, and Michael never once crossed my mind. I'm a horrible wife."

Pamela handed me another tissue.

"There's no forgiving me not being available when my husband needed me most. I never even thought about getting my phone. I spent the rest of the afternoon convincing myself we were two old friends having lunch together and there was nothing wrong with that."

"You are not responsible for Curtis's headaches," Alicia said.

"I understand that. But I was supposed to be there for my family when they needed me. And I wasn't. Why didn't I have my phone with me? Why did I feel the need to be totally cut off? That's why I don't deserve them. And God took one of them away from me. I couldn't handle him taking the rest. Now, it took them not wanting to live with me to finally understand how much I love them and need them."

Nausea rose as I ran into my bedroom and slammed the door. The truth was out, and I knew then that to move on, I needed to tell Michael where I was that day.

Chapter 47

Two days after my confession to Pamela and Alicia, I garnered the courage to ask Michael to come to the cottage so we could talk.

"Do you want me to bring the girls?" he asked.

"No, just you."

"I'll be there in an hour or so," he said. "And Julie, we need to discuss Thanksgiving." There it was. He brought it up. Hopefully, he and the girls had a plan. And I so desired to be part of it.

Michael's car sat in the driveway as I rounded the corner from my beach walk. He stepped out of the car, and Roger made a beeline straight for him.

"Sorry. Time stands still when I walk the beach," I said, looking at my phone and realizing I had spent over forty-five minutes staring at the horizon. "Come in, where it's warmer."

We settled in the kitchen, Michael with a coffee, me a hot chocolate.

"How's the cottage?" Michael asked.

I thanked him with a hug. "I love it here. I didn't know I dreamed of owning our very own beach cottage, but now I know it's something I've always wanted."

"You signed the papers?"

"I did, just yesterday."

He smiled. "You always said the salt air fed your soul."

I did use to say that, years ago, before the kids nourished my soul. Good for me, he remembered. All week, I had thought about what would change when I told Michael about the day Curtis died. He couldn't kick me out of the house nor be more upset with me than he had been since that day. But freeing the words to Pamela and Alicia got me closer to understanding me. And they seemed to think by telling Michael the truth, I would have no more guilt hidden in the crevices of my mind. I would be free to think of what I truly wanted from life.

"How was it so easy for you to watch me leave?" I started. My wringing hands were as tight as my fretting gut.

"My therapist helped me accept Curtis's death, but I couldn't get over my loss of trust in you. I could never have thought there'd be a time I couldn't contact you, never thought we'd never be there for each other. I had never dreamed you weren't around during the day, any day."

"That's just it, Michael. You never asked where I was or what I did on any given day."

He nodded his head as he gathered understanding. "Are you ever going to tell me where you were?"

I dug my fist into my forehead. I knew it. I had added to his grief by pretending all this time I hadn't done anything wrong.

"After that fight in the garage," he continued, "I realized how much I needed some time to myself, at least away from you and your rules, to sort things out in my head. I couldn't do it with you in the house, pushing everyone forward and acting like everything would be okay. So later, when you packed up and said you needed time to yourself, I got it. I knew how important that would be for both of us."

"What did you tell the girls?"

"I explained exactly what I just said to you. I knew how important it was to be on your own so you could search and find what you truly needed to move on in life," Michael said. "Have you found it?"

"I think I have, but it's complicated," I said with a hesitant grin, knowing that wouldn't surprise him. I wouldn't be able to see a future with him, without all my cards on the table. "Michael, before Curtis's incident. I hadn't been myself for a while. Not since before that last Thanksgiving, actually. I felt like a shell of a human going through the motions. Like a zombie with no intention and no purpose. Every day was the same, every week, month, holiday."

Michael's eyebrows raised. I could tell this was news to him. He tilted his head but said nothing.

"I know, ironic coming from me, Mrs. Forever Home, dedicating her life to a dream of raising her family and establishing traditions. But things got stale. I got stale. I couldn't find joy in anything anymore. And so, when Chad Knight…"

"Chad?" Michael's mouth fell open, and his face turned red. His eyes glazed over as if he was hit from behind. He stumbled, getting out of his chair.

I stayed seated but reached out my hand. When he didn't reciprocate, it dropped on the table. "Wait, please, Michael. Please listen, and if you want to leave when I'm done, I won't stop you."

After a moment, he leaned on the back of his chair for support. It was apparent he wasn't going to sit and get comfortable in case he wanted to walk out the door.

I started with the morning when the girls needed pancakes for school, and no one, not even Michael, told me I was still in my housecoat when we left. I explained feeling invisible, unappreciated, and taken for granted. I explained how I forgot to say I love you to Curtis in all the commotion and assumed I would see him after baseball practice. Then I told Michael about receiving messages from Chad and felt no one cared what I did with my time, so I agreed to meet him for lunch. Michael's watery eyes never left mine, and I owed him the same. I never looked away while I told the whole story, every detail.

"I left that beach with a renewed lease on life," I said, getting up to pour myself a glass of wine. "I had such an appreciation for all you and I had built together. I've since realized that by keeping everything so hammered down, I had taken the fun and spontaneity out of our lives. But then, after Curtis…" I shook the hospital images out of my head. "Having taken that afternoon for myself validated my life with you and our children. It renewed my faith in you and our family. I'm just sorry I had to see Chad to realize it."

The impact when he took a seat forced Michael to break our gaze. "Why didn't you tell me? Why did you lie and say you were going out with Pamela? Did she know this all along?"

"No. I *was* supposed to go to lunch with Pamela. She was in the dark as much as you. But when I got Chad's messages, I canceled on her at the last minute. Don't you see, I wanted to take a break from being me."

Michael dropped his head in his hands. He rubbed his face and left his hands in prayer at his lips. "I didn't know you were so unhappy,"

"I didn't either. I wasn't. Ugh." I sounded crazy. "I just didn't know how good I had it."

"And now what? You need forgiveness from me so you can move forward?" His sarcasm hit home, and I deserved it. I let him continue. "I had to go to that hospital without you and face what that doctor had to say alone. All because you were with Chad Knight, your ex-boyfriend?" He began to pace, a few steps at first, and then to the front door and back as his anger built.

"It was just supposed to be lunch with an old friend," I begged.

"He was my friend too. Why didn't you invite me?"

He missed the point. "I didn't want to be a wife, mother, chef, house cleaner, or taxi driver just for a few hours. I wanted to do something for me alone. I know it sounds crazy, and it wasn't a secret, it's just…"

"It's just your family needed you, and wait, why did you never answer your phone if you were just having lunch?"

"I had put it in the glove compartment. I knew Pamela would keep calling and…"

"I'm sorry, Julie. But I have to go," he said as he pulled his jacket over his left arm. His phone rang before he got to the door.

"But we're not finished," I said, blocking his way out.

"Hi, honey. I'm on my way home now. What's up?"

I could tell it was one of the girls on the other end of the phone by his sudden change of demeanor. He continued talking and reached around me for the doorknob. I stepped out of the way, and he left without a goodbye.

I grabbed the door before it swung shut, and he said, "That's fantastic, honey. I'm so proud of you. We'll celebrate when I get home."

I followed him to his car, still pleading for him to stay. His car door shut, and the rest of the conversation left with him. My family would celebrate an achievement of sorts, and I wasn't invited.

Unable to see through my tears, I tripped over Roger sitting on the mat with his ears and tail tucked. As I hit the tiled floor, I cursed myself for messing everything up so badly. I dragged myself to bed, crossed my arms over my eyes, and prayed that, with time, Michael could forgive me so I could forgive myself.

The next morning at 5:00 a.m., I rolled out of bed less refreshed than I should have been after ten hours of sleep. I threw on a sweat-shirt and thanked Roger for letting me sleep. We sat on the back deck, in the dark, contemplating my future. Michael and I had never talked about Thanksgiving. I guessed it was a nonissue. It was time for me to move forward by myself. I grabbed pen and paper and walked room to room, deciding how to update the cottage and truly make it my own. Fresh wall colors, beachy fabrics, new flooring, and current furniture all made the list. I did decide to keep the kitchen table set and the bunk beds. Now all I had to do was earn the money to get all this done.

On my morning walk with Roger, I found the flyer in my jacket pocket for the 7:00 a.m. yoga classes in the back of the hardware store. No time like the present. I changed my clothes and walked downtown, pleased to begin my journey with yoga. After an arduous yet enlightening class, the teacher offered a couple of free private lessons, confirming my clumsy undertaking. But her sweet commit-ment to making me feel comfortable in her class was just the thing I needed to make sure I would return.

Nora Amberly had left a message explaining she got all my paperwork and I could start volunteering at the center the second Tuesday after Thanksgiving. Happy that that was in place, I called Alicia and asked her if she could meet me tomorrow at my local Ace Hardware to help me pick out wall colors. I might know what I thought I wanted, but there was no way I would redecorate the cot-tage without her input.

With two things checked off my list, I unwrapped leftover pizza and heated it up. My phone rang, and Michael's face popped up on the screen. I shut off the ringer and turned the phone facedown on the table. I was celebrating me and didn't want to hear him say he no longer wanted me in his life.

I took a shower after I raked the backyard with Roger until I couldn't feel my toes then crawled into bed with a new novel. Before I began reading, thoughts of Curtis, the girls, and Michael traipsed across my mind as they did each night before falling asleep as a kind of prayer. I plugged my phone in for a night of charging and saw Michael did indeed leave me a message.

Hearing the tears in his voice broke my heart. "Julie, I'm sorry you were so unhappy, and I didn't see it. I guess I had been going through the motions too. But I'm sorrier that it took seeing Chad for you to appreciate our family. We need some time, but hopefully we can fix this."

Epilogue

Thanksgiving morning arrived, and I couldn't have been more excited. I hadn't seen the girls since the fundraiser and looked forward to spending the day with them. The weight of past holidays had melted away with great relief when Heather suggested we begin a new tradition and have the family share our holiday by serving meals to the hungry and lonely.

I bumbled through my yoga class and reveled in my morning beach walk with Roger. I showered after I straightened up my studio and made the bunk beds with new sheets and covers. I cleared out the back of the van, which had become a catchall as Alicia and I renovated the cottage. Nicole was coming home with me for the long weekend, and I wanted everything to go smoothly.

The past four nights, over a glass of wine and a beer, Michael and I had a 5:00 p.m. tête-à-tête, a phone date, as he called it, where we talked about our future and our past. The only thing the two of us had agreed on so far was a real date the following week—movie and dinner or the likes. Neither of us were in a rush.

I pulled into the New Castle County Food Pantry and Soup Kitchen parking lot fifteen minutes behind schedule.

Nicole ran up to the van and opened my door for me. She couldn't pull me out of my seat fast enough.

"I'm sorry I'm late," I said, reaching into the back seat for the four Thanksgiving aprons I had painted just yesterday. I handed the brown apron with a colorful turkey on the front to Michael. I tossed two to the girls to sort out. Heather tied the orange apron with autumn leaves around her neck, and Nicole took the yellow one with fall gourds. That left me with the forest-green apron with a cornucopia of fruit.

"And I have something to show you," Nicole said, handing me a piece of paper.

After reading it, I looked up into three sets of eyes. All antici-pated my reaction.

"Congratulations, sweetie."

Nicole had been accepted into the New York Institute of Photography. I wrapped both my arms around Nicole and fixed my eyes on Michael.

His shoulders dropped, and the corners of his lips curved up, a smile long forgotten, clearly relieved with my reaction. Nicole and I pulled Heather into our hug fest.

"Let me grab my stuff," Nicole said and ran to their car and grabbed her suitcase and overnight bag. Heather grabbed a hard-shell carry-on too.

"All that for one girl for three nights?" I laughed and offered to take her overnight bag from her.

"No," Heather said. "Two girls for three nights."

I reached to hug her, but she let go of her bag, and it tipped over as she ran back to the car. "Hold on. I forgot something," she yelled over her shoulder. She returned and handed me a thousand-piece puzzle of a José van Gool's *Three Women in White on the Beach*.

The end

About the Author

Kyle Ann is a "fingers crossed, jump right in" kinda girl. Just sink your teeth into her years of journal entries and poetry for details. (Actually, please don't!) Born in Japan, Kyle traveled around the world and east coast of the United States as a Navy brat. She mostly grew up in Virginia Beach, Virginia, traveled through Kentucky, Massachusetts, Georgia, and Florida before retiring from the world of physical therapy and turning to a second career in creative writing. She has successfully raised four wonderful kids who are presently out living their own adventures. She now lives in Florida with her husband and enjoys visiting with her six (and counting) grandkids, golfing, gardening, and of course, writing honest and heartfelt family stories.

CPSIA information can be obtained
at www.ICGtesting.com
Printed in the USA
BVHW030320280223
659275BV00002B/5